WHEN LOVE BLOOMS

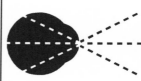 This Large Print Book carries the
Seal of Approval of N.A.V.H.

WHEN LOVE BLOOMS

ROBIN LEE HATCHER

THORNDIKE PRESS
A part of Gale, Cengage Learning

GALE
CENGAGE Learning™

Detroit • New York • San Francisco • New Haven, Conn • Waterville, Maine • London

GALE
CENGAGE Learning™

LIBRARY OF CONGRESS CATALOGING-IN-PUBLICATION DATA

Hatcher, Robin Lee.
  When love blooms / by Robin Lee Hatcher.
    p. cm. — (Thorndike Press large print Christian romance)
  ISBN-13: 978-1-4104-1562-2 (alk. paper)
  ISBN-10: 1-4104-1562-7 (alk. paper)
  1. Governesses—Fiction. 2. Idaho—Fiction. 3. Large type
books. I. Title.
PS3558.A73574W47 2009
813'.54—dc22   2009007732

Published in 2009 by arrangement with The Zondervan Corporation LLC.

*The fig trees are budding, and the
grapevines are in blossom.
How delicious they smell!
Yes, spring is here!
Arise, my beloved, my fair one,
and come away.*
Song of Songs 2:13, NLT

Prologue

Washington, D.C., February 1883

Emily Harris pressed the telegram from her brother-in-law against her chest and felt the rapid beating of her heart beneath her palm. Maggie and little Sheridan. She couldn't bear it if anything were to happen to her sister and her youngest nephew.

Please, God. Please don't let them die.

She looked again at the brief message.

MAGGIE AND SHERIDAN SICK. DOCTOR SAYS PNEUMONIA. MAGGIE ASKING FOR YOU. PLEASE COME HOME. TUCKER.

Emily couldn't imagine not having Maggie to turn to when she needed help or advice. Her sister had raised her, loved her, protected her, been as much a mother as a sister to her.

Please, God. Please don't let her die.

She must find Professor Abraham at once. Arrangements must be made to return to Idaho as quickly as possible. If Maggie was asking for her, it had to be serious. She hadn't a moment to waste.

ONE

It was mid-afternoon when Gavin Blake drove the wagon down Boise City's Main Street. The territorial capital had grown in the years since his last visit. There had to be several good physicians living here these days. One of them would be able to help Drucilla. If he didn't believe that, he never would have agreed to undertake this trip.

He turned toward his wife. A tall and plain woman, her kind and giving spirit more than made up for whatever outward beauty she lacked. Everyone who knew Dru loved her. Which only made it harder on Gavin, seeing her as she was now — too thin, too frail, exhaustion from a week of travel written in her hazel eyes.

I shouldn't have let her come.

Not that she'd given him much choice. Dru's will hadn't weakened along with her body. It was still hard as flint.

At least the weather had been warm for their trip. He'd made her a comfortable bed in the back of the wagon so she could rest whenever she wanted, and at night they'd lain beneath the blankets, staring at the stars and talking about what Dru wanted for Sabrina and Petula. Sometimes listening to her — hearing the calm acceptance in her voice — made him angry. He wanted to rail against her illness — and against God for letting her get sick in the first place. Hadn't she suffered enough?

Gavin stopped the wagon in front of the Overland Hotel. After setting the brake, he hopped to the ground.

"Come on." He held his arms toward her. "Let's get you into a nice, soft bed."

"Shouldn't we go to the newspaper office first?"

"I'll take care of that later."

"Gavin, I —"

"You heard me. Come on."

Dru acquiesced with a nod. "I suppose you're right, but we came all this way to —"

"I know why we came." His tone was gruff, though he didn't mean for it to be. He wasn't angry at her.

It never failed to alarm him when he lifted her down from the wagon and his fingers overlapped around her waist. He remembered when she was pregnant, her body ripe and round like a pumpkin, her face rosy, her eyes shining with happiness. That seemed a lifetime ago. Look at what had happened in the few years since then. First her son was stillborn, then Charlie died, and now this. If only he could take her back East to one of those fine hospitals. If only he were wealthy. If only there was more he could do for her.

"Gavin?" Her cool fingers touched his cheek. "Let's go inside."

Without a word, he placed a solicitous arm around her back and guided her into the lobby of the hotel.

Wanted: Governess and teacher for two young girls on mountain ranch. Separate living quarters. Apply Mrs. Blake, Overland Hotel, after 2:00 PM Friday.

Emily set down the newspaper and stared out the window at the tall poplars, cottonwoods, and willows growing alongside the river. A warm breeze lifted wisps of hair across her forehead and caressed her skin with the last breath of summer. A large blowfly buzzed beneath the porch awning, bumping into the window, then flying away before returning to try again.

Perhaps the insect seemed noisy because the house was so silent. Kevin, Colleen, Tara Maureen, and Colin — Maggie's four oldest children — were all in school. Sheridan, at four the baby of the family, had gone into town with his mother for some shopping. And Emily was here alone with time weighing heavy on her mind.

She left the dining room and wandered into the parlor. There, her fingers caressed the photographs and knickknacks as she moved about the room. Memories. Lots of memories. Happy ones too. And yet she felt out of place here. She was restless and impatient with her life. Nothing seemed to be going as she wanted.

Not that she was entirely sure what that entailed. What *did* she want?

For many weeks after her hasty return last winter from Washington, D.C., she had gladly cared for her sister and young nephew, nursing them back to health, praying for their recovery, seeing to their every need. She had mothered the older children, reassuring them that all would be well. And she'd spent many a late evening sitting with Tucker in this very room, offering her brother-in-law what comfort she could.

12

But the Branigan household had long since returned to normal. Although wanted, she knew, Emily wasn't needed any longer.

Should she return to Washington? Despite how much she had enjoyed her work, that option no longer felt right. But what awaited her here? Marriage? A family of her own? She didn't feel ready for those things yet. In fact, she had turned down a proposal from Matthew Foreman only one week before.

No, she wanted to *do* something before she married. She wanted to make some sort of difference in the world. If only she knew what.

She shook her head and walked back toward the dining room, pausing by the window and staring across the yard toward the river. Bed sheets fluttered in the golden September sunlight. Tucker's old collie lay in the shade of a poplar, his tail slapping the dried grass in a lazy, steady rhythm.

God, what is it I'm to do? I'll die of boredom if you don't show me something soon.

She sighed as she turned from the window. Her gaze fell upon the folded newspaper, lying on the oak table where she'd left it moments ago.

Look at it, her heart seemed to say.

She took up the paper and read the ad a second time.

Wanted: Governess and teacher for two young girls on mountain ranch. Separate living quarters. Apply Mrs. Blake, Overland Hotel, after 2:00 PM Friday.

Her pulse quickened. This could be it. This was something she could do. She'd lived on a ranch since she was six, so that prospect didn't daunt her. Cattle and horses and cowhands were a part of her history.

She certainly knew how to teach. She'd received a wonderful education and had countless things she could share with two young girls. And after living all these years with Maggie's brood, she knew a thing or two about acting like a governess to children, even if she'd never been employed as one.

Yes, this was something she could do. She was sure of it.

Did she dare apply for the job?

Drucilla Blake awakened slowly from her nap. On days like this, when she felt no pain, it was hard to believe she was dying. Tired, yes. Dying, no.

She pushed herself up on the pillows, then swept her hair back from her face as she looked at the watch pinned to the bodice of her dress, 1:15. She would have to get up if she was to meet people at two o'clock.

A cold feeling engulfed her chest, and she closed her eyes, her fingers still clutching the watch. What if no one came? Or what if they came and no one was right? It was important to find the right woman. Not just for Sabrina and Petula, but for Gavin too.

It wasn't right what she'd done to him. When that old sawbones told her she was dying, she should have left the ranch. She should have taken the children and gone. But to where? She had no other family, no way to support herself. What would have happened to Sabrina and Petula if she'd left the basin and taken them to a strange place? No, she'd had to stay. The Idaho mountains were where she would end her days, where she would be buried beside Charlie and her stillborn son.

She filled her lungs with a deep breath, then straightened and lowered her legs over the side of the bed. There was no time to feel sorry for herself. She had come to terms with her illness months ago. Gavin would love and care for the children. He was that sort of man. She had only this one last detail to attend to, and then she would be able to die in peace.

She rose from the bed and walked toward the bureau, glancing into the mirror as she

15

picked up the hairbrush. That was a mistake. Her reflection depressed her. She looked far older than her thirty-five years. Her illness had taken its toll, turning her brown hair gray and leaving her eyes dull and lifeless.

Lowering her gaze, she tidied her hair and smoothed her dress with the flat of her hands, then left the bedroom.

In the small sitting room, Gavin stood at the window, gazing down at the busy street below. Dru paused a moment to look at him. His black hair was shaggy around his shirt collar, badly in need of trimming. She should have seen to that before they left the basin.

He must have heard something, for he turned to face her. "Did you sleep?"

She nodded.

"Are you hungry?"

"No. I don't think I could eat anything."

"You barely touched your breakfast." It was a tender admonishment.

She shook her head and turned toward the nearby sofa. She hated to see that look in his eyes. It made her feel guilty for all she had put him through, all she had yet to put him through.

"I wonder what the girls are doing this afternoon," Gavin said.

She understood the motive behind his

words. He wanted to cheer her with thoughts of the children. She loved him for it.

"Probably out riding with Stubs," he continued. "The boys ought to have the cows rounded up by the time we get back."

"I wish we didn't have to leave the summer range so soon." Dru imagined the majestic peaks of the rugged Sawtooth Mountains and the log house that lay in their shadows. No one needed to tell her she wouldn't see another spring in the Stanley Basin.

Her husband came to sit beside her. "Dru, I want you to see the doctor before we leave Boise."

She offered a faint smile. "Don't, Gavin. We both know it won't make any difference."

Before he could contradict her, they were interrupted by a knock. Dru's gaze snapped toward the door.

"They're early," she whispered.

Dear God, please bring us the right woman.

TWO

Standing beside the buggy, Emily ran the palms of her hands over her blue-and-white striped skirt. Nerves fluttered in her stomach as she looked across the street at the Overland Hotel. Was she foolish to have come? Was there even a remote chance Mrs. Blake would consider her for the position?

She was tempted to climb back into the buggy, but she didn't allow herself to succumb. If God wanted her to be a governess to these children, she would get the job. If not? Then so be it.

Maggie would call Emily mad if she left Boise to tend to another woman's children. If she wanted to do that, Maggie would say, she could stay at home and watch after Maggie's five. Maybe she would be right.

But Emily couldn't ignore the feeling that she was supposed to be here. This could be the change she needed. No more boring cotillions. No more listening to gossip. No

18

more marriage proposals from men she didn't — and couldn't — love. Besides, as much as she loved Tucker and Maggie, she longed for her independence.

Emily wrapped the reins around the hitching rail, patted the gelding's neck, and walked across the street and into the hotel lobby.

The clerk behind the desk raised his head as she approached. "Good day, Miss Harris." His greeting was bright, his look hopeful. "I haven't seen you in town for a while. Is Judge Branigan with you? Will you be dining with us?"

"No, Mr. Samuels. My brother-in-law isn't with me." She gave him a half-hearted smile. Mark Samuels was one of her erstwhile suitors and a terrible gossip. She didn't want him knowing her business, but there was nothing to be done about it. "I've come to see Mrs. Blake. Can you tell me what room she's in, please?"

Disappointment tightened his mouth. "Mrs. Blake?" He glanced at the registry before him. "Oh, yes. Mrs. Blake." His gaze lifted to meet hers. "She's in room 210. But I'm afraid now isn't a good time for a visit. She's interviewing for a governess to care for her children. There's already been three ladies come and gone."

"Three? But it's not even 2:30." What if she was too late? She at least wanted a chance.

"First one come more'n a half hour ago. Mrs. Blake's a good friend of yours, I take it?"

Emily ignored the question. "Did you say room 210?"

"Yes, but —"

"Thank you, Mr. Samuels."

Squaring her shoulders, she headed for the stairs.

Gavin left his chair near the window to answer the knock on the door. This would be the last one, no matter what Dru said. She was too tired to continue with these interviews — especially since she'd found the first applicants unsuitable.

He pulled open the door expecting to find another woman in her late thirties or early forties with a dour face and reading glasses perched on her nose. That was a far cry from the young lady he saw.

From beneath a bonnet made of plush blue felt, trimmed with a white ostrich feather, a fringe of pale blonde hair kissed the woman's forehead and curled in wisps around her temples and ears. Her eyes were the color of a robin's egg, and her mouth was shaped like a bow.

"I'm here to see Mrs. Blake? About the position of governess."

No, she was nothing like the others — but she was even more unsuitable than the three before her. One look told him that. "I'm Mr. Blake. Come in."

As she moved past him, he caught the faint scent of her cologne. Like wild honeysuckle.

Dru motioned to the chair across from her. "Come in, Miss . . ."

"Harris," the young woman supplied as she crossed the sitting room. "Emily Harris."

"Please sit down, Miss Harris. I'm Drucilla Blake."

Gavin watched as the young woman settled onto the edge of the chair. Her back was ramrod stiff, her gloved hands clasped in the folds of her blue-and-white skirt. This was no penniless spinster in search of much-needed employment.

He closed the door and returned to his place by the window.

"I won't beat around the bush, Miss Harris," Dru began. "Mr. Blake and I have a ranch near Challis up along the Salmon River. We spend most of the year there. For the past two summers, we've trailed our cows into a more remote area known as the Stanley Basin. That's where you'd be for a few more weeks, then up the Salmon. It's beautiful country. We live a simple life, and sometimes it's a hard one."

When Dru paused, Emily Harris nodded, acknowledging that she listened.

"I've got two girls. Sabrina, she's nine. Petula's five. They're bright but in need of more schooling than I can give them. Have you done any teaching?"

"No." The young woman lifted her chin. "But I'm fully qualified to teach. I excelled in my academic studies, both in Boise and at the college I attended in the East. At present, I live with my sister and her husband. They have five children. I've helped raise them. There isn't much I haven't done to care for them over the years."

Dru leaned forward, her hazel eyes narrowing. "Why would someone as . . . pretty as you want to leave the capital city with all of its diversions? Are you running away from something, Miss Harris? Or perhaps some-*one?*"

Gavin's gaze fastened on the petite blonde. He'd wondered the same thing.

"No, Mrs. Blake, I'm not." Her voice was firm. "I am twenty-two years old and living with my sister and her family. As much as I love them all, it's time that I made my own way. Being a governess is something I can do. Something I would enjoy doing."

"The wages wouldn't be much. Only a few dollars a month. You'd have your own small cabin at the main ranch, and you could take your meals with us. If we hire you, we'd want your pledge that you would stay through spring. At least until the cattle return to the summer range in June. Could you make that promise?"

Emily nodded.

His wife's eyes took on a faraway look. Gavin recognized it. That look came over her whenever she thought about her girls and wondered what would happen to them after she was gone. He'd seen it often since the night she'd told him she was dying.

Dru's voice was soft, almost inaudible, when she spoke again. "Miss Harris, you must know one thing more. I'm not a well woman. I need someone who won't mind caring for me as well as the children, when the need arises."

As if searching for a proper reply, Emily Harris looked toward Gavin. Their gazes held for the breadth of a heartbeat, then she turned away.

"I'm not afraid, if that's what you're asking. I returned from my work in Washington because my sister and nephew were deathly ill. I nursed them back to health. I'll do the same for you, as needs be."

Rich, young, spoiled, and much too sure of herself. Emily Harris would be more trouble than help. Gavin had seen her type before. For now she would make promises, but she would do whatever she wanted when things got difficult. That's how it was with women like her.

Dru was silent as she studied the other woman. Perhaps she shared Gavin's reservations. Perhaps she could see the girl wasn't suitable for the work she would be required to do.

At long last, Dru smiled, the tension gone from her face. "Tell me more about you and your family, Miss Harris."

With a sinking feeling, Gavin realized his wife had made up her mind.

Emily walked toward her buggy, Gavin Blake at her side.

"We'll want to get an early start in the morning," he said. "Can you be here by eight?"

She had the distinct feeling he didn't like her. "I will be here before you're ready to leave." She lifted the hem of her dress and stepped into the buggy, settling onto the seat before taking up the reins. "Good day to you, Mr. Blake."

He stepped back from the buggy and Emily slapped the reins against the gelding's rump. The horse jumped forward, quieting into a comfortable trot as they traversed Main Street.

It had been a strange interview, she thought. Not at all what she'd expected. Drucilla Blake had encouraged her to talk about herself — about Maggie and Tucker, about her nieces and nephews, about her experiences in Washington. The other woman had had many questions, but none of them seemed to have anything to do with Emily's qualifications as a governess. Emily had wondered if the woman was only making polite conversation and would still not hire her. But it hadn't happened that way. In the end, Emily was offered the position, and she'd accepted.

Maggie won't like this.

She clucked her tongue in her cheek and slapped the reins against the gelding's backside. The sooner she got home, the sooner she could convince her sister that she'd done the right thing.

"I'm afraid your wife is right, Mr. Blake." The doctor closed the door to the bedroom.

"We can minimize the pain with laudanum, but there's little else we can do for her. There is no treatment that will spare or lengthen her life."

"But she's seemed better. Except for her lack of appetite, I thought —"

"A cancer will often go into a period of remission. The tumor, for some reason we don't understand, will simply stop growing. Patients may think they are cured when they are not."

Gavin rubbed his forehead with his finger-tips. "Maybe it will last a few more years? When the girls are older . . ." His words trailed into silence as he met the physician's gaze.

"I wouldn't pin my hopes on it." The doctor picked up his hat from a nearby chair. "I'm sorry, sir. Very sorry."

The snap of the closing door echoed in Gavin's head. There was no denying the truth any longer. Dru wasn't going to get better. No matter what he did for her, she would die. She'd long since accepted it. Now he must do the same.

Sinking into the chair by the door, he thought of Sabrina and Petula. What kind of father would he be to them without Dru's wisdom and guidance? Would he fail? Would he turn to bitterness, like his own father? In most of his memories, the man who had sired him was lost in a drunken stupor. Mean and surly to boot. It had been a relief when he died. Gavin didn't want to imagine Sabrina and Petula having that same feeling about him.

As for his mother . . . Well, Gavin tried never to think about her. Those memories left a sour taste in his mouth that was hard to get rid of.

Gavin had been on his own since he was fourteen and had little knowledge of what it meant to be a husband and father. What he did know about love, home, and family, he'd learned from Charlie Porter, Dru, Sabrina, and Petula. But things were changing. Again. Charlie had died over two years ago, gored by a bull not long after Dru lost the baby. Now she was dying too, leaving him to raise the girls.

How would he manage?

"Gavin?"

He looked up to find his wife standing in the bedroom doorway. A billowy white nightgown engulfed her bony frame.

"I want to stay in the basin as long as we can. Let Stubs and Jess take the cows to the Lucky Strike. A few more weeks won't matter much."

"It might matter, Dru. The weather's

unpredictable in the basin. Winter can come on mighty fast."

"Please. I won't ask for more than a few weeks."

He rose from the chair and strode across the sitting room, stopping within arm's reach of her. *I'm scared, Dru. I don't know how to raise the girls without you.*

As if she understood his thoughts, she reached up and touched his cheek. "You're going to do fine by them. And Miss Harris will help. You'll see."

"You just met her. She may be worthless as a governess."

"I have a feeling about her, Gavin. Please give her a chance. I asked God to send the right woman, and I'm sure that he did."

He took her in his arms and pressed her cheek against his chest. "All right, Dru. I'll give her a chance."

Dru stood at the open window, her left shoulder leaned against the frame, enjoying the kiss of the evening breeze against her skin. Somewhere on the street below, Gavin was walking. Walking and worrying, as he did far too often. If only she could help him release his worries to God. If only he could accept that the God of the universe had it all in control.

Lord, I pray that I made the right choice today. I pray that Miss Harris was the one you sent to me. I think she is. I saw something in her eyes. I don't know what exactly, but something. I believe she'll be good for the girls. And maybe, if it be your will, good for Gavin too.

She closed her eyes and envisioned the beautiful summer range, cattle grazing in belly-high grass, her daughters running and playing and laughing. Oh, her beautiful daughters. God had been so good to allow her to be their mother for a time. It would be so hard to say good-bye to them, but say good-bye she must.

Please, Lord. Help me instill in them a strong belief and trust in you. Protect their hearts and minds so that the enemy of their souls cannot turn their sorrow over losing me into anger toward you. You have provided them with a good man to be their father, to love and to guide them. Thank you for Gavin. Help them to remain a strong family.

Once again she looked down at the street below. The gloaming had brushed the town with varying shades of gray. In the distance, she heard laughter and voices talking. Perhaps people on their way home from supper in one of the restaurants. Perhaps businessmen who had worked late into the evening.

Father, open Gavin's heart to love. He needs your love. He needs the love of Brina and Pet. And he needs a woman's love too.

She pictured Emily Harris. Beautiful, fair, intelligent. Something told Dru that Emily had a great capacity for love — both to give and to receive.

If it be your will, Lord. If it be your will.

"You can't mean to go through with this."

Emily turned from her packing to face her sister. "I do mean to go through with it."

"But you don't know these people. They're strangers to us."

"Mrs. Blake is an acquaintance of Reverend Cook. He can vouch for the family."

"You'll be so far away. It will be harder to reach you in Challis than it was in Washington. Especially during the winter months. What if you get injured or fall ill? What if —"

"Maggie, I'm not six anymore. I don't need you to mother me." She sighed, recognizing how harsh her words must sound. "I'm sorry. I know you only want what's best. But my heart tells me to do this. I can't explain why. I just believe it's true."

"I shall do nothing but worry about you. This won't be the same as living and working in Washington. You were with your friend and her family. You enjoyed every comfort. You're too young to —"

"You weren't even eighteen when we came west. You didn't know anyone on the wagon train. You had to trust Mrs. Foster when she said we could travel with them. You didn't know where we were going. Not really. You just did what you believed was for the best."

Maggie's face registered defeat. "But I don't *want* you to go."

In unison, they moved forward to embrace each other.

"I know," Emily whispered. "I'll miss you too. Honest, I will. And Tucker and the children and Fiona and my other friends. I'll miss you all. But it's only until May or June. That isn't so very long. And I'll write. Mrs. Blake told me the post goes up to Challis every week, even in winter."

Maggie sniffed as she pulled back. "I don't understand why you feel the need to do this."

"I'll be all right."

Her sister was silent for a long while. Finally, she leaned forward and kissed Emily's forehead. "Then God go with you, kitten."

Tears sprang to Emily's eyes. It had been

a long time since her sister called her by her pet name. It brought back a rush of memories, all of them filled with Maggie's image.

"We'll take you into town in the morning," Maggie said, tears glittering in her eyes too. "But I still think you're making a mistake."

THREE

Tightly held emotions burned the back of Emily's throat as she looked at the gathering of family and friends waiting outside the Overland. Maggie must have sent messages with several of the Branigan ranch hands to all of Emily's friends yesterday afternoon, telling them that she was leaving in the morning.

Each one of her well-wishers hugged and kissed her in turn. She managed not to cry until almost the end. The trouble began when her best friend, Fiona Whittier — Tucker's younger sister — embraced her. Fiona was entering her ninth month of pregnancy, and her belly was so large the two young women found it hard to draw each other close. They laughed about it, even as their tears fell.

"I thought you would be here when the baby was born," Fiona said as she dried her eyes with a handkerchief. "I *wanted* you here."

"I wanted it too, but spring will be here before you know it. The baby won't be so very grown by then."

"You'll write to me?"

"Of course," Emily answered. "Just like I did while I was away at school."

"Be sure that you do."

Emily turned toward her sister, and a small sob escaped her throat.

Maggie took hold of her by the shoulders. "I'll pray for you every day, Emily. We all will."

"I know. Thank you. Please don't worry about me."

Emily had her tears under control by the time Gavin Blake brought his wagon around from the livery and halted the team in front of the hotel. He hopped down from the seat and his gaze swept the large gathering until he found her.

She swallowed the lump in her throat. "Good morning, Mr. Blake."

He stepped onto the sidewalk and touched the brim of his battered hat. "Morning, Miss Harris." His eyes flicked once more over the group of friends and family, then returned to her. "Where are your bags?"

Stepping forward, Tucker said, "I've got her trunk in my carriage." He held out his hand toward Gavin. "I'm Judge Branigan, Emily's brother-in-law."

"Gavin Blake." His hand clasped Tucker's.

Emily had the feeling there was some sort of testing going on between the two men as they stared into each other's eyes. She held her breath until Tucker's expression relaxed.

"We can't say we're glad to have Emily leaving us this way," her brother-in-law said.

Gavin nodded. "She won't come to any harm while staying with us."

"We're counting on that. Kevin?" Tucker turned toward his oldest son. "Get one of the twins to help you bring Emily's trunk over to the wagon."

"Sure, Dad."

"Put it in the back of the wagon there. I'll get my wife." Gavin turned on his boot heel and disappeared through the hotel doors.

Frowning, Maggie placed her hand on Emily's shoulder. "You can still change your mind and come home with us."

Emily shook her head. "No. I'm going with the Blakes." Despite the nerves churning in her stomach, she meant it. She was going. She wouldn't be dissuaded. Not by her sister, nor by Mr. Blake's cool reception.

Moments later, Gavin and Dru came out of the hotel. Dru's smile was warm, very different from her husband's stern expression. "Good morning, Miss Harris. Is this your family?"

"Most of them."

Gavin moved his wife closer to the wagon. "We've got a long trip ahead of us. We'd best go." With that, he lifted her onto the wagon seat.

Emily turned toward Maggie, her heart thundering in her chest. "I'll write you every week, but don't be alarmed if you don't hear from me right away. They told me the summer range is quite remote."

"I'll write you too. And I'll worry when I don't hear from you, no matter what you tell me."

Another flurry of good-byes erupted. As she was engulfed in a final round of embraces, Emily sensed Gavin Blake's mounting tension.

"Miss Harris, we need to be on our way." His words were tinged with impatience.

Emily kissed Maggie's cheek one last time, then turned. "I'm ready, sir."

He met her at the back of the wagon, put his hands around her waist, and lifted her effortlessly into the wagon bed. Besides Emily, it held two trunks — hers and another smaller one — a tick mattress, and numerous blankets.

"Make yourself comfortable, Miss Harris. It'll be a while before we stop."

She sat on the larger trunk, twisting so she could look at Maggie and Tucker again.

Gavin took his place next to his wife. "Do you need anything before we leave?" he asked softly.

"I'm fine, Gavin. Let's go home."

With the rattle of harness and braces, the wagon jerked forward. Emily stared at her loved ones until the wagon turned a corner and they were hidden from view.

They didn't stop to rest until it was time for their midday meal. When they resumed their journey, Dru joined Emily in the back of the wagon.

"Tell me more about your time in the East," she said. "Why did you stay there so long when all your family is here?"

"After I graduated, I went home with a friend to visit her parents in Washington. Her father, Professor Abraham, saw how interested I was in his historical research, and he asked if I would stay and assist him in his work. I was thrilled by his offer, especially because he seemed to value my opinions and ideas. He didn't put me off just because I'm a woman, the way some men do."

"It sounds like you were happy there."

"I was."

"So why didn't you go back to Washington after your sister was restored to health?"

Emily shrugged. "I'm not sure why. For some reason, it never seemed right to go back. I guess I missed living in Idaho more than I realized."

"Perhaps there's a young man in Boise?" Dru smiled at her. "Someone you hope to marry one day?"

"No, there's no one."

Dru lifted an eyebrow. "You don't want a family of your own?"

"Someday, perhaps. But not yet."

"Then I guess it is safe to assume that you've never been in love."

She thought about Maggie and Tucker, of the way they seemed to be two parts of one whole. She thought of their tender glances, of the way they touched each other — a brief brushing of hair from the other's forehead, a light caress of the cheek — of the smiles they exchanged that said they shared a secret, of the sweet words of endearment they whispered.

She also thought of Fiona and her husband, James. Still in the first blush of newlywed joy, Fiona thought the sun rose and set with James Whittier. Fiona's face almost glowed when she spoke of her husband, and James was solicitous whenever he was with his wife, even more so now that she was expecting their child.

No, Emily had never been in love, but from these examples and others, she had a good idea what it would look, sound, and feel like when it happened.

"Am I right, Miss Harris?"

"Yes, you're right."

Dru leaned back on the makeshift bed and closed her eyes. "Someday you'll meet the right man, and love will take you by surprise . . . as it so often does."

On the first evening they were on the trail, after they'd eaten their supper and the women retired for the night, Gavin sat beside the dying embers of the campfire, a worn piece of harness in his hands. He would have to repair it before long. If the cattle prices were good come spring, maybe —

"Mr. Blake?"

He glanced up, surprised that he hadn't heard Emily's approach.

"May I speak with you a moment?"

He motioned to the stool on the opposite side of the fire. As she settled onto it, he couldn't help noticing that she looked lovely, despite the long, dusty day. Such a contrast to Dru's wan appearance when she'd retired.

"Is there some reason you disapprove of me?" she asked, her gaze lifting to meet his.

"Dru chose you, Miss Harris. That's good enough for me."

"That isn't an answer."

He supposed she deserved the truth. "I don't think you're cut out for the place we're going."

"Why is that?"

"You're not headed for another city like Washington, D.C., or even one like Boise. Our nearest neighbors in the basin are more than likely a small band of Sheepeater Indians or some of their kin. There won't be any tea parties to be shared with other womenfolk or dances to go to on Saturday nights, all decked out in a pretty dress. Winters are hard and long." He lowered his gaze to the harness in his hands, then set it on the ground beside his feet. "I built the cabin at our summer range with my own two hands, and the house at the main ranch isn't much different from it. There's no money for luxuries, that's for certain."

"I can do this job, Mr. Blake, and I don't need luxuries."

He leaned forward and took hold of her

right hand, turning it palm up. "Look at your hand. You haven't done a real day's work in your life. You may have been raised on a ranch, but it's a gentleman's ranch. That brother-in-law of yours hires all the help he needs to run it. Right? You've never had to —"

She pulled away from him. "That's not so. My family worked hard for everything we have. Like you, Tucker built our first house himself. I remember what it was like when we left the wagon train and settled in Boise. We worked from sun up to sun down. In some ways, it was even harder than being on the trail." She stood. "Maybe Tucker does have others managing his ranch now, but he's earned it. And maybe because of his success I haven't faced much hardship, but I can do everything I was hired to do. I can take care of your wife and daughters."

"I guess we'll soon find out, won't we?"

"Yes, I guess we will." She turned away. "Goodnight, Mr. Blake."

"Goodnight, Miss Harris."

When she was gone, Gavin returned his gaze to the dying embers. She wouldn't last. She would wilt like a rose without water. Just see if she didn't.

The days on the trail were long and exhausting. Yet Emily felt a growing sense of adventure as Dru shared more about their summer range in the Stanley Basin. Still, despite the other woman's glowing reports about the place she loved, Emily wasn't prepared for the breathtaking panorama that met her gaze late in the afternoon a week after they left Boise.

In the valley, a carpet of green grasses waved like the sea while late summer wildflowers bobbed their colorful heads. Sage and pine scented the breeze. Winding its way across the valley floor flowed a ribbon of water, and beyond it pine trees climbed the mountainsides as far as possible, then admitted defeat before reaching the rocky peaks of the Sawtooths.

"Is that snow?" she asked, eyeing the splotches of white on the high crags.

"Glaciers," Gavin replied. "They're there year-round."

"Can we see your house from here?"

Dru shook her head. "Not yet. The basin's northwest of here. We'll be there tomorrow."

Gavin hopped from the wagon seat and walked across the narrow dirt road. His brows drew together as his gaze swept the nearby wooded area. Moments later, he returned to the wagon and pulled a long, heavy-looking chain from beneath the seat.

Emily watched as he carried the chain over to a fallen tree, dropped it on the ground, rolled up his sleeves, then bent over to slip the heavy links beneath the log. His muscles bulged as he leaned forward, pulling on the chain.

"What is he doing?" she asked Dru.

"It's to help check our speed. Gavin fastens one end of the chain around a large log and the other to the undercarriage. The log helps create drag on the steep grade so the wagon won't get away from the horses."

Twenty minutes later, they started down the mountainside. Behind them, the dead tree carved a groove in the earth. It soon became apparent to Emily why Gavin had taken this precaution. Even with it, the horses leaned back over their hind legs, straining against the weight of the wagon pushing against them. The narrow track — too primitive to be called a road — wound back and forth across the side of the mountain but still the descent seemed too swift. The drop to the valley floor was frightening. What if the animals bolted? They would all plunge to their deaths.

"Easy there," Gavin murmured to the horses. "Easy now."

Emily looked up at him from her spot in the wagon bed. He was leaning back on the seat, his boots braced against the footboard, the reins woven through his fingers. Sweat stained the back of his shirt along his spine.

"That's it. Easy now. Take it slow. That's it."

His words might have been meant to calm only the horses, but they served to calm Emily as well. It surprised her to find that, despite his obnoxious attitude toward her, he made her feel safe.

FOUR

Patches of brown and white dotted the landscape across a wide sweep of meadowland where cattle grazed along the banks of the river, the lush grasses tickling their bellies.

"We're home," Dru whispered.

Emily rose to her knees and leaned over the side to see what was ahead. As she did so, she saw a horse and rider break away from the cattle and canter toward them. Gavin drew back on the reins, stopping the team, and waited for the cowboy to arrive.

"It's good to see you folks. Your girls ain't stopped asking when you'd be back since the day you left."

"There's nothing wrong, is there, Stubs?" Dru's voice was anxious.

The cowboy's grizzled face broke into a grin. "No, ma'am. Nothin' that their ma being home won't cure."

"Where are they now?"

"Jess and Brina are whipping up some grub for supper. I imagine Pet's trying to help. Better get up there so they can throw in a bit more." Stubs removed his hat and drew his arm across his forehead, glancing toward Emily as he did so. "Got your teacher, I see."

Gavin looked over his shoulder. "Miss Harris, this is Stubs Martin. He's the foreman for the Lucky Strike Ranch."

"How do you do, Mr. Martin." Emily stood, her hand on the back of the wagon seat for balance. "It's a pleasure to meet you."

"Well, doggies, if you ain't a pretty little thing. You just call me Stubs and we'll get on fine." He winked at her. "Yes, sir. She's a right pretty little thing."

Emily felt the warm blush spreading up from her neck. She'd received fancier compliments in her life, but this one, coming in front of her employer, seemed too much by half. The last thing she wanted was for Gavin Blake to think she was just a pretty face and nothing more. He already expected her to fail.

"You'd better sit down, Miss Harris." Gavin slapped the reins against the horses' rumps, and the wagon jerked forward, nearly toppling Emily.

He'd done it on purpose. The rude, ill-mannered man.

Stubs fell in beside them. "We got all the cattle in. Lost only a handful over the summer. A couple to wolves, looked like, the rest more'n likely to Indians. They should bring a good price, fat as they are. How soon'll you be ready to drive 'em out? It's getting a mite late in the season. First snows could fall any time now."

"Dru wants to stay in the basin for a few more weeks, but you'd better start the drive tomorrow or the next day. The buyers will be expecting us."

"You think you oughta —" Stubs began.

Two shrill cries interrupted his question. "Ma! Ma!"

Once again, Emily got to her knees and leaned over for a better view, and once again, Gavin stopped the wagon.

"Ma!"

Dark brown hair streamed out behind the girls as they ran. The older one was tall and slender. The younger was plump and rosy. Both wore big grins.

Gavin hopped down from the wagon seat, then lifted his wife to the ground. Dru turned just in time to receive the two girls into her arms.

"Ma, you're back! You were gone so long."

"I know, Brina. It seemed like forever to me too."

Sabrina had her mother's hazel eyes as well as the same long, narrow face. Her complexion was fair except for the spattering of freckles across her nose and cheeks. Her dress barely covered her knees. She would soon be grown clear out of it.

"Ma." Petula tugged on her mother's sleeve. "Look." She opened her mouth, pointing into it.

The younger girl's eyes were a dark chocolate brown and were capped by chestnut brows. Her complexion was dark, her mouth wide and full. Emily saw little resemblance to either Gavin or Dru in the child.

"My goodness, Pet. Where did your tooth go?" Her mother feigned amazement.

"It came loose when I was ridin' this morning." The girl's eyes widened. "I swallowed it."

"Well then, you probably won't be hungry for supper, will you?" Gavin swooped Petula into his arms.

The girl promptly threw her arms around his neck and gave him a kiss on the cheek. "Will too. Mr. Chamberlain's fixing pie for dessert, and I helped."

With his other arm, Gavin lifted Sabrina against his side. "What about you? Stubs tells me you're doing the cooking."

Sabrina mimicked her sister's actions by hugging his neck and kissing his cheek. As she pulled back, she nodded. "I made the stew."

What an amazing smile he gave the children. Emily would have sworn he was incapable of such a joyous expression. She certainly hadn't seen its like from him before. Although he'd been tender and solicitous with his wife throughout the journey home, the most frequent look on his face had been frowns and scowls. She'd come to think him a dour sort.

He must love them very much.

Dru touched Emily's hand on the side of the wagon. "Come meet my daughters."

"Yes, of course." She jumped to the ground. *Oh, please let them like me,* she prayed.

"Brina . . . Pet . . ." Dru waited while Gavin set the girls on their feet. "Come say hello to Miss Harris."

Holding hands, they came forward to stand next to their mother. Two sets of eyes stared up at Emily, curious and skeptical at the same time.

Her throat felt dry. "Hello, Sabrina. Hello, Petula."

They didn't say a word.

"I'm glad to meet you at last. Your mother's told me so much about you."

Still no response.

Emily swallowed hard. Her stomach churned. If the children took a dislike to her as quickly as their father had, she wouldn't stand a chance.

Petula turned and tugged on her mother's skirt, then motioned for Dru to lean closer. "I like her hair," she whispered. "Don't you, Ma?"

"Yes, Pet, I do."

The baying of hounds interrupted the introductions. Emily turned to see three huge brown and gray dogs barreling toward them. The first two slid to a halt at Gavin's feet. The third didn't stop until he'd risen on hind legs and thrust muddy paws against Emily's shoulders.

Thrown off balance, she flailed the air with her arms. But it was a lost cause — the dog gave her another push and she dropped like a rock onto her backside, hitting the ground with a hard *thump.* Before she could close her mouth, the dog's long tongue smacked her across the face. She sputtered, closing her eyes and raising her arm to ward off the beast, hoping all the while he wouldn't decide she was tasty enough for a bite.

She heard the children's laughter.

"Get back, Joker," Gavin said. "That's no way to greet a lady."

Emily opened her eyes as he dragged the overzealous wolfhound away by the scruff of his neck. Obviously Gavin Blake didn't share his daughters' amusement. His gaze was hard and unflinching as he offered his hand.

She accepted reluctantly. "He's your dog, no doubt."

"Joker's still a pup." He pulled her to her feet. "He hasn't learned any manners yet."

"A *pup?*" She turned to stare at the dog — large square head, thick wiry coat, muddy paws. "He's almost as big as a horse." She brushed at the dirty prints on her bodice.

"Duke. Duchess. Come." In response to Gavin's quiet command, the other two dogs sprang to their feet and trotted over. Without a word from their master, they sat next to him. "Miss Harris, meet Joker's parents, Duke and Duchess."

The larger of the two dogs lifted his right paw. Large black eyes perused her. She almost believed the canine understood what his master had said.

"He's pleased to meet you, Miss Harris." Gavin motioned toward Duke. "Go on.

Shake his hand."

Was he hoping to humiliate her further? Couldn't he see she was already wearing enough mud? She was about to refuse, but then she saw Sabrina and Petula watching her, waiting to see what she would do. This was a test she didn't want to fail.

Tugging on her bodice, she straightened her dress, then bent forward and took hold of Duke's paw. "How do you do, your grace." She moved the dog's leg up and down three times, then let go as her gaze moved to the female wolfhound. She held her skirts and executed a perfect curtsey. "It's a pleasure to meet you, Duchess." Her voice dropped to a stage whisper. "But, my lady, that son of yours is a disgrace. You must take him in hand at once or there'll be no redeeming him. He'll prove himself a fool at court."

The girls burst into laughter once again and hurried forward to throw their arms around the dogs. Joker pushed his way into the happy group, his tongue lapping everyone in reach. A warm thrill surged through Emily as she watched them. The girls were going to like her, even if their father didn't.

Her gaze met Gavin's as she straightened. Was that grudging approval she saw in his eyes? She hoped so. She was determined to change his opinion of her before she returned to Boise in the spring. She would make him admit that she was well suited for the work he'd hired her to do. So help her she would, even if it killed her.

"Come along, girls," Dru said. "Let's show Miss Harris to her room."

Petula came to stand beside Emily, without a word slipping her small, sweaty hand into Emily's and pulling her toward the house.

Emily Harris had spunk. Gavin had to give her that. She could have burst into tears or railed at the dog for ruining her dress. Instead, she'd been a good sport and had even played along when he introduced her to the dogs. Maybe it wouldn't be so awful having her here. Maybe she wouldn't wilt as fast as he'd thought. Maybe she wasn't completely spoiled and self-centered.

"Something botherin' you, Gavin?"

He didn't look at Stubs as he shook his head.

"Is it Dru? Is she feeling bad again?"

"No. You wouldn't even know she's sick except she doesn't eat enough to keep a bird alive."

"She seems to like Miss Harris, and Miss Harris seems taken with the girls. That's what Dru was wantin'."

Gavin didn't reply.

"Mighty pretty to look at too. Matter of fact, she kinda reminds me of your —"

"Don't." Gavin glared a warning at his foreman.

Stubs Martin had worked as a hired hand on the Blake farm back in Ohio when Gavin was a boy. Fate had brought them together again years later, and they'd been good friends ever since. But every friendship had boundaries, and Stubs had just about crossed the line.

"Sorry, boss. I won't mention it again."

With a grunt, Gavin climbed into the wagon and drove the team toward the barn.

FIVE

Emily pressed her face against the pillow and tried to recapture her dream. She was at a masked ball. Couples in dazzling costumes twirled around a mirrored ballroom, the women's gowns sweeping out in wide arcs in time to the music. She danced in the arms of a tall stranger, his face hidden behind a black mask. Eyes like steel stared at her through narrow slits. He held her close, so close his breath seemed to be hers.

The fingers of her left hand tightened on his shoulder, and he whimpered.

Whimpered?

She opened her eyes and found herself staring into Joker's fuzzy face, his shiny black nose mere inches from hers. The dog was beside her in the bed, crowding her to the edge of the mattress. Before she could move, the wolfhound slapped her with another of his affectionate licks. She lifted her hand to ward him off — and promptly fell to the floor.

"We're going to come to terms, dog." She stood, hands on hips. "Now get off my bed."

His tail slapped the heavy patchwork quilt.

"I said, get off." She pointed at the floor.

Joker stepped down from the bed and flopped at her feet, rolling onto his back to expose his belly.

"Oh, no. You'll get no reward from me. How did you get in here anyway? Don't you belong outside, protecting us from wolves or something?"

He whimpered again.

Emily moved toward the door of her bedroom and eased it open. The main room was empty. "Get out," she whispered. Tail between his legs and head slung low — she almost felt sorry for him — Joker obeyed. Sounds from elsewhere in the house met her ears a second before the door snapped closed.

She glanced at the bed with longing. Oh, for another hour of slumber. But there would be no return to sleep now, not with the household stirring. She didn't want them to think her a lazybones.

Emily walked to her trunk and pulled out clean undergarments. She'd hung her dresses the night before on wooden pegs pounded into the log walls of her room.

Now she chose one of her favorite day dresses and laid it on the bed. The sky-blue gown had a simple bodice, pointed front and back, and an overskirt that was draped back to form short side panniers with fullness behind.

After removing her long-sleeved nightgown, she completed her morning ablutions with haste. A chill in the morning air didn't invite her to linger.

She fastened the last button of her bodice and settled onto the edge of the bed, reaching for the hairbrush on the bedside table. The brush had belonged to her mother. Maggie had kept it hidden when their uncle was selling off everything of value from their New York home, and she had brought it with them when they came west on the wagon train. It had been Maggie's gift to Emily on her eighteenth birthday. Fingering the intricate design on the silver brush, she wondered if her parents could see her from heaven. Would they be proud of the woman she'd become?

Tears pricked her eyes. How she wished she could remember her mother and father. But she'd been so young — only a year old — when they died. What memories she had of them belonged to Maggie first. They'd become hers as her sister told her the stories, over and over again through the years. When their uncle had one of his cruel moods, they used to hide from his wrath, and Maggie would tell her stories of their parents, of their mother's beautiful hair, of their father's great laugh, of how very much they'd loved Maggie and Emily.

Her thoughts turned to Dru. She wasn't well, but at least she was here with her daughters. Sabrina and Petula wouldn't have to take another person's word about the love their mother felt for them. They would know it firsthand. Fortunate girls.

On the heels of that thought came shame. How awful to feel envious. Maggie had raised her, loved her, protected her. Emily couldn't have asked for more. She gave her head a shake, chasing away her thoughts. She had too much to do to spend her time woolgathering in her bedroom.

With practiced movements, she brushed her hair, caught it back from her face with a pair of ivory combs. A quick glance in the small hand mirror she'd brought from home told her she was presentable.

She finished tidying her room, then found Dru in the kitchen, standing over a black iron stove.

"Good morning, Miss Harris. Would you like some coffee? It's hot."

"Yes. Thank you. I would like some."

Dru plucked a tin cup from a shelf above the stove and filled it with the dark brew. She carried it to the rough-hewn table, then settled onto the bench opposite Emily. "It's good to be home. This cabin isn't much, but it's got wood floors and keeps out the wind and rain. Charlie wanted us to have as good a house here as at the main ranch, but he said this would do until he and Gavin could build it."

"Who's Charlie?"

The woman stared at her hands, folded atop the table. "Charlie was my husband. He died two years ago, up in Challis." She stared toward the fireplace at the far end of the main room, and Emily saw the quickly hidden expression of grief that crossed her face. "Pet looks a lot like him. Everyone says so."

"But I thought . . . Gavin isn't her father?"

"No." She returned her gaze to Emily. "When Gavin and I married, he adopted my daughters."

If Emily hadn't seen Gavin and Dru together, if she hadn't heard them talking, seen the tender way he treated her and the affection in her eyes when she looked at him, she might have thought Dru was still in love with Charlie . . .

Before she could sort things out in her mind, the girls climbed down the ladder from their room in the loft.

"Where's Pa?" Sabrina asked as her feet touched the floor.

"He rode out with Stubs at daybreak."

Sabrina's face fell. "I wanted to show him the calf I found. I helped Jess rope him."

"Well, you can show him later. He'll be back for breakfast."

Dru rose from the table as her daughters approached. She gave them each a hug, kissed both their cheeks, then reached for a bucket hanging on a hook. "Say good morning to Miss Harris."

"Morning," the girls said in unison.

"Here's the bucket. You two gather the eggs, and I'll fry the bacon. Hurry now."

"Is there anything I can do to help?" Emily asked as the door closed behind them.

"Just talk with me. It's been a long time since I've had another woman to visit with the way we've been doing this past week."

"Aren't there any other women in the area?"

"A few up in Sawtooth City. The sort who follow the miners from gold rush to gold rush, if you understand my meaning. But we're the only ranchers who summer our cattle here."

"Why only for the summer?"

"Winters are too harsh. There are four mountain ranges that circle this valley, and they hold the cold in. We'd lose too many of the herd if we stayed." She shook her head. "Not that we don't have hard winters at the Lucky Strike. I don't want you thinking that. But it's much worse here."

"Why come at all, then? From what you've told me of the Lucky Strike, it sounds like you would do well enough there."

Dru tossed a few pieces of wood inside the stove, then pulled a heavy frying pan from its hook on the wall. "I suppose the real reason is because I fell in love with this place the first time I saw it. I had a yearning to live here. So Charlie, Gavin, and Stubs came in that first spring and built this cabin, and then we trailed in our herd. The cattle thrived that summer, and they brought a good price when we sold them to feed the miners in Bonanza and Custer."

Dru worked as she talked, putting butter into the skillet, then adding sliced potatoes and onions. The room soon filled with delicious odors, and Emily's stomach began to growl.

Not long after, the door opened, and the girls spilled inside, followed by Gavin, Stubs, and Jess Chamberlain. Sabrina carried the bucket of eggs to her mother as the two ranch hands sat down at the table.

Gavin crossed to the stove and placed his hand on Dru's shoulder. "How are you feeling?"

"Much better this morning." She smiled at him. "I always feel better when we're here."

Gavin's fingers squeezed her shoulder before he turned and reached for the dishes on the shelf to the right of the stove. Before he could ask for help, Sabrina and Petula joined him, and he handed the plates to the two girls.

Emily felt uncomfortable, sitting idle while Dru cracked the eggs over another hot skillet and her daughters set the table. She knew what Gavin must think of her. She wanted to explain that she'd asked if she could help and had been turned down, but she feared doing so would only make her look worse in his eyes.

Thankfully it wasn't long before everyone was seated around the big table, their heads bowed as Dru blessed the food. "And thank you, Father, for bringing Miss Harris to stay with us. We ask you to bless her work and make her feel at home with our family. Amen."

Emily's heart plummeted in response to

the prayer. What if she failed as a teacher and governess? What if Gavin Blake was right about her?

As if reading her mind, Dru addressed her from across the table. "After the men are out from underfoot, I'll show you the school primers I bought for the girls. Brina reads well and is very good with her numbers, but Pet's only started to learn her ABCs."

"I'd like to see the primers." Emily glanced at the girls. "I brought some books with me too. Some of them were my nieces' favorites when they were your age."

Dru said, "That's wonderful. Isn't it, girls?"

Sabrina and Petula nodded.

Emily returned her gaze to Dru. "Shall I give them their first lessons today?"

"I think we should wait a day or two. After the boys leave with the herd will be soon enough. In the meantime, you and the girls can get better acquainted."

Conversation died as everyone turned their attention to breakfast. As she ate, Emily surreptitiously studied the others at the table.

Jess Chamberlain looked to be about her age. Long and lanky, he was what people called a beanpole. He never looked up from his plate. Unless she missed her guess, Jess was shy around females.

Stubs Martin, on the other hand, had winked at her twice since sitting down at the table. Though not a tall man, he was built like a rock. She supposed he was close to fifty but knew his grizzled jaw and graying hair might make him look older than he was.

Next, her glance fell on Gavin. He was handsome enough, she supposed, although not as good-looking as many of her past suitors. But when he smiled and laughed with the girls, she found herself thinking he was the most handsome of all.

Too bad all she ever garnered was his frown.

Watching the family interaction, though, she wondered — why had Gavin married Dru so soon after the death of his friend? Had he been in love with her even before Charlie died? And if Gavin was as surly with others as he'd been with Emily, she was surprised that Dru agreed to marry him at all.

She lowered her gaze to her plate, silently scolding herself. She was here to teach and look after the children, not to speculate on their parents' marriage. Gossip was an ugly pastime, even in one's own mind.

Gavin's chair scraped against the floor as

he pushed away from the table and stood. A split second later, Stubs and Jess rose too.

"Pa?" Sabrina said as he turned from the table, plate and utensils in hand.

He stopped and looked at the girl.

"Did you see my calf? I helped Jess rope him."

"You roped a calf?"

"Yes, sir," Jess said. "She done all right. I reckon she'll be ridin' with us regular in another year or two."

"He's in the barn, Pa. Will you come see him?"

Gavin carried his dirty dishes to the washbasin. "I guess I can take the time for that." He grabbed his hat from a peg near the door. "Let's go."

Sabrina, her father, and the other men went outside, trailed by Petula who stopped at the door and asked, "Are you coming, Ma?"

"Not right now, Pet. I need to do the dishes first. But why don't you take Miss Harris? I'm sure she'd love to see Brina's calf."

"Shouldn't I stay and help you?"

"No." Dru shook her head. "I think you should go with the children."

Petula smiled, showing her missing tooth, as she returned to the table and held out her hand to Emily. "There's kittens in the barn too, but we don't want Duke and Duchess to know."

"I should think not." She took hold of Petula's hand and allowed herself to be led from the house.

The barn was warm and filled with earthy scents — hay and straw, dung and sweat. Sunlight streamed through the open hay door in the loft, creating a swirl of light below.

"Over here," Sabrina called.

They moved toward the stall where Gavin and Sabrina stood. Inside was a reddish-brown calf with a white-blazed face and enormous brown eyes. It was lying down, its legs curled underneath its body.

"He's an orphan." Sabrina's gaze shifted to Gavin. "He won't have to be sold yet, will he?"

Her father shook his head. "He's a bit young."

"May I . . . may I keep him, Pa?"

Gavin knelt in the straw, one hand on Sabrina's shoulder. "Cows aren't pets, Brina. We raise them to sell. You know that."

Emily heard the tenderness in his words. He loved this child. There was no mistaking it. Sabrina and Petula might not be his by blood, but they were certainly his by heart.

"But if you'll promise to take good care of him through the winter, see that he's fed and kept clean and stays healthy, whatever money he brings when he does go to market will be yours."

Emily half-expected the girl to burst into tears, but she didn't. "I'll take real good care of him. I promise. And I'll share the money with Pet."

Gavin patted her shoulder as he stood. "That's a good plan, Brina. Sharing's always a good thing."

He seemed a different man from the one who had escorted Emily from the hotel a week earlier. Less gruff. Less disagreeable. More prone to smile.

Petula tugged on her hand. "Now come see what I got."

Emily was pulled across the barn to a ladder that led to the loft. She looked at it with misgiving. She was terrified of heights. Had been since she was a child. Could she climb to the loft without falling?

Petula obviously didn't share her fear. She scampered up the ladder like a monkey up a tree. No hesitation. No doubt.

"You don't have to go up, Miss Harris," Gavin said. "You'd probably get your dress dirty."

Ah, there was the Gavin she knew. She

heard the challenge in his voice, knew he still thought his wife had made a mistake in her choice of governess. It was unfair of him and it made her angry.

"My dress will wash, Mr. Blake." She grasped a rung on the ladder. "It certainly won't keep me from seeing whatever it is Pet wants to show me."

She began to climb. *Don't look down. Don't look down.* As soon as she reached the loft, she whispered a prayer of thanks to God for her safe ascent.

"Over here. Come look."

She joined Petula in the corner near the hay door. There, nearly hidden in a nest of straw, a gray-striped cat bathed a kitten with her tongue while three more nursed at her belly.

"That's Countess," Petula said, pointing to the cat. "Ma thought up her name. Says it's next best to Duchess."

Emily leaned forward for a better look. "Duke, Duchess, Countess. Such fancy names for all your pets."

"Dru's always wanted to visit England."

She looked behind her to see Gavin standing on the ladder, his head and shoulders above the loft floor.

"She's got a fascination for royalty," he finished.

Petula asked, "Would you like to hold one, Miss Harris?"

Emily took the proffered kitten into one hand, cupping her other hand over it as she brought it close and brushed its fur against her cheek. "Perhaps you and Dru will get to go one day. My sister and her husband visited England and the Continent a number of years ago and had a wonderful time." She turned toward him again. "It was the honeymoon they never had."

One look at Gavin told her she'd said the wrong thing. His eyes grew cool and his expression hardened like flint.

"Brina —" he started down the ladder — "you and your sister get inside and help your ma with the dishes. Right now. We've dawdled enough for one morning."

Six

"You weren't employed to be a laundress, Miss Harris."

Emily looked up from the clothing she was sorting and gave Dru a smile. "No, but I was employed to help care for you until you're well again. You're still tired from the trip back from Boise. I can see it in your face so don't bother to deny it."

Following Dru's instructions, Emily put the heavier and dirtier things to soak in lye. Afterward, she dropped them into the copper kettle to boil. The more delicate articles were given to Dru, at her insistence, to wash in a tub of lukewarm water.

Steam filled the kitchen, leaving Emily's face beaded with perspiration. Wisps of hair — all of it that wasn't hidden beneath a scarf — curled across her forehead and nape, sticking to her skin. Bent over the washtub, she scrubbed the clothes and linens on the fluted washboard. It wasn't long before the muscles across the back of her neck and shoulders complained, but she gritted her teeth and kept at it. As each article was completed, she dropped it into a barrel-shaped tub to await rinsing. The girls were kept busy hauling clean water into the house and dirty water out.

"Here, Miss Harris." Dru came around the washtub. "Let me take over while you get those things rinsed and hung out to dry. It would be a shame to waste the sunshine. Days are short now that autumn's here."

Short? This day felt like an eternity, and it wasn't yet noon. Perhaps Gavin Blake had been right about her. She might not have what it took to live on a ranch like this one. Her brother-in-law's good fortune had given her a life of privilege, and she'd grown soft because of it. Over time, those early years after they'd settled in Idaho had become romanticized in her mind.

Wringing water from the clean laundry took longer than she'd imagined it would. By the time she had her first basket filled with clothes, her hands hurt, the skin raw and chapped. Gavin couldn't call them lily-white today.

As she carried the basket toward the door, she paused to whisper in Sabrina's ear.

"Help your mother. She is tired and should rest."

The girl nodded, and Emily continued outside.

The Stanley Basin was blessed that day with the warm breath of Indian summer. A gentle breeze stirred the trees and grass, bringing with it the sweet scent of pine. Aspens applauded with leaves turned gold by cooling nights.

Emily paused for a moment to take in the beauty that surrounded her, and familiar words bubbled up from her heart, demanding to be spoken aloud. "I will lift up mine eyes unto the hills, from whence cometh my help. My help cometh from the Lord, which made heaven and earth. He will not suffer thy foot to be moved: he that keepeth thee will not slumber."

She smiled. How good to know that God watched over her, even in this remote valley. How good to know he didn't slumber, even in the darkest hours of night.

Drawing a deep breath, she moved toward the clothesline that was stretched between two trees and supported in the middle with a wooden prop. She set the basket on the ground, then placed her hands on the small of her spine and bent backward. When she straightened, she found Gavin leaning against the corner of the cabin, watching her.

"Not as much fun as a fancy dress ball, is it?" He pushed off from the house and walked toward her.

She turned away and grabbed the shirt on top of the basket of clothes. "I told you before that I'm not afraid of hard work."

"I can see that."

His tone caused her to look at him again. Was that an apology of sorts? She couldn't be sure. And what did it matter, even if it was?

Only it *did* matter. She wanted him to think better of her.

She gave the shirt in her hands a good shake, wanting to slough off thoughts of Gavin Blake at the same time, then held it against the clothesline and slipped the split wood pin over one sleeve. As she reached to fasten the other sleeve in place, the pin dropped into the thick grass at her feet.

Without a word, he leaned down, picked up the clothespin, and held it out to her.

"Thank you." She closed her fingers around it, feeling suddenly clumsy beneath his gaze.

He didn't release the clothespin immediately, and after a moment she was forced to look at him a third time. His hard, searching gaze made her feel like a bug under a microscope. How she wished he would go study someone else for a while and leave her in peace.

"Thank you," she said again.

He let go at last. "You're welcome, Miss Harris. And just so you'll know, I'm grateful for the help you're giving Dru." With a tip of his head, he turned and walked away.

It took several seconds more before Emily could breathe easily again.

Twilight had settled over the basin, bringing with it a bank of clouds in the west.

"Looks like we're in for some rain." Gavin turned from the window. "You girls better get your animals in the barn fed."

"Okay, Pa." Sabrina set aside the square of embroidery fabric. "Come on, Pet."

"Put on your jackets," Dru said before the girls reached the door.

Gavin sat on a chair near the fireplace. "Where's Miss Harris?"

"Lying down. She's exhausted after all she did today." Dru leveled a reproachful gaze on him. "It's your fault, you know. She's trying to prove she can do *everything* because you don't think she can do *anything*."

"Wait a minute. I never said —"

"Don't argue with me. You know it's true.

I didn't hire her to clean house or wash clothes. I want her to teach the children, to get them to trust and care for her so that when I . . . when I'm not here, they'll have a woman they can turn to. They'll need her. More than you know."

His jaw tightened. Despite his words of thanks today, he didn't think Emily Harris would last a month, let alone stay around after Dru passed on.

"It's not like you to be unfair, Gavin."

Unfair? He hadn't been unfair. Had he? Well, maybe he had. She might prove him wrong. There could be more to her than he'd first thought.

He pictured her as he'd seen her earlier. There she'd stood by the clothesline in that yellow dress — fitted bodice and flounced skirt — her hair hidden beneath a matching scarf. She'd looked like a wilting sunflower. Her face had been flushed, damp wisps of hair clinging to her nape. Her hands had looked like the hands of a rancher's wife, red and rough.

"All right, Dru. Maybe I haven't been fair."

He turned his gaze on the fire, wishing he'd never let his wife talk him into hiring a governess. Especially not Emily Harris. Bitter experience had taught him not to trust a beautiful woman just because she did one good deed. And whatever else Emily was, she was first of all beautiful.

Gavin would be wise to remain on guard.

SEVEN

Dru closed the cabin door behind her and walked to the center of the yard, pulling the shawl close across her chest. The air was still. Nothing stirred. All was quiet. Overhead, stars winked down upon the earth, but she wouldn't be able to see them for long. A storm was coming. She could feel it. She could smell the rain. Soon the wind would rise and clouds would roil across the sky.

If only the storm would blow away her cancer. If only the number of times she would see these storms had not been cut short. If only she could live long enough to see her daughters grown and settled and happy.

If only this cup could pass.

But heaven called to her too. No more sorrow. No more sighing. No more pain. Charlie was there, waiting for her, and she would at long last see the Savior face to face. She would no longer be an alien in a strange land. She would be in her true home, her eternal home.

Father God, Brina and Pet need someone in their lives who loves you. Emily knows you, Lord. Perhaps she can do what I haven't been able to do. Perhaps she can help Gavin discover your saving grace.

Two tears moved slowly down her cheeks.

I don't want to leave them. Why must I leave them?

In the distance, she saw a flash of light, followed by the low rumble of thunder. It wouldn't be long now. A breeze caressed Dru's damp cheeks and tugged at the hem of her nightgown.

Rest, her heart seemed to say. *Rest and trust. Fear not.*

She drew in a shuddery breath.

Yes, Lord. I will trust in you. I will rest. Therefore I will not fear, though the earth be removed, and though the mountains be carried into the midst of the sea.

Gavin opened his eyes, his body alert. The room he shared with Dru was dark, but he sensed his wife's bed was empty. As he sat up, he reached for his trousers and slipped into them, then pulled on his boots. A few quick steps across the bedroom and he was opening the door. A faint glimmer of light from the red coals in the hearth revealed the front door ajar. He moved toward it, his concern growing.

Outside he was met with a flash of lightning that lit up the sky, followed seconds later by a crack of thunder, splitting the silence. Before the sound faded, the heavens sparked again and then again.

Dru stood in the yard between the house and barn. A dark shawl was draped over her narrow frame, so slight it seemed a breeze could blow her away. As if in response to his observation, the wind rose, billowing the white fabric of her nightgown.

He moved toward her. "Dru?"

She didn't turn. "I felt the storm coming." Her voice was soft, barely audible above the peals of thunder. "The air was so still when I awoke. Thick, like you could cut it with a knife. I wanted to see it for myself."

He stopped beside her, almost put his arm around her shoulders, then didn't. Something told him she didn't wish to be held.

"I'll miss these storms." She turned her head, her face spotlighted by another flash of lightning. "I yearn for heaven, but I'll miss all I've loved on earth."

His chest grew tight. He hated it when

she spoke about dying this way.

"I'll be with Charlie in heaven. With Charlie and our baby son who never got to take his first breath. They're waiting for me now." She was silent a moment, then added, "There won't be any tears or sorrow or sighing where I'm going. Do you know that's true?"

No, he didn't know. He'd tried to believe, but he couldn't find it in him.

The wind increased. Dru's hair whipped about her face while black clouds, turned silver by the lightning, rolled overhead.

"It wasn't right to ask you to marry me, Gavin. You should have had a chance to find the kind of love Charlie and I shared. If it weren't for my girls . . ." She let her words trail into silence.

"I wanted to do it. I'll do my best by Brina and Pet. They'll never want for anything. I'll tell them what a fine woman their mother was, and they'll never have cause to doubt it. Not ever."

"Loving God and loving others are the only things that make sense in this world, Gavin. It's what we're made for, to love and be loved." She turned toward him. "If you let him, God can heal that broken heart of yours. If you let him heal you, you could find a woman to love."

His gut tightened. "I care about you, Dru."

She placed her hand on his forearm. "I know you care." Her voice was softer now, her look pleading. "You care because I was Charlie's wife and we were a family. You care for me as you would a sister if you'd had one. But that's not the kind of love I mean, Gavin. You deserve more."

"I like things the way they are."

Dru leaned her head against his chest, whispering, "No you don't. You only think you do."

Emily was awakened by Joker's scratching at her door. The moment she opened it, the young wolfhound leapt onto her bed and burrowed his head under the covers. She would have joined him but for the flash of lightning that revealed the open front door. She rushed across the room to close it against the storm.

And there they were, standing in the middle of the yard, Dru's head resting against Gavin's chest, his arm around her back as he stared up at the sky. Poignant, powerful, the scene caught at Emily's throat and made her heart ache. Her eyes burned as an unbearable weight threatened to crush her chest.

She returned to her room and lay on the bed, pulling the covers up beneath her chin. Loneliness rolled over her in waves, punctuated by the flashes of light and cracks of thunder. It was a feeling as severe as it was unexpected.

She envisioned them again — Gavin and Dru, standing together, united against the elements — and she wondered what it must be like to have that kind of bond with a man. The image in her mind changed, and it was she who stood beneath the crashing heavens. It was she who felt the hardness of a man's chest beneath her cheek, who heard the steady beating of his heart. It was she who knew that he loved her and would take care of her.

In her mind, she looked up at her husband's face. Into Gavin's face —

No! She couldn't imagine such a thing. Not about Gavin Blake, of all men. Why, she didn't even like him much. And he was married to Dru. What on earth was wrong with her, to let her imagination run so wild?

"Go away," she whispered, squeezing her eyes closed.

Joker whined and inched his way up until his muzzle was near her face. Emily pressed her forehead against his ear.

"Please go away."

But she didn't mean the dog.

Dru listened to her husband's steady breathing and knew he slept at last. She turned her head on her pillow to gaze in the direction of Gavin's cot, even though she couldn't see him in the darkness.

She had known him for over five years now. Much more than a friend, he'd been an important part of the Porter family. Charlie and Gavin had been like brothers. When things had been at their blackest after Charlie died, he'd been there to support and comfort her. He'd been her rock when she learned of her cancer, and he'd married her when she asked him so that her daughters would have a home when she was gone. Other than Charlie, she knew no better man than Gavin Blake.

And yet much of his past remained a mystery to her. What little she knew, she'd pried out of Stubs. It was the ranch foreman who'd told her that Gavin's mother had deserted her husband and son when Gavin was a boy. There was more that Stubs hadn't told her, and Dru knew whatever had gone unspoken was even worse than what had been said. There was a world of hurt inside the man Gavin had become. His distrust of women ran deep. And yet there was a great capacity to love inside that wounded heart of his. Look at how he was with Sabrina and Petula.

Her thoughts strayed to the bedroom next door where Emily Harris slept. With all her heart, she hoped she'd rightly discerned the Lord's voice. There was no time left to allow for mistakes.

Dru rolled onto her side and hugged the pillow to her breast as she pictured Emily in her mind. She was more than pretty. She was young, strong, and determined, kindhearted and bright. She had faith in God, and a lot of love to give to those around her. All this Dru had perceived as she'd listened to Emily in that hotel room in Boise City. The days that followed had only served to confirm her first impressions.

Lord, if it be your will, help them learn to love each other. Give my girls a home with a mother and father who will cherish each other.

A lump welled in her throat, and her tears dampened her pillow.

And Lord, please let me love my girls awhile longer.

Emily awakened after a long restless night filled with disturbing dreams. Wearily, she pushed aside the blankets and rose from the bed. The previous night's thunderstorm had been followed by a drenching rain, and the air in her room felt chill and damp. She shivered as she hurried toward the makeshift dresser, wasting no time selecting what to wear. The first dress her hand touched would be good enough.

Tying her hair at the nape with a narrow scarf, she slipped from her bedroom and out the front door, hoping the cool morning air would clear her troubled thoughts. Dawn had painted the lingering clouds the color of grapes, poppies, and dandelions. Moisture, crystallized by the crisp morning air, sparkled from every tree limb and fence pole. The horses in the corral huddled together, their heads drooping toward the ground, their breath forming white clouds beneath their muzzles.

Emily wrapped her arms around her middle as she hurried toward the barn, her teeth chattering with cold. She paused as the door closed behind her and drew a deep breath. There. That was better. The quick walk across the yard had helped.

"Morning, Miss Harris."

She gasped in surprise.

Gavin stood inside a stall, looking at her over the top rail. "You're up mighty early."

He opened the gate and stepped out.

"I . . . I wanted to see Sabrina's calf."

He wore a dubious expression. "I had no idea you were so fond of the little guy."

She felt a blush rising into her cheeks and hated herself for it. "Sabrina's fond of him, and anything that interests the children interests me." She moved toward the stall that held the calf, head high, eyes avoiding his.

"I believe you mean that, Miss Harris," Gavin said as he joined her.

"I do mean it or I wouldn't have taken this job." She risked looking at him then, daring him to disagree with her.

He didn't. "You must be cold. You'd better get back to the house."

"I'm fine. It's not cold in the barn."

"Go back to the house, Miss Harris," he said in a low voice. "It's colder out here than you think."

She recalled the moment she'd imagined herself in his arms and felt a frisson of dread run through her. "Yes," she whispered. "I'm afraid you're right. I'll go."

She forced her feet to walk slowly, but in her heart she fled.

■ ■ ■ ■

October 3, 1883

My dearest Maggie,

I'm sorry it has taken me so long to put pen to paper, but I have been very busy since arriving in this valley. Without the slightest danger of overstatement, I can say that this is the most beautiful place I have ever seen. The mountains cut a jagged swath against the sky, trees and rocks and even some glaciers in the highest peaks. Although the days are pleasant, the nights are already cold.

The journey to this summer range took a week. It reminded me of the months we spent on the Oregon Trail, sleeping under the stars, cooking over a campfire. I confess I was heartily glad to spend a night in a real bed once we reached the basin, but those days on the trail were a perfect time to get to know my employers better.

Mrs. Blake is warm and easy to like. She isn't a strong woman. Whatever her illness is, it has sapped her energy. But there is life in her eyes, and when she talks about her daughters, joy can be seen on her face. Rather like you and your children, Maggie dear.

Mr. Blake, I'm sorry to say, is nothing like his wife. He doesn't approve of me at all, and despite my assertion that I am up to the task, he believes I will fail and want to return to Boise. With me he is rather taciturn, but when he is with the children or caring for his wife, I see a totally different person. At those times he can be likeable.

I cannot imagine anyone not loving my young charges. Sabrina is nine and Petula is five. They are so bright and cheerful. Upon our arrival I was introduced to Sabrina's calf as well as to the new litter of kittens in the loft of the barn. Yes, Maggie, I actually climbed the ladder to the loft. I do not exaggerate when I say I was terrified, although I would not show it for all the world. Not with Mr. Blake watching me.

The Blakes own several wolfhounds, the youngest of which has decided to become my close companion. Joker is almost as big as a small pony, but I'm told he is still a pup, which explains his clumsiness as well as his total lack of manners.

Mr. Blake and the ranch hands are going to drive the cattle up to the main ranch soon, and the family will leave in a couple more weeks. I will send this letter with the men when they go so that it can be posted from Challis. Mrs. Blake is reluctant to leave. Every time it is mentioned, I see the sadness in her eyes. And now that I've been here a few days, I suppose I can understand.

It grows late, and I had better close this letter and get some sleep. Our days begin before daybreak.

Please pray that I will be a good teacher for the children and a caring companion for Mrs. Blake. And also that Mr. Blake wouldn't object to me quite so much as he does. I do so want to prove myself.

Your loving sister,
Emily

EIGHT

Emily looked up from the book. The room was wrapped in silence while the usually boisterous girls concentrated on their studies.

Petula leaned over her slate, a piece of chalk pinched between chubby fingers, copying her letters while frowning in concentration. The girl would have the alphabet conquered in no time. She was determined and eager to learn.

Emily's gaze shifted to the opposite end of the table where Sabrina sat. The tip of her tongue could be seen in the corner of her mouth as she worked on her math lesson. Sabrina had made it clear that she disliked arithmetic, but she never gave up before she found the right answers.

Satisfaction washed over Emily. She hadn't dreamed she would enjoy teaching this much. If she had, she would have made it her vocation long ago. It was exciting to see the children's eyes light with under-standing, to answer their questions, to expand their horizons. When she returned to Boise in the spring, she would seek another teaching position at once.

When she returned to Boise. The words saddened her more than they should. She'd grown attached to these girls, to this family, in the short time she'd been here. Spring would come too quickly.

A door closed softly behind Emily, and she turned toward the sound. Dru smiled as their eyes met, then she placed an index finger to her lips, indicating she didn't want to disturb the children. With silent footsteps, she made her way across the living room to a chair near the fireplace. Once there, she sat, pulled a lap rug over her knees, and closed her eyes.

In the four days since Gavin and the other men drove the cattle from the valley, Emily had begun to understand how ill Dru was. The moment her husband rode away, she had wilted before Emily's eyes. Her face looked older, more tired. Her shoulders were stooped. She smiled less often; only her daughters brought a look of joy into her eyes.

Emily wished she could ask the exact nature of her illness, but something in the woman's demeanor forbade her from doing so. She would have to wait until the information was offered.

"Miss Harris." An index finger poked her arm.

Emily looked at Petula.

"I did 'em." The girl held out the slate. "I did 'em all. Just like yours."

"Yes, Pet. You've done a fine job. You learn things fast. Your mother wasn't exaggerating when she said you were bright."

Petula cocked her head to one side. "What's exag . . . exagger . . ."

"Exaggerating." She printed the word on the slate. "It means to make things seem bigger or better than they really are."

The girl's eyes widened. "You mean *lie?* Ma wouldn't ever tell a lie."

Emily laughed as she smoothed Petula's hair back from her face. "Of course she wouldn't. Your mother is a very honest woman."

"Girls?"

They all turned at the sound of Dru's voice.

"Why don't you take a break from your lessons and get some fresh air? You could take Miss Harris for a ride up to the ridge. There might not be another chance before we leave the basin, as cold as the nights are turning."

Sabrina pushed her pencil and paper toward the center of the table. "Will you come too, Ma? We could take a picnic lunch."

"No, darling. I think I'll stay here and rest. I'm feeling quite tired today. But a picnic seems a good idea for all of you."

"Maybe we shouldn't go, Mrs. Blake." Emily rose from her chair and walked toward the fireplace.

"Nonsense. I could use some peace and quiet." Dru's smile never reached her eyes. It was there and gone in an instant. "Go on and have some fun. It's good for the children to get to know you better. You should be more than their teacher. I want you to be their friend too."

"Well, if you're sure. I hate leaving you all alone. With the men gone, I —"

"I'll be fine." Dru flicked her fingers. "Go on with you. And have a good time."

Their faces wreathed in grins, the girls climbed the ladder to the loft and returned a short while later with britches on beneath their skirts.

"We'll get the horses into the barn and brush 'em down," Sabrina told Emily. "But you'll have to help with the saddles. I can get the saddle on the horses' backs, but I'm not very good with the cinches." A shadow of doubt darkened her eyes. "Can you do that?"

"I'm an excellent horsewoman, Sabrina Blake. I can certainly help you with the saddles. I'll change into riding attire and join you in the barn."

After the front door swung closed, Emily looked at Dru. "Is there anything I can get you before we go?"

The woman shook her head, her eyes closed once again. "Just take care of my girls. When I'm not around, take care of my girls."

"Mrs. Blake?" Emily took another step forward. "Are you certain —"

"Yes, I'm certain." She drew in a breath and released it. "I'll enjoy having the house all to myself for a spell. Take some dried apples and slices of cheese and bread. You'll be hungry by the time you reach the ridge." Her smile looked strangely sad. "It's one of my favorite places in the world," she added in a whisper. Then she was silent. Perhaps she even slept.

Emily hesitated a moment longer before she turned and walked to her bedroom, careful not to make a sound.

Gavin slowed his horse as he approached

the cabin. He'd left Stubs and Jess with the herd along the Salmon River yesterday. With the aid of Duke and Duchess — two of the best cow dogs he'd owned — the cowboys would drive the herd the rest of the way to the Lucky Strike.

It hadn't taken much encouragement from Stubs for Gavin to turn around and head back to the basin. Things had been quiet on the summer range this year, but he didn't like leaving the women and children alone for long. The Bannock tribes had caused trouble on occasion, plus there were always a few strangers — most of them miners — wandering through the valley. Even though he'd only been gone a few days, he needed to know all was well with Dru and the girls . . . and Emily.

As if summoned by his thoughts, Emily Harris stepped out the front door of the cabin. She wore a powder-blue riding habit with a matching bonnet swathed in darker blue netting. For all the world a woman of society, wealth, and beauty.

He pulled his gelding to a halt.

Although loathe to admit it, it had been her image that haunted his thoughts during the past four days. Emily smiling. Emily laughing. Emily hanging laundry. Emily with the children. Emily speaking with Dru.

She had been in his thoughts when he rose in the morning and in them when he bedded down for the night.

As he watched, she checked the cinch of the saddle on the stocky mare the girls always rode. That's when Sabrina and Petula stepped into view from the opposite side of the horse. Emily said something to them, and Sabrina laughed before slipping her foot into the stirrup and swinging onto the saddle. Then Emily lifted Petula onto the mare behind her sister. More laughter carried to him across the distance. The sound had been all too scarce in recent months. For all the reasons he had — good reasons too — for not wanting the young woman here, he had to admit she'd brought laughter back to Dru and the girls. For that he was grateful.

Emily moved aside the train of her riding habit with a tiny kick as she turned toward Dru's palomino. It was an easy, graceful movement, much like everything she did. She mounted the horse with practiced ease, hooking her right knee over the pommel and ignoring the extra stirrup.

Fool woman. This wasn't some fancy park like the ones gentlewomen rode in back east, and that wasn't a sidesaddle on her horse either.

He nudged his gelding forward. Dru came outside as he rode into the yard.

"Gavin." She moved toward him. "We didn't expect you back until tomorrow or the next day." She laid her hand on his knee. "You're just in time to go with Miss Harris and the girls up to the ridge. They're taking a picnic lunch with them."

His gaze flicked to Emily, then back to Dru. "You coming too?"

"No."

"I'd better stay here."

"Please come, Pa," Sabrina said.

"Yes, please," Petula chimed in.

"Perhaps your father is too tired," Emily offered. "He can join us another time."

It was true. He was tired. But he didn't like her being the one to say so.

"Go with them." There was a pleading tone in Dru's words. "It'll be good for the girls to have some time with you."

His chest tightened as he was reminded again of what was ahead. "All right. I'll go, but we won't be long."

"Take all the time you want." Dru smiled at each one of them in turn. "Enjoy yourselves."

Gavin glanced at Emily in her fancy riding attire, the kind of clothes Dru would never wear, the kind that he could never provide for her daughters either. It irritated him, just to look at her. "We won't enjoy it much if Miss Harris falls off her horse and breaks her neck."

She sat a little straighter. "I won't fall off."

"That saddle's meant to be used astride." He pointed at the palomino. "And that mare's not used to being ridden sidesaddle."

"I assure you, Mr. Blake, that I can handle both this horse and this saddle." With that, she clucked her tongue and touched her heel to the mare's side. "Come along, Brina."

Before Gavin could follow, Dru touched his leg a second time. "Give her a chance. Whatever's stuck in your craw, it isn't Emily's fault. There's a lot about that young woman to like, and you will see it if you only try."

He nodded but didn't reply as he tightened his heels against the gelding's ribs and started after the other three.

Emily felt Gavin's gaze on her back, as tangible as a touch of his fingers would be. Knowing he watched made her nervous, made it hard to concentrate on anything the children said. If only he had returned half an hour later . . .

"Look, Miss Harris." Sabrina pointed

toward the tree line, where green forest stopped and the jutting crags of the Sawtooth peaks began. "The sheep. Up there. See it?"

"Sheep?" Emily squinted as her gaze swept the mountainside.

The heavy-bodied animal didn't look like any sheep she had seen before. It reminded her of a short, squat deer with its brown coat and white rump. It could have been a deer except for its head. Even from this distance, she saw the pair of massive, spiraling horns.

"It's a bighorn sheep." Gavin rode up beside her. "The Sheepeater Indians were named for them because the bighorn are a staple of their diet. Better than mutton. We eat them regular in the summer. They're easy to hunt except when they climb up that high."

His nearness increased her anxiety. What if she fell off this saddle, as he'd warned? That would please him no end.

But it was silly of her to think it. She'd sat more high-spirited horses than this docile mare. She wasn't in danger of falling, with or without Gavin Blake's company. She drew a deep breath as she nudged the mare to the right, putting some space between her horse and his.

A short while later, the trail led them into the forest, tall pines towering over them, filtering the sunlight. She heard the breathing of the horses and the crunch of their hooves on the carpet of dried needles. Doing his part to break the mountain silence, Joker barked as he raced ahead of them.

A line from the Psalms came to her, and she spoke it aloud. "Let the field be joyful, and all that is therein: then shall all the trees of the wood rejoice." That's what it was like, here in this forest. As if the trees themselves were rejoicing in their Creator.

She would do the same. She would set her thoughts on the Lord rather than the ofttimes surly Gavin Blake, and she would be the better for it.

Gavin hadn't much knowledge of the Scriptures, but unless he missed his guess, Emily had been quoting from the Bible. Perhaps it had been the soft reverence in her voice that gave it away.

Dru wanted her daughters raised in a Christian home. He supposed that was one reason she was so keen on Miss Harris. Emily shared Dru's faith, and she would make sure Sabrina and Petula remembered all that their mother had taught them. If she stuck it out. If she lasted long enough. He still wasn't convinced she would. She was young and inexperienced. Wait until winter set in. Wait until Dru's health worsened.

Emily's horse pulled ahead of his as the trail narrowed. She sat her horse with ease, her body swaying with the horse's gait, her posture straight and sure. Watching her almost mesmerized him.

He gave his head a slow shake and forced his gaze in another direction. He had no business letting his thoughts get caught up on that young woman. He had a sick wife and two stepdaughters who would soon be motherless. Those were the people he should be thinking about. In fact, he should turn his horse around and go back to Dru right now.

The trail spilled out of the forest and into the clearing on the ridge. As soon as they all brought their horses to a halt, Emily looked over her shoulder at Gavin. "It's spectacular!" She clapped her hands together. "I never imagined it would be so beautiful. No wonder Dru loves to come here." She faced forward again, taking in the panoramic scene.

From this vantage point, they had a clear view of the rocky mountain sentinels that surrounded the basin. Through the dense woods below them, they caught glimpses of the crystal-clear lakes that dotted the area, the icy waters fed by melting glaciers, and the Salmon River that wove through the tall, drying grass on the valley floor. The colors of autumn were everywhere. Reds and oranges and yellows were splashed among the forest greens, aspen and birch trees quivering in the breeze.

"It's so . . . so untouched," Emily said, her tone reverent.

Gavin dismounted and walked to her horse. "Let me help you down. There's a spot over there where you can see even more."

Their eyes met, and he saw the wariness there. Did she think he would drop her? She might, given how coolly he'd treated her from the beginning. At last, she leaned forward and placed her hands on his shoulders, allowing him to lower her to the ground. She was light, yet there was something real and solid about her. Not like Dru, who was wasting away to nothing.

The breeze ruffled the net of her bonnet and teased him with whiffs of her honeysuckle cologne.

"Thank you, Mr. Blake."

It wasn't until she pulled away that he realized he'd held onto her waist after her feet touched the ground. He rubbed his palms on his trouser legs and turned toward the children, hoping they could distract him from the unwelcome sense of loss that had filled him after Emily moved from his grasp.

NINE

Sabrina didn't always like being the oldest. Sometimes it was hard. She knew things her little sister didn't know. Sometimes she heard the adults talking when they thought she was asleep. Other times they thought she wasn't smart enough to understand what they were saying. But she *was* smart enough. She *did* understand. She longed to be able to talk to somebody about the things she heard and the things she knew. But who? She couldn't talk to her little sister about any of it because it might scare her. She couldn't talk to Ma because Ma didn't want her to know.

Sabrina remembered when their pa was gored by the bull. Not Gavin, their new pa, but their real pa. She'd heard her ma weeping after Mr. Martin and Mr. Chamberlain brought him home in the wagon, and she'd known he was gonna die. Nobody had to tell her. She'd just known. And now she knew their ma was gonna die too. Ma tried to hide it, tried real hard, but Sabrina still knew.

Some days it was nice to pretend she didn't know. Days like today, up there on the ridge with her pa and Miss Harris and Petula. Days when she could play games, like she and her sister were doing now. The two girls stood with their backs pressed against a tree, waiting to see if Miss Harris would find them in their game of hide and seek.

"Brina?" Petula tugged on her skirt. "What're those?" She pointed at large prints carved into the hardened earth.

Sabrina studied the prints, then answered, "Bear tracks, I think."

"Is there a bear around here now?" Her little sister scooted closer to Sabrina's side.

"Shh." She put an index finger to her lips. "We don't want Miss Harris to hear us."

"But is the bear around?"

"No, those tracks are old. They were made when the ground was muddy. See? It's hard now."

"I'm scared of bears, Brina. I think we oughta go back. Miss Harris would be scared too if she knew there was a bear around here."

As if summoned, Miss Harris called for

them. "Brina! Pet! Game's over. You win. Your father says it's time to go."

Sabrina squeezed Petula's hand. "Let's see if it scares her." She grinned. "Let's pretend there's a bear chasing us."

"Come on, girls." Miss Harris's voice was closer now. "We don't want to be gone so long that it worries your mother."

Sabrina let go of her sister's hand and ran from their hiding place. "A bear! There's a bear after us!"

Petula shrieked as she followed right behind.

Sabrina had expected their governess to turn and run away with them.

Instead, Miss Harris grabbed each of them by their hands before they could rush past her, drawing them to a sudden halt. "I've never seen a bear before. Let's wait and have a look at him. Is he very big? What color is he?"

Sabrina felt a flash of panic. What if there was a bear? What if the prints weren't old?

"You know, girls." Miss Harris leaned down, her tone ominous. "When you want to play a trick on someone, make sure they're not listening on the other side of the tree. It spoils the surprise." She dropped their hands and tapped Sabrina and Petula on the tops of their heads. "Tag!

You're both it."

Lifting the hem of her riding habit, her laughter trailing behind her, Miss Harris raced away from them. Sabrina turned a startled expression on her sister, then took out after their governess.

Gavin turned from the horses in time to see Emily run out of the trees. She had removed her hat earlier and now her hair had tumbled free of its pinnings. It flew out behind her like pale gold wings, and her laughter rang like bells in a mountain cathedral.

Sabrina appeared a moment later, intent on catching her governess. Petula's shouts were heard long before her short legs carried her into the clearing. But Emily was too quick for either of them.

Joker evened the field. The young hound bounded into Emily's path. She tried to stop, but it was too late. Over the dog she went. Sabrina, in hot pursuit, fell onto her governess, then the two of them tumbled head over heels down a grassy incline. Seconds later, Petula threw herself after them.

Gavin hurried forward, but by the time he reached them, their giggles told him no one was hurt.

"You're it, Miss Harris," Sabrina said.

"Yeah, you're it, Miss Harris."

Emily's cheeks were flushed, and her tangled hair was decorated with dried grass. A smudge of dirt accented the tip of her chin. "Where is he?"

Gavin thought she meant him and almost answered her.

Then she swung around. "Ah! So there you are."

Joker lay on the ground a few feet away, his head flat against the ground, a paw on either side of his muzzle, a look of contrition in his dark eyes. His tail slapped the ground in a slow beat.

"Benedict Arnold."

Joker whined and inched his way forward.

"Don't think you'll win my forgiveness so easily." Emily turned away, her nose pointed into the air.

The dog slinked across the remaining distance and placed his chin on her thigh. His whimper pleaded for absolution.

Gavin stepped forward, wondering how she would respond.

"This time, you mangy hound." She stroked the wiry hair on top of dog's head. "But don't you turn traitor on me again."

Joker sat up and barked.

Laughter filled the air again as the girls

each gave the dog a tight hug. Then Joker was up and running, Sabrina and Petula racing after him.

Gratitude washed over Gavin. It was good to see the children acting carefree. He might not want Emily Harris around, but he had to concede that the girls and Dru liked her. She had brought happiness back into the Blake home.

He moved to stand above Emily. "Let me help you up." He took her by the hand and pulled her to her feet. "I'm afraid Joker's antics may have ruined your dress." He pointed to a ragged tear in her sleeve.

She inspected the damage, then shook her head. "It will mend." With her eyes, she sought out the girls, who were by then rolling in the grass with Joker. "It's worth it."

An odd sensation twisted in his chest, a feeling he didn't much like nor wish to understand. "Like I said, we need to be heading back." He turned toward the horses. "We've been up here too long as it is."

On the ride down the mountain, Emily found herself watching Gavin as he led the way. He rode his horse with a relaxed ease, but she suspected he was alert for hidden dangers. There was something about him that made her feel protected.

In fact there were many reasons to like Gavin Blake, his gentleness with his wife and his affection for his stepdaughters chief among them. If only he weren't so cantankerous with her. She'd given him no reason to be. None at all.

There had been a moment, when he'd helped her to her feet up on the ridge, that she'd almost felt she had earned his approval. Or at least a little respect. But then he'd spoken to her in that same abrupt and clipped manner of his. The manner he only seemed to use with her. She felt so frustrated she wanted to scream.

Miserable, impossible man.

Guilt pierced her heart. It wasn't right to think that way about another person, no matter how he had offended her. Christ called her to love her enemies, and from all appearances, Gavin Blake fit that bill. No matter how he treated her, she mustn't respond to him in kind. If he sued her for her coat, she must give her cloak as well. If he smite her one cheek, she was told to offer him the other one.

You will not drive me away with your brusque behavior and ill humors, Mr. Blake. Before the spring, you will acknowledge you were wrong about me. Before I go home, you will realize that your wife hired the right person for the job. So help me, you will.

Gavin stopped his horse when they reached the valley floor. Sabrina nudged her horse into a trot, and she and Petula giggled as they rode past him. Emily wasn't sure if she should do the same or not, but as she drew close, he clucked to his horse and fell in beside her.

"We'll leave for the main ranch in a couple more weeks," he said, his gaze searching the clear blue sky. "Weather's going to change soon."

"You would rather go now, wouldn't you?"

A frown furrowed his brow. "Yes. I'm worried about Dru. She doesn't look good. I'd rather we were home."

Again Emily wanted to ask what was wrong with Dru. Again she bit back the question. It should be up to Dru to tell her.

"How did you all get along while I was gone?" he asked, intruding on her thoughts.

"Fine. The children are working hard at their lessons. They're inquisitive, both of them, and they're a great help to their mother."

"Dru's brought them up well." His voice cracked with emotion. "I've never known a better mother than she is."

Emily was tempted to reach over to him,

to cover his hand where it rested on the pommel, to tell him everything would be all right. But it wasn't her place to try to comfort him. And it surprised her that she wanted to do it anyway.

TEN

The temperature took a sharp drop before the sun set. By nightfall, the sky was hidden behind low-slung clouds. Stillness blanketed the basin, making every sound inside the log house seem an intrusion upon nature.

Emily pulled the warm quilt up from the foot of the bed. "Snuggle close," she told the girls. "It's going to be cold tonight." She leaned down to kiss their foreheads, their hair hidden beneath white nightcaps. How had they claimed her heart so completely in such a short time?

"Miss Harris?"

"What is it, Pet?"

"I'm glad you wasn't scared about the bear. You're lots of fun."

She swallowed the lump in her throat. "Thanks, Pet. Good night, Brina."

"Night, Miss Harris."

Holding her skirt out of the way, she climbed down the ladder from the loft. Her fear of heights always caused her to breathe a sigh of relief when her feet touched the floor again. As she turned around, the front door swung open before Gavin. His hat and shoulders were dusted with snow. He frowned when he saw her, and even from across the room, she could see concern in his eyes.

"Good thing we got the herd out when we did. That's quite the storm blowing in." He removed his hat and slapped it against his leg. "I don't like the looks of it."

Again she felt that desire to offer him respite from his many worries. But what could she say? What had she the right to say?

He shucked off his heavy coat. "Where's Dru?"

"She went to bed already. The girls too."

Gavin met her gaze a second time. "I'd better check on her."

After he went into the bedroom and closed the door behind him, Emily crossed to the window, moving aside the curtain with her hand. Snowflakes, chased by an icy wind, had carpeted the yard with a thin blanket of white. The barn was hidden from view by the blowing snow. How was it possible it could change so abruptly? Only this afternoon they had been riding with the warm kiss of sunshine on their faces.

She heard the bedroom door close a second time and knew that Gavin had returned to the living room. "How's Mrs. Blake?" she asked, her back still to him.

"Asleep."

The lid of the wood box creaked open. She heard the crackle of fire and pitch as new logs were added to the flames. A chair scraped against the floor. She let the curtain fall into place and turned. Gavin sat on the spindle-backed chair, leaning forward, his forearms braced on his thighs. He stared into the fire, the firelight dancing across his face. Light that revealed the worry that was still in his eyes. She moved toward the fireplace, drawn by its warmth — and by the man beside it.

"It doesn't snow this early in Boise," she said softly.

"It won't last long. A few days, a week maybe." He glanced up as she sat on the rocker opposite him.

"A week?"

Gavin raked his fingers through his hair. "Could be longer, but I imagine we'll be up to the Lucky Strike before the end of October." A frown furrowed his brow. "I never should've let Dru talk me into staying. No way to get a doctor to her now if she needs one."

"Mr. Blake . . ." She hadn't wanted to ask, had wanted to wait until the information was offered. But now she felt she had to know. "What's wrong with Dru?"

Pain and defeat filled his eyes, and her heart ached in response. He looked vulnerable in this moment, so unlike the man whose dislike for her was evident at every turn. For the third time today, she wished she could offer solace. She wished she could ease his anxieties.

"She's got a cancer. The doctors we've seen . . . none think she'll live much longer."

Tears burned her throat. Emily had feared it was something bad, but she hadn't expected this. She hadn't known Dru's illness was fatal. It made her irritation with Gavin seem small and petty. No wonder he was concerned with hiring the right person to tend his daughters. They would soon be motherless. No wonder he was moody. So would she be in his place. She'd judged him too harshly.

"I thought you knew," he added. "I thought she'd told you."

"No, she never told me. I knew she was ill but not how serious it was." She released a soft breath. "I should have guessed, but I didn't. I'm so sorry, Mr. Blake." She reached out and touched the back of his hands, folded between his knees.

He looked up at her, and something tightened and twisted inside Emily's chest. Something in his eyes. Something in the way he watched her. Her breathing felt suddenly labored as she drew back her hand.

"I'll pray for her," she whispered as she rose from the chair. "And for you and the children." She moved away from him, hurrying toward the safety of her room.

Before the door swung closed behind her, she heard him say, "Thank you, Miss Harris."

Gavin closed his eyes and rubbed his fingers in tiny circles over his temples, his head throbbing.

He never should have agreed to stay in the basin, despite Dru's wishes. He'd told Emily Harris that the snow wouldn't last long, but he could be wrong about that. And if he was? That didn't bear thinking about.

Women. He never should listen to them. Never. Not even to Dru.

Agitated, he rose and went to the window. By this time, there was more than an inch of snow on the ground, and the storm showed no sign of letting up.

Like the falling snow swirling before the

windowpane, unwelcome memories from his boyhood sifted through his mind. Twenty years had passed, and yet he could still hear his mother's voice as she'd screamed at his father, *"I hate you, and I hate everything here. I'm leaving with Mr. Hannah and I'm never coming back."* Snow had fallen on that day too. It had blanketed the carriage that carried her away.

His mother was as good as her word. She didn't return to the farm. Her hatred must have run deep, for she never asked to see her son again, never even wrote him a letter. Not long after she was granted a divorce, she married her lover, the wealthy Mr. Hannah. Gavin's father turned to whiskey for comfort and drank himself into an early grave.

In the years it took his father to die, Gavin learned to hate the woman who gave birth to him.

He remembered another snowy day not long after he buried his father. The farm was lost, anything of value sold. With nothing to hold him there, Gavin wrapped the framed photograph of his parents on their wedding day in an old newspaper and — carrying all his worldly possessions in a canvas bag slung over his shoulder — made his way to the city where his mother lived.

He couldn't have imagined her home if he'd tried. It was a mansion, and she was a pillar of society. It seemed enough money and distance could make people forget that she'd deserted a good husband and her only son for this life she lived. Or perhaps society didn't know and didn't want to know.

He remembered every detail of how she looked that day. She wore a blue gown, jewels sparkling at her throat and on her ears, and her cool eyes perused him for the longest time before she said, "You look like your father."

Gavin handed her the photo wrapped in newspaper.

She lifted an imperious brow, then opened the package. Her expression didn't change a bit as she stared at the photograph. At last she said, "Too bad he wasn't as rich as he was handsome." Then she dropped the frame unceremoniously into a wastebasket.

Gavin had never forgotten nor forgiven what his mother did. He never would.

And because Emily somewhat resembled Christina Blake — blonde, blue-eyed, and beautiful — he resented her too.

There. He'd acknowledged it. That's why he didn't want to like her. That's why he didn't like any beautiful woman, especially if they were wealthy. Trouble was, Emily was nothing like his mother. She kept surprising him, doing and saying things he never would have expected from her.

He turned from the window, his gaze moving toward Emily's bedroom. A thin spray of light fanned out beneath the door. She was still awake.

His mouth felt suddenly dry. His breath quickened as he recognized what he felt. He not only liked her against his will — he wanted to be *with* her.

He made a sound of disgust in his throat as the realization washed over him. It wasn't Emily, with her beauty and privileged lifestyle, who was like his mother. He was the guilty one. He was like his mother — married to Dru and desiring Emily. The discovery sickened him. It didn't matter that his was a marriage in name only, that he'd married in order to provide for two girls who would soon be orphaned. No matter the reason for the vows he'd given, he was still married, and he didn't mean to forget it.

No matter how many things Emily said or did to surprise him.

ELEVEN

By morning there was at least a foot of snow on the ground, and snowflakes continued to fall.

As Emily stood at the window, watching the falling snow, she wondered when they would be able to leave. It looked like winter was here to stay. What would that mean for Dru? She needed a doctor. No wonder Gavin had been reluctant to honor his wife's request.

Lord, please grant this family a miracle. They will all be so lost without Dru. Extend her life beyond what the doctors have told them. And Father, if it is your will to call her home to heaven, help me to help them deal with their loss. May I be of some small comfort to them.

She thought of Gavin, sitting by the fire, his face creased with tension. She recalled the moment she'd covered his hands with her own, and she felt that same strange disturbance in her chest. The sensation that had made her leave his presence in such haste.

Lord, grant me wisdom.

"You're up early."

Emily turned to find Dru standing outside her bedroom, clothed in nightgown and robe. Her hair hung in a single braid over her shoulder. Dark circles marred her eyes.

"So are you. Did you rest well?"

Dru sighed. "Well enough." She crossed the room. "How bad was the storm?"

Emily stepped aside to reveal the snow-blanketed yard. "It isn't over yet."

"This will keep us here awhile."

"You don't want to leave, do you? You would stay all winter if you could."

"It's true. I love it here more than anywhere in the world. It's my true home."

"Mr. Blake is worried. About the weather and about you."

"You two talked last night."

Emily felt a stab of guilt — almost as if she'd done something wrong. Utter foolishness. "I'll start breakfast. Why don't you sit next to the fire and keep warm. Would you like some coffee or would you prefer tea?"

"Tea, I think."

Emily put the kettle on the stove, then gathered the ingredients for flapjacks while she waited for the water to come to a boil. Minutes later, she carried a cup of brewed tea to Dru.

"Thank you, Miss Harris. You've been very kind to me. I'm thankful God brought you to be with us."

"It's I who should thank you," she replied. "I adore Brina and Pet and have discovered how much I love teaching. I wouldn't have, apart from this opportunity." She turned toward the kitchen.

That was the moment Gavin stepped out of the bedroom. His gaze met briefly with hers and then moved to Dru. "I didn't expect you to be up this soon," he said to his wife.

Dru lifted the cup in her hand. "Miss Harris made me some tea."

His eyes — filled with the familiar chill he often directed at her — returned to Emily, and he gave her a nod. "I'll check on the livestock." He crossed the room, pulled on his coat, and opened the door, letting in a gust of wind and a flurry of snow. "We're in for another blow. Don't anyone venture out. This looks like it could get nasty." He exited without a backward glance.

What was wrong with him? He hadn't been rude to her last night. Why did he have to be so now? Why couldn't he treat her with the same kindness he showed his wife?

Am I such a horrid person that he can't be civil to me even for a day? Isn't there anything about me that he can find to like?

Emily tried to ignore the feelings of hurt and rejection as she mixed the pancake batter while the skillet heated on the stove.

From the loft, Sabrina called, "Ma! Ma, did you see the snow?" She hurried down the ladder, Petula right behind.

"Yes, I saw," Dru answered.

Sabrina turned toward the kitchen. "Mmm. Flapjacks. I'm hungry."

"Me too," echoed her sister.

Emily smiled. "Good, because I made lots of batter."

"I want six," Sabrina said.

"Me too," Petula parroted.

Oh, how she would miss these girls when her time with them was over. She hadn't known she would feel such love for her charges when she accepted this job.

Feeling the threat of unexpected tears, she returned her attention to the skillet, scooped two pancakes each onto two plates, and set them on the table. When she had control of her emotions, she turned. "Breakfast is ready."

Sabrina and Petula took their places at once.

"Mrs. Blake?"

Dru shook her head. "I believe I'll stay here by the fire. My tea is enough for now." A tired smile tweaked the corners of her mouth. "It's time you called me Dru. I like to think we've become friends."

A lump thickened in Emily's throat. "I would like that . . . Dru. And you must call me Emily."

"Can we go play in the snow after breakfast, Ma?" Sabrina asked before stuffing a large bite of hotcakes into her mouth.

"Not until the storm is over. When it stops snowing, you can go out."

As if in response, a gust of wind slammed against the house, rattling the windows and whistling beneath the door. Emily poured more batter into the skillet, then walked over to the window to look outside. The steady snowfall of earlier had become a blizzard. There was no earth or sky to be discerned. All was white, the barn obscured by snowflakes driven sideways by the wind. She hugged her arms against her chest.

"How will Mr. Blake find his way back?" She glanced over her shoulder at Dru. "He can't possibly see."

"He'll wait it out in the barn."

Time passed slowly after that. The girls finished eating, and Emily washed the dishes. All but the skillet. She would wait until Gavin had his breakfast before she washed it. Surely it wouldn't be much longer before he returned.

Every time the house creaked she looked toward the door. Dru looked too, and Emily knew the woman shared her concern. She tried to hide her growing anxiety from the children, but despite her best efforts, the air was thick with it.

"Ma?" Petula crawled into her mother's lap. "Is Pa okay?"

"Of course he is. He's tending the animals, like he does every morning."

"He's been gone a long time."

"He'll be in soon, Pet. Don't you worry." As she stroked her daughter's hair with one hand, she glanced at Emily.

It was bad enough for the women to worry. Worse yet for the children to be afraid. Emily nodded, communicating her understanding. Then she said, "Girls, it's time for your studies. If we get our work done now, we can play in the snow when the storm is over. Get your books and slates." She clapped her hands twice. "Hurry now."

Gavin groaned as consciousness returned, bringing with it a terrible throbbing in his head. Was that straw scratching his face? Yes, it was. Why was he lying facedown in the barn?

He rolled onto his back. A horse snorted nearby. Then he remembered.

"If I didn't need you to pull the wagon," he said through gritted teeth, "I'd plug you between the eyes right here and now."

It wasn't the first time the big workhorse had kicked at him. It *was* the first time the gelding had connected — a glancing blow to the head that had actually knocked him out.

The barn spun around him as he sat up, another groan escaping his lips.

"You'd make great buzzard feed."

The piebald looked at him with unrepentant eyes.

How long had he been unconscious? Long enough to feel the cold in his bones. And from the sound of the wind outside, the storm hadn't let up any. Gingerly he touched the back of his head, finding a hoof-sized lump with his fingers.

"I may shoot you yet."

Emily tightened the rope around her waist as she repeated the instructions Dru had given her. "Two tugs mean I need you to pull me back. Four tugs means I'm in the barn and you can tie off the rope for us to use to find our way back when Gavin agrees it's safe." She tried to sound confident.

She wasn't confident, of course, but she had to go out into the blizzard anyway. Gavin had been outside too long now. They needed to know why he hadn't returned. They all needed to know — Dru, Sabrina, Petula, and Emily.

She tightened the knitted scarf around her head and pulled open the door. Snow stung her cheeks as she leaned forward and stepped outside.

"We'll be back soon," she called over the wind.

A few steps was all it took for the house to disappear from sight. Emily was surrounded by nothing but white. She held onto the rope for all she was worth as she forged ahead. Her feet sank into drifts of snow, and she stumbled more than once. All sense of direction vanished. There was no up or down, right or left, forward or back, night or day. There was only snow. Snow, snow, and more snow.

Was she still going in the right direction? What if she was lost out here? Panic rose like bile in her throat.

Turn back. Turn back now!

She couldn't turn back. Dru and the girls

were counting on her. Maybe Gavin was counting on her too. She had to reach the barn. She had to find it soon.

For courage, she silently quoted one of Maggie's favorite verses: *For God hath not given us the spirit of fear; but of power, and of love, and of a sound mind.*

She pressed on.

The barn seemed to loom out of nowhere, mere inches away by the time she saw it. She felt almost giddy with relief as she touched it with her hands, making sure it wasn't a mirage. Then she pressed her forehead against the board siding and whispered, "Thank you, God. Thank you."

Drawing a steadying breath, she felt her way toward where she thought the door should be. Not finding it, she turned and moved the other direction until her hand fell upon the latch. She pulled on the door, but the snowdrift was too high. It wouldn't budge. She would have to clear away the snow before she could open it enough to slip inside. Using both hands, she scooped and tossed, scooped and tossed, scooped and tossed. It took forever. Despair threatened, but she wouldn't allow herself to give into it.

By the time she opened the door and stepped into the dark, pungent air of the barn, her hands were stiff with the cold.

"Mr. Blake?"

She remembered to give the four tugs on the rope to let Dru know she was in the barn. Then she untied the rope from around her waist and secured it to a rail near the door.

"Mr. Blake?" she called again.

No reply. Where was he? Could he have tried to return to the house and been lost in the storm? Her heart raced with fear at the thought.

She made her way slowly toward the stalls that held the animals, the dim light of the barn making it difficult to see. She found Gavin in the third stall, his back against the rails.

"Mr. Blake?"

He didn't answer. Didn't look at her.

She knelt in the straw beside him and placed her hand on his shoulder. "Gavin?"

He groaned, his eyes closed.

She gave him a little shake. "Gavin? What happened?"

At last he looked at her, but his eyes seemed unfocused.

"What happened to you?"

"Nothing much," he answered slowly. "I just got the sense knocked out of me . . . by a horse." His eyes rolled back in his head,

and she had to catch him in her arms before
he could topple over into the straw.

Twelve

Emily wasn't sure how much time passed before he regained consciousness again. It seemed like forever. The silence of the barn and the whistling wind from beyond it made the waiting sheer agony. She didn't know what to do for Gavin. He was obviously hurt or sick, but she had no way of knowing what was wrong. So she continued to hold him, his head on her shoulder, and waited.

At long last he stirred, releasing another long groan.

"Be careful, Mr. Blake," she cautioned.

He drew slowly back from her, his eyes filled with confusion and surprise. "What happened?"

"I was hoping you could tell me."

Another groan, then, "I'm gonna kill him."

"Kill who?"

"Patch." He turned the back of his head toward her. "How bad is it?"

She leaned closer and saw that his dark

hair was matted with blood. "What did Patch do?"

"I leaned down to pick up the bucket, and he kicked me in the head. Knocked me out cold."

She gingerly moved his hair out of the way so she could see the wound.

He grunted but didn't pull away from her.

"It's hard to tell in this light, but I don't think you'll need stitches. Head wounds always seem to bleed a lot. My nieces and nephews taught me that."

Gavin pushed himself up from the floor. "I take it it's stopped snowing." He steadied himself against the top railing of the stall.

"Not yet." She stood and brushed the straw from her skirt. "The wind is still driving the snow very hard. At least it was when I came to the barn."

"You came out here through that blizzard?"

"I had to. We knew something was wrong when you didn't return."

Moving with care, Gavin walked across the barn to the door. Reaching it, he saw the rope tied to the rail and looked back at Emily.

"We tied it around my waist so I wouldn't get lost. We can follow it back to the house."

With a nod, he lifted the latch and tried

to open the door. It barely moved.

She followed him across the barn. "I cleared away the snow so I could get in. It can't be covered over already."

"You're wrong about that, Miss Harris." He looked toward the loft. "We'll have to go out through the loft."

"Through the loft?" Her heart thudded as she sank onto a nearby storage bin, her frantic pulse pounding in her ears. He couldn't possibly expect her to jump from up there.

Gavin hadn't seen a snowstorm like this one this early in the year since he'd settled in Idaho. In December and January, plenty of times, but never in October.

He closed the loft door and returned to the ladder, stopping at the edge to look down. Emily hadn't moved from the storage bin. Even from up here he could see her shivering as she hugged herself.

"No sign of it stopping yet." His head throbbing, he lowered himself down the ladder. "And my guess is that rope of yours is under a foot of snow already."

She nodded, misery written on her pretty face.

"Come over here," Gavin said, motioning with his hand. "We need to warm you up."

She rose from the bin and moved toward him, her arms still folded across her chest. When she reached him, he placed his hand on the small of her back and steered her toward the stall holding Sabrina's calf.

"Wait here," he commanded.

In the tack room at the back of the barn, he grabbed several saddle blankets. On his return trip, he took the lantern from its hook and carried it with him to the stall.

"Hold this." He handed her the light.

With his boot, he kicked straw into a pile in the corner, then made a nest in the center of it. Afterward he placed one of the blankets over the bed of straw and smoothed out the wrinkles as best he could.

"Come on in."

"Mr. Blake, I —"

"Don't argue with me, Miss Harris. Look at you. You're shivering so hard I can almost hear your teeth rattle."

When she drew near, he took the lantern from her. She lifted her eyes to meet his, and he felt his gut tighten. Vulnerable. Sweet. Uncertain. Fearful. There was something about her that made him want to —

He gritted his teeth and willed the incomplete thought away. "Go on. Sit down on that bed of straw and pull those other blankets over you."

She skittered away from him.

Smart girl.

When she was covered with the saddle blankets, Gavin hung the lantern on another hook nearby, turning up the flame as high as it would go, then led the calf over to Emily. With a little encouragement, he got the calf to lie down close to her.

"He'll throw off some body heat," he explained without looking at her. "It should help warm you."

The blustering wind whistled around the corner of the barn. A horse blew dust from its nostrils. Another stomped its hoof. The calf curled into a tight ball, making the straw rustle as he buried his nose against his belly.

Gavin felt their isolation. They might have been the only two people in the world. One man. One woman. Alone together.

He moved to the opposite side of the stall and slid to the floor, hugging his arms around his chest. If he were a praying man, he would definitely be asking God to bring the storm to an end — and soon.

Emily was cold and scared. Scared of staying in the barn while the storm raged. Scared of the thought of being lowered out of the hay door in the loft or worse, having to jump.

"It'll be all right, Miss Harris."

She looked across the stall at him. His face was hidden in shadows — the light from the lantern falling upon her and not him — but she took comfort in his presence. She took even more comfort knowing he hadn't fallen unconscious again.

"I've waited out my share of blizzards. It won't last much longer."

How could he be sure? Still, she appreciated his attempt to reassure her.

"Put your hands on the calf. That'll help warm them, and then the rest of you will start feeling warmer."

She did as he suggested. "I hope Dru won't be too worried about us."

"That woman's got a lot of faith in her God. I imagine she'll trust him with us too."

Emily nodded, drawing even more comfort from that thought than from Gavin's presence. "I guess I should do the same, shouldn't I? I'm sorry for letting my fear take over."

"I'd say you didn't let fear take over, Miss Harris. Otherwise, you wouldn't be out here in this barn, and I might still be unconscious."

Warmth at his unexpected praise spread through her.

He chuckled softly. "I bet you didn't foresee anything like this when you decided to take a job as governess."

She smiled. "No, I didn't imagine this."

He said nothing more, and although she couldn't see his eyes, she was certain he watched her. The silence stretched out, and the air felt thick between them. Emily remembered when she'd touched his hands in front of the fire last night. She remembered the strange feelings that had caused her to go to her room, to get as far from him as she could.

It was almost as if . . . as if she were attracted to him. As if she wished —

No! She felt no such thing. He was a married man. Married to a woman she considered her friend. Besides, he'd been beastly to her from the first day they met. She had no reason to be attracted to him.

And yet —

Covering her mouth, she drew in a little gasp of air as she squeezed her eyes closed.

No . . . no . . . no . . .

Gavin said, "Listen. The storm's over."

She heard him stand and leave the stall. Only then did she dare open her eyes. Only then did she realize the wind no longer blew, that snow was no longer being driven into the side of the barn.

His footsteps told her he was in the loft above her head. "Dru," she heard him call. Then, after a short wait, he said, "We're all right. Miss Harris is here with me."

Dru must have said something, but Emily couldn't hear her.

"No. Stay inside," Gavin continued. "We can manage. I'll dig things out later." Silence, and then his voice was directed toward her. "Miss Harris, we can go now."

Emily stood and brushed straw from her skirt and plucked it from her hair. Then she leaned down and stroked the calf's muzzle. "Thanks for keeping me warm."

"Miss Harris?"

"I'm coming."

She climbed the ladder, but forgot to be afraid. Heights were the least of her problems now.

Dru watched from the window as Gavin used the rope on the pulley to lower Emily from the hay door to the ground. She saw the wary expression on Emily's face as Gavin untied the rope from around her waist, saw the awkward way she leaned away from him, as if trying to escape his touch. As they made their way toward the cabin, Emily stumbled in the deep snow, but Gavin caught her by the elbow before she could fall. He let go as soon as she was steady.

Dru let the curtain fall back into place and went to the door. Snow spilled into the house.

"Brina, bring some towels to wipe up the snow. Pet, are the blankets ready?"

"They're ready, Ma."

"Bring them to me."

She opened the door wider as Gavin and Emily took the last few steps to reach the house.

"You must be frozen to the core," she said as she took Emily's arm and drew her inside. "Take off your coat. We've warmed blankets by the fire."

Emily did as she was told, and very soon Dru had her wrapped in a warm blanket and seated next to the fire. At Dru's insistence, Gavin was soon seated beside her. Neither of them said a word. Neither of them looked at the other. They didn't seem angry, but tension crackled between them.

Dru felt a flutter of joy. It was happening. What she'd hoped for from the beginning was happening. They were attracted to each other. Attracted and resisting it — because of her. Gracious. She hadn't considered that she would be an impediment while she was alive, although she should have. Gavin was a principled man, and Emily was a virtuous young woman. How was she to nurture their growing affection in these days or weeks before the Lord took her home while still preserving their honor? How was she to help them fall in love so that after she was gone . . .

Give me wisdom, Lord.

THIRTEEN

After two days of being snowbound, everyone felt restless, the children especially so. Emily had done her best to keep their minds occupied, but even she felt taxed to the limit. She wanted to be anywhere but here, kept in such close quarters with the Blake family. No, it wasn't the family that made her nerves scream. It was being in such close proximity to Gavin. Whenever he was in the same room, she found it difficult to breathe.

Thankfully, he wasn't in the room at present.

Emily turned from the window to look at the two girls seated at the table. "I'll bet there isn't a bit of snow in Boise. The weather's almost always warm for the Howard Clive Ball. It's *the* social event of the fall season."

"What's a ball?" Petula asked.

Sabrina answered, "It's a dance, silly."

"Don't call your sister names," Dru cautioned.

Petula stuck out her tongue at Sabrina in a so-there expression.

If Emily didn't do something, they would be fighting in a few seconds. "I do love to waltz," she said, hoping to distract them. She twirled in a circle, arms out as if holding a dance partner.

Sabrina and Petula pushed aside their schoolbooks, waiting for her to continue.

"Tell us more," Sabrina encouraged.

Emily was only too happy to oblige. "The first year we were in Idaho — that was a long, long time ago — my sister attended the event. It's where my brother-in-law proposed to her. I was only six, but I remember how she looked that night. Her gown was silvery-blue and there were little puffed sleeves right here." She pointed to the spot on her upper arms. "The dress had a big skirt, held out by lots of stiff petticoats. Well, maybe they weren't petticoats. Maybe she had a hooped skirt. Dresses were so different back then."

Emily sat across from the children and rested her chin in the palms of her hands, elbows on the table. "My first ball gown was very different from Maggie's. It was apple green and embroidered with red poppies, and it had a square neck edged with white lace. I wore long white gloves that had gold bands at the wrists. The vogue was for long trains then, and my first ball gown had a very long one, indeed. I felt so grown up in it. I danced and danced and danced that night. Mr. Clive had an orchestra up in a loft above the ballroom, and they hardly ever stopped playing. It was magical."

"I bet you were the prettiest girl there."

"Thank you, Pet. That's very sweet of you to say." Her gaze flicked to the far end of the parlor where Dru sat near the fireplace, knitting a scarf.

Emily closed her eyes, envisioning herself in that same dress, and she wondered: Would Gavin have wanted to dance with her if he'd been there? The moment the question formed in her mind, she willed it to go away. She couldn't think about him like that. She mustn't think about him like that.

Sabrina leaned forward. "Do you suppose, when I'm old enough, I could go to the ball? Do you think anybody'd want to dance with me?"

Eyes open again, Emily reached across the table and clasped the girl's hand. "If you lived in Boise, you would most assuredly be invited, and all the young men would want to dance with you."

"I don't know how to dance." Sabrina looked crestfallen.

The girl's expression squeezed Emily's heart. "Then we must teach you at once. Put your book down and stand up." She shoved chairs against the walls as she spoke, clearing a wide space in the middle of the parlor. Satisfied, she turned toward Sabrina. "Come here."

In short order, she instructed the child how to stand, how to hold her partner's hand, how to follow the man's lead. "And you should smile all the while, as if you know a secret that your partner doesn't know." She laughed, then hummed a tune, swaying with the melody.

Sabrina gripped Emily's hand as the two began to slowly turn about the room.

"Relax, Brina. It's supposed to be fun."

The girl tripped over her own feet, bringing them to a halt. She looked as if she might burst into tears.

"No one gets it right the first time," Emily said in a low, encouraging voice. "It's easier when you see others dancing."

From across the room, Dru said, "Let your pa show you. Gavin, dance with Miss Harris."

Emily caught her breath. When had Gavin

returned? She kept her eyes trained on Dru, answering, "I . . . I think it would be better if Mr. Blake danced with Brina."

Sabrina said, "But you said it's easier to learn if I see others dancing. I can't see when I'm dancing with Pa."

"Gavin," Dru said softly. "Dance with Miss Harris. Show Brina how it's done."

Gavin answered, "I think they're doing fine."

Emily felt herself relax a little. He didn't want to dance with her. That was all for the best.

But Dru didn't let it go. "Please, Gavin. Do it for me."

A long silence followed. Emily was tempted to glance in the direction of his voice, but she was afraid to look. What should she do? What could she say to —

"All right, Dru," he said. Then, "May I, Miss Harris?"

This shouldn't be happening. This shouldn't be happening.

She turned to face him. "Perhaps you shouldn't. Your head —"

"My head is fine." He held out his arms for her, but she could see his reluctance matched her own.

Emily had promised herself that she wouldn't feel anything more for this man than the proper regard for an employer. Surely she could dance with him, at his wife's request, and remain emotionally withdrawn.

She stepped into his arms.

He began to sway from side to side, then, as he hummed the same melody she had hummed a short while before, they began to twirl around the parlor. Emily stared at the base of his throat, afraid to look up, afraid to look into his eyes, afraid he might see what she was feeling — feelings she didn't want to have. It was the most torturous dance of her young life.

Gavin.

They spun to a halt in the middle of the room. Her skirts swished around her ankles, then stilled. Emily withdrew her hand from his and stepped away, her pulse pounding in her ears.

"Thank you for the dance, Miss Harris."

She had to look at him then. Couldn't keep from it.

He bowed his head.

Dru and the girls applauded. "That was wonderful," Dru said. "Absolutely charming."

Emily had never felt this way before. She longed to step back into his embrace. She wanted to be in his arms, to be there even when she knew she shouldn't want to be there.

Thou shalt not covet thy neighbor's wife. Recalling that commandment made her want to groan, because surely it meant her neighbor's husband as well.

She turned away from him. "Your turn, Brina. Dance with your father."

Without waiting to see what happened, she went to the table, fighting for composure and praying no one had seen the storm that battered her from within. *I don't belong here. I must leave. I must.*

As suddenly as the temperature had dropped and the blizzard blew through, warming winds arrived the next day to melt the snowfall. Water dripped from the eaves of the house and barn. Brown, muddy spots of earth appeared in the yard. In a few days, all traces of snow would be gone, and they would leave the basin.

Gavin tossed another flake of hay over the side of the stall, then leaned on the top rail as the black gelding buried his nose in the feed, searching for the most delectable shoots.

They needed to get out of this valley. They needed to see some other people, say howdy to their Challis neighbors. He'd like to play a few games of checkers with Patrick O'Donnell and take the girls to the mercantile where they could buy a new hair ribbon or a new doll. Things were too close here, too secluded. He needed to keep busy, get his mind back to the business of ranching instead of thinking so much on —

He didn't allow himself to finish that train of thought. It could only lead to trouble.

Gavin left the barn and returned to the cabin. Inside, he took off his coat and hung it on the nearest peg. "It's warming up out there." He turned around.

Dru sat in her rocking chair near the fireplace, a bundle of mending on the rug near her feet, needle and thread in her hands.

"We'll be out of here in a couple of days or so."

She nodded, but it was easy to see the thought didn't make her happy.

He moved toward her. "Spring will be here before you know it."

"Spring." Her expression grew wistful. "I always loved to see spring come. It's so beautiful when the wildflowers are in bloom."

He rested his hand on her shoulder, squeezing his fingers in wordless acknowledgment of what she hadn't said. Time was growing short.

The door to Emily's room opened, and she stepped into the parlor. She wore another pretty gown, one he hadn't seen before. Both she and the dress were out of place in this rustic cabin.

"Where are the girls?" she asked.

Dru set aside her mending. "Outside playing."

"May I speak with the two of you a moment?" Emily moved toward them, the hem of her dress swishing against the floor as she walked, her hands clasped at her waist.

Gavin remembered the feel of her small hand within his as they'd waltzed in this room yesterday. He remembered it too well.

Emily looked straight at Dru. "Mrs. Blake, I'm very fond of Brina and Pet. You know I am. They're wonderful girls, so bright and easy to teach." She talked fast, her words almost running together. "But you see, I realized last night how much I miss my family. I think I should go home. I . . . I miss all the social events in Boise and my friends and the theater and . . ." Her words faded into silence, and her gaze dropped to the floor.

Gavin felt as if he'd been punched. He'd always known she didn't belong here, but he'd almost forgotten. He'd almost begun to believe she would stay. He was a fool. As big a fool as his father ever was.

"I think I should return to Boise as soon as we're able to leave the basin," Emily ended.

Gavin stepped away from Dru and strode toward the door. "You'll have to wait for the stage in Challis, Miss Harris." He slipped his arms into his coat sleeves. "I'll check on the girls." He slammed the door behind him.

He never should have let down his guard. He never should have let himself believe that Emily might be different from other beautiful women of means. He never should have taken her in his arms and danced with her. Never . . . never . . . never.

He should have refused Dru when she first made the suggestion to hire a governess. He should have told her he could take care of everything. He could have taught the girls their lessons. He could be Dru's nurse and companion. They hadn't needed someone else, but because he hadn't stuck by his guns, Dru and the girls would be hurt when Emily left.

Giggles filtered down from the loft as he stepped into the barn, and he knew Sabrina and Petula were playing with the kittens. He was in no mood for laughter or children's banter. Without a word, he turned on his heel. Swift strides carried him away from the barn and off toward a copse of aspens.

He remembered again the day his mother had left them, the way she rode away without a backward glance. Then he imagined Sabrina and Petula watching Emily Harris leave. They would be heartbroken. They adored her, and she was leaving because life here was too hard.

Or was she leaving because of him? The thought stopped him in his tracks.

Was it possible that she'd guessed that he'd begun to care for her — even as he'd tried to deny it to himself?

Dru tapped lightly on the door to Emily's bedroom. "May I come in?"

"Of course," came the soft reply.

She opened the door.

Emily was seated on the edge of her bed, her hands clenched in her lap. Her cheeks were damp with her tears. "I'm sorry, Dru. I thought I could do this, but I was wrong. I can't help it."

Dru sat beside her and took hold of her left hand. "What has really upset you, Emily? I don't believe it is because you miss the social activities in Boise City."

"But it is. I —"

"When you took this job, you promised to stay through spring. I must hold you to that."

"But —"

"I'm ill, Emily, and I'm going to get worse. My daughters love you already. They trust you. They're going to need you more than you know. You can't leave them now. They've suffered enough loss in their short lives. Please. Keep your promise to me and to them."

Emily drew her hand from Dru's grasp, rose, and began to pace the floor.

Dru saw the turmoil written on the young woman's face, and for a moment, she felt ashamed of herself. Ashamed for using both Gavin and Emily the way she had done, the way she still meant to do. But if they could learn to love each other the way she hoped they would, the way she thought they were already beginning to, wouldn't it all be for the best? Ruthlessly she pushed away her doubts. She had believed with all her heart that God had ordained this plan. She would not falter now.

"Emily, I cannot allow you to leave," she repeated, more forcefully this time. "You must abide by your word of honor. I beg of you. You must stay in our employ until spring. The girls will need you when I am gone." She paused, then added, "Gavin will need you too."

Emily stopped her pacing and turned to face Dru. Defeat was written in her eyes. "I wish you understood," she whispered.

"I understand much more than you know. Please, Emily. You must stay."

She released a deep sigh. "All right, Dru. I'll stay."

October 12, 1883

My dear Maggie,

I write this letter while we are still in the basin, but it won't be posted until we arrive at the main ranch and I can send it to Challis. Mr. Blake believes we should be able to leave in three or four days. Perhaps I will have more news to share by then that I can send at the same time.

We had quite the snowstorm earlier this week. You would have thought we were in the dead of winter instead of the middle of October. The heavy snow has delayed our departure. Fortunately, Mr. Blake had returned from the cattle drive before the storm began.

Maggie, I almost decided to come

home. Although I love the children and Mrs. Blake has become like a sister to me, there are some things that make being here more difficult than I expected. But I cannot leave. I gave my word, and I am needed here. I hope I shall prove myself worthy of Mrs. Blake's trust.

Emily laid the pen on the table and hid her face with her hands. She wanted her sister's advice, but she couldn't bring herself to write all that she felt, all that had happened. She couldn't write that there was no place she would rather be than dancing in the arms of Gavin Blake.

God forgive me.

Gavin had been angry when she told them she wanted to go home. She'd *wanted* him to be angry. She wanted him to stay angry. Only then might she be all right.

She took up the pen again.

I will have my own cabin when we arrive at the main ranch. I believe that will make my job a little easier. Here in the basin, I have a room of my own, but that provides too little privacy.

Maggie dearest, please pray that I shall prove myself worthy of the trust that's been given to me. Pray that I will be strong and able to handle whatever comes my way. It comforts me to know you are already praying for me.

Give my love to Tucker and the children, and tell them I am missing you all so very much. I will write again soon, and I look forward to the letters that I'm sure are awaiting me in Challis.

Your devoted sister,
Emily

FOURTEEN

The journey to the main ranch, located ten miles outside of Challis, took six days. The trail — it couldn't be called a road — was often narrow, sometimes squeezed between a rising mountain on one side and a steep drop-off on the other, sometimes following creeks and rivers through flats and draws. The team and wagon were often slowed to a near halt by the difficult terrain.

They were an odd-looking group, Emily thought. Gavin drove the wagon with Dru either at his side or resting on the makeshift bed behind the seat. In addition, the wagon held several trunks, a basket containing an unhappy Countess and her mewing kittens, and a wooden cage full of squawking chickens. The two milk cows were tied to the back of the wagon, and Sabrina's orphaned calf trotted along beside them. Emily and the girls brought up the rear on horseback.

Twilight had spread a gray mantle over

the countryside by the time Gavin brought his tired band of travelers into the yard of the Lucky Strike on the sixth day after they departed the Stanley Basin. Emily was too weary to give anything more than a cursory glance at the house and outbuildings before sliding from the palomino's back. Every part of her body ached. Her backside. Her thighs. Her arms. Her head. She longed for a bath and a night in a real bed. She would have to settle for the latter for now.

Gavin hopped down from the wagon seat, then turned to hold his arms out for his wife. Emily watched as Dru slipped into his strong embrace, her head nestled in the curve of his shoulder and neck. For a moment, Emily forgot her resolve and wished he might hold her in the same manner. How wonderful to be cared for so tenderly.

Gavin looked her way. "I'll need your help getting everyone settled."

There was no tenderness about his tone of voice, no doubt about the coldness of his feelings for her. No, her request to leave the Blake family, her wish to return to Boise, had brought about its desired effect. If there had ever been a warming of feelings between them, it was gone now. Gavin felt nothing but disdain for her. And that was what Emily had wanted, to keep him at arm's length.

Wasn't it?

Early the following morning, Emily sat up in bed, the blankets tucked around her, the room as cold as ice. Perhaps it wouldn't be nice having a cabin to herself as she'd once thought. Not if it meant freezing to death.

And it wouldn't get any warmer unless she did something about it.

With a swift motion, she threw back the covers and hurried across the room to the black iron stove. A nearby box held wood and kindling, and she tossed some of both into the stove's belly. Shivers raced through her, making it difficult to strike a match.

"Come on. Come on."

On the fourth try, the match flickered to life, and she held it to the kindling, watching and hoping until it began to burn.

"Please don't go out." She stomped her bare feet and hugged herself.

When it was clear she'd succeeded, she dashed back to bed and burrowed beneath the blankets. After a short while, with the chill losing its grip, she appraised her new lodgings, something she'd been too tired to do the previous night.

The one-room cabin was plain but of a comfortable size. In addition to the stove and bed, there was a table and two chairs, as well as a sideboard for dishes and a cupboard for storing a few food supplies. Curtains adorned the lone window, and a rag rug covered the board floor.

This had been Gavin's home before he married Dru.

She closed her eyes, wanting to shut out thoughts of him. At least the wrong kind of thoughts. Her feelings for him would be no different than what she felt for Dru and their daughters. She would make sure of it. She would take her thoughts captive. She would get through the coming months and not forget herself again. Once spring came and Gavin was ready to take his family and his cattle back into the basin, Emily would return to Boise. She would find employment as a teacher. Maybe she would marry one of her former suitors. She would make a new life for herself — far from Challis, far from the Lucky Strike.

Far from Gavin Blake.

Half an hour later, dressed and ready to begin her day, she opened her cabin door to the chilled mountain air. Ribbons of smoke curled skyward from the chimneys of both the main house and the bunkhouse, and the scent of frying bacon teased her nostrils. Tardy again. Chagrined, she hurried across the yard. Her knock on the back door was answered by Gavin.

"Come in, Miss Harris." As she entered, he returned to his place by the stove where pork sizzled and spat in a frying pan. "No need to knock." He waved a fork toward the shelf that held the dishes. "There's breakfast if you want it."

Emily shrugged out of her coat and tossed it over a nearby chair before crossing the room. She grabbed a blue-and-white platter from the shelf and held it out to him.

As he scooped the bacon from the frying pan, he said, "Dru tells me you've changed your mind. You're going to stay." His voice was empty of emotion.

"Yes, I . . . I gave my word."

"Wouldn't want to put you out any."

Emily met his hard gaze. "For as long as I'm needed, I'll stay." She read the doubt in his eyes before he turned his attention back to the stove.

"Why don't you check on Dru, see if she's ready to have a bite to eat?" he suggested. "She's still in the bedroom." He jerked his head toward the far end of the house.

"All right." She set the platter on the sideboard and walked to the bedroom, rapping on the door before pushing it open. "Dru? Are you awake?"

"Come in, Emily."

"Mr. Blake's prepared breakfast. Are you hungry?"

Dru shook her head, her eyes closed. "Not right now." She drew a deep breath. "Are the girls up yet?"

"I haven't seen them." Emily went to stand beside the bed.

"We're all a bit tired, I suppose." Dru looked at Emily, smiling weakly. "As much as I hated to leave the basin, it is good to be home." She patted the edge of the bed. "Sit with me a spell."

Emily did as she was asked.

Dru reached out and took hold of her hand. "I wanted to thank you again for agreeing to stay. I hope you understand how important you are to this family now."

A lump formed in Emily's throat, making it hard to speak.

"Gavin is a good man, Emily. I know he hasn't always made you feel welcome, but it's only because he is unsure of the future. He married me so that my children would have a father when I'm gone. He married me because I asked him to, not out of some great passion."

Emily felt her cheeks growing warm. It didn't seem right that she should know such things. She already had more than enough on her conscience.

"Gavin has a big heart." Dru released a long sigh. "So much room for love."

She couldn't bear it. She couldn't listen to Dru continue to sing Gavin's praises. "I'd better tell him you aren't ready to eat yet."

Dru's hold on Emily's hand tightened. "Tell Gavin he needs to take you to town. We need supplies before winter sets in hard, and I'm sure you must have mail waiting for you from your sister."

"Shouldn't Stubs go with Mr. Blake? I should stay here in case you need me."

"No." Dru released her hand. "You go with Gavin. You should see the town, and there may be things you'll want at the mercantile. Yes, you go with Gavin. The girls will look after me while you're gone."

With the completion in 1880 of the toll road from Challis into the mining district, miners, their families, hangers-on, and enterprising merchants had poured into the area. Bonanza City and Custer had become bustling towns complete with general stores, meat markets, livery and feed stables, restaurants, laundries, and hotels. Challis, located in a more bucolic section of the mountain country, had thrived as well.

As Gavin drove the wagon toward town, he ruminated on the series of events that had brought him to the Salmon River country. He and Stubs had finished a long cattle drive up from Texas and collected their pay in Miles City, Montana, then headed west to find wealth in the gold-laden hills of Idaho Territory. Except they'd found, as had many others, that riches were more apt to come to those selling goods to the miners than to the miners themselves. But they'd kept looking, moving from camp to camp, always hoping their luck would change.

It was in Idaho City that they'd met the Porter family. From the start, Charlie Porter had felt like Gavin's long-lost brother. But it was Dru who made them into a family. Dru with her warm laughter, her enjoyment of life, and her strong faith. Later, when Petula was born in Bonanza City, Dru had asked Gavin to be the baby's godfather. Even now, remembering, it created a warm spot in his heart. It had hurt more than he'd thought possible when Charlie died. And now Dru —

The right front wagon wheel dropped into a deep rut in the road, almost unseating Gavin. A moment later, the rear wheel followed suit. He heard Emily's gasp and looked in her direction in time to see her jostle from side to side.

"Sorry," he said.

She touched the crown of her hat, as if to make certain it hadn't fallen off as she'd been jerked about. "Are we nearly there?"

He nodded — and resisted the urge to help straighten her hat, which was now slightly askew on her pretty head.

He clenched his jaw. It wasn't right, this infernal attraction he felt for her. Worse yet, it wasn't smart. She had her place and he had his, and there would never be a time when those two places were one and the same.

Emily released a sigh of relief as the wagon rolled down the main street of Challis. The trip into town had seemed hours long. Gavin hadn't spoken more than a half dozen words, and those few words had been clipped. She would be glad to be down from this wagon seat and away from him.

Challis, Idaho, looked much like hundreds of other small Western towns. Not that Emily had seen hundreds, but she imagined them all the same. There was a mercantile, a saloon, a dry goods store, a livery stable, a Wells Fargo office, and a Chinese laundry all within easy view. A few small homes could be seen down a side street. The wagon drew to a halt in front of the Challis Mercantile.

Gavin wrapped the reins around the brake handle, then hopped to the ground and walked around to the opposite side. Wordlessly, he held out his right hand to Emily. With some misgiving, she slipped her gloved fingers into his. Better to take his hand than risk a fall and possibly ruining her dress as she climbed down.

"Gavin! Sure and I'm glad to see you're back."

Emily turned along with Gavin toward the deep male voice with the soft Irish burr. The man who stepped onto the boardwalk was well over six feet tall and wore a stylish suit coat over his broad shoulders. His feet were clad in shiny leather boots. Without hesitation, he threw his arms around Gavin and gave him a hug and a few slaps on the back before releasing him.

"Saints be praised. It's far too long since we've seen you, mate. How are the wee lasses? How is Dru?"

Gavin grinned. "We're well enough, Patrick. The girls have grown like weeds over the summer. You'll hardly know them when you see them. How are you and your family?"

"Right as rain, mate." He turned toward Emily, flashing a wide grin. "I see you've brought a bit of beauty out of the basin with you." His gaze appraised her. "Perhaps I should be summering my cattle there too."

And just like that, Gavin's smile vanished.

"What are you waiting for, man? Introduce me to the lady." The man called Patrick gave Gavin a lighthearted punch on the arm, then said, "Oh, the devil with you." He doffed his felt derby in Emily's direction, revealing a shock of carrot-red hair. "Patrick O'Donnell, at your service, miss." He bowed. "It's glad I am to make your acquaintance."

There was no resisting that charming grin. She tilted her head, acknowledging his greeting. "I'm Emily Harris. Pleased to meet you, Mr. O'Donnell."

"Emily. A name that must make the angels rejoice." He bowed a second time.

Gavin made a disgusted noise in the back of his throat.

"Ignore the blighter." Patrick slipped Emily's hand into the crook of his arm and drew her toward the door of the mercantile. "Now tell me, Miss Harris. What brought you to our fair community?"

"I am governess for the Blake children."

Patrick opened the door. As she moved

past him, he offered an exaggerated wink. "Then you'll be staying. Must be the luck of the Irish I'm having today."

Emily laughed. It seemed ages since a man had flirted with her so outrageously. After languishing too often under Gavin Blake's disapproving glare, it did lift her spirits to be with someone who actually seemed taken with her.

"Unfortunately, Miss Harris, I have an appointment at the bank and so cannot stay to make your further acquaintance. But we will see each other again. Soon, I hope." Patrick turned toward Gavin who had followed them into the store. "You'll be giving my best to Dru and the lasses."

"I'll do it, Patrick."

"It is good to have you back. I've missed beating you at checkers." He laughed again, then stepped outside and disappeared down the boardwalk.

"Be warned, Miss Harris," Gavin said, a note of reluctant humor in his voice. "Patrick O'Donnell is full of blarney, if ever an Irishman was."

Maybe so, but Emily had already decided that she liked him.

FIFTEEN

Emily watched as Dru pulled her best dress over her head. Three weeks of rest had done wonders for the woman, but she was far from being strong. Feisty, yes. Strong, no.

"Would you stop looking at me like that?" Dru said. "I am well enough to attend the wedding, and nothing you say will keep me from it."

Emily shook her head, defeated. "Mr. Blake won't like this. I was supposed to convince you to stay home."

"I know." Dru settled onto a stool in front of the dresser. "But it doesn't serve any purpose for me to stop living before I die."

Emily sucked in a breath. It hurt to hear those words, even if they were true.

Dru's eyes met Emily's in the mirror. "We all know what's coming, and it will come at its appointed time, no matter what I do." She twisted on the stool to look at Emily. "I don't want my girls' last memories of me to

169

be sad ones. I want them to remember me happy at a wedding. Maybe even dancing. Can you understand that?"

"Yes," Emily whispered, her throat tight. She picked up the brush and selected a ribbon from a box on the dresser. "How would you like your hair?"

"Anything to make it look halfway pretty will do."

Emily ran the brush through the gray-brown hair, wishing there was something special she could do. "I know!" She dropped the brush onto the dresser. "Don't move, Dru. Stay right there. I won't be but a few minutes."

She rushed out of the bedroom, not even pausing to pull on her coat before heading outside. Hugging her arms over her chest, she ran toward her cabin. Once inside, she rummaged through her trunk, tossing things onto her bed until she found the small box she sought.

"It will be perfect," she whispered to herself.

Her heart felt lighter as she hurried back to the main house. Dru waited at her dressing table, just as she'd been told to do.

"Look. Isn't it wonderful?" Emily opened the box. "It will go perfectly with your dress." She held up a spray of satin tiger lilies and brown ostrich feathers on a comb, the orange flowers interspersed with burnt-sienna leaves of the same shiny fabric.

Dru held out her hands, cradling the satin and feathers as if they were fragile glassware. "This is much too fine for me. It's meant for someone young and pretty . . . like you."

"What nonsense." Emily took the brush in hand once again and quickly swept Dru's hair into a smooth twist at the back of her head.

"What if I lose it? I couldn't replace —"

"I'm not lending it, Dru. It's yours to keep. A gift from me to you."

"Oh, Emily. That's too —"

"It's much prettier with your coloring. You'll see." As she spoke, she slipped the comb into the hair above and behind Dru's right ear, then leaned down and met the woman's gaze in the mirror. "See? I was right. It's perfect. Look at the color it brings to your cheeks. You look beautiful."

"She's right, Dru," Gavin said from the doorway. "You do look beautiful."

Emily straightened and turned, but his gaze was on his wife's reflection, a tender smile on his mouth, a soft look in his eyes. In that moment, Emily felt like an intruder. She slowly backed away from Dru. But she stopped when Gavin's gaze shifted to her.

When the tenderness didn't alter or disappear, she felt a wonderful warmth rush through her veins. Her mouth went as dry as dust.

"It's a gift from Emily," Dru said.

"I heard." He crossed the bedroom in several easy strides. "I guess this means you won't stay home."

"I haven't seen my friends and neighbors since last May. This may be my last chance before . . . before winter sets in hard. Please don't argue with me."

He shook his head. "Since when did it do me any good to argue with you, Drucilla Blake?" He rested a hand on her shoulder.

Her hand came up to cover his. "Never."

Once again, Emily felt like an interloper and sought to leave the room. And once again, she was stopped by a single glance from Gavin.

A maelstrom of feelings swept through her. Pleasure, confusion, bewilderment, satisfaction. Warm and cold at the same time. Joy and sorrow mingled together. Hope for what could be, despair for what could never be.

She found her voice at last. "I'd better get ready too." She retreated to her cabin as quickly as her feet would carry her.

■ ■ ■ ■

Gavin drew the wagon to a stop on the crest of a hill. "What do you think of it, Miss Harris?" He motioned with his head toward the valley below.

The two-story stone house, U-shaped and sprawling, resembled a medieval castle. It was set against a tree-covered mountain and surrounded by a sloping lawn. Threads of smoke drifted above numerous chimneys jutting up from the steep-pitched roof. Green shutters bordered the many windows that looked over the panoramic countryside.

"Who lives there?"

Gavin answered, "The O'Donnells. They call it Killarney Hall. Impressive, isn't it? The Johansen girl didn't do too bad for herself, I'd say."

Dru jabbed him in the ribs with her elbow, and he regretted his comment. From all reports, Pearl Johansen was head over heels in love with her intended. He had no cause to assume she married for money.

Emily leaned forward on the wagon seat to look at him. "I thought we were going into town."

"There'll be too many people at this wedding for the little Episcopal church in Challis," Dru answered. "It's not every day one of the O'Donnell boys gets married. Folks from miles around will be here today."

"Mr. O'Donnell is the groom," Sabrina said with an air of authority.

"Patrick O'Donnell? The man I met when we went to town for supplies?"

Was that disappointment Gavin heard in Emily's voice? "No. His brother, Shane."

Sabrina stood and leaned her head between her mother and Emily. "Patrick O'Donnell is the oldest brother. He's older, like Pa. Shane O'Donnell, the one who's getting married, is next. Then comes Jamie and then Trevor. Trevor's sixteen, and I'm going to marry him when I grow up."

Dru and Emily exchanged amused glances but didn't contradict the girl.

Gavin found nothing humorous about it. What would he do when Sabrina became a young woman? How would he know if she was ready to marry? What would he do if she chose unwisely? The questions sent a chill through him.

He slapped the reins against the horses' backsides, and the wagon started down the hillside toward Killarney Hall and the many outbuildings that were part of the estate. As soon as they pulled into the yard a short while later, the front door of the house opened and three of the O'Donnell brothers — strapping, tall men with matching thatches of red hair — came outside.

"Gavin!" Patrick called to him, his usual grin in place. "I told Shane you wouldn't miss seeing him trussed up in holy wedlock." He strode toward the wagon and lifted Petula from the bed, swinging her high in the air before setting her on her feet. "This can't be the wee lass, can it?"

"I'm Pet!" she answered with a giggle.

"And can this be Sabrina? Faith, but she's become a young lady over the summer." He lifted the older girl to the ground as he had her sister.

Sabrina looked toward the two younger men still standing near the entrance to the house. "Hello, Trevor," she called to him.

Gavin felt that same chill again.

"Puppy love," Dru whispered as her hand touched his knee. "You needn't worry."

Patrick stepped to the opposite side of the wagon, his arms outstretched toward Emily. "It's pleased I am to see you again, Miss Harris. Allow me to help you down." And with that, he lifted her to the ground as easily as he had the children.

Gavin jumped down from the wagon seat, then helped Dru descend.

Patrick let out a low whistle. "Drucilla

Blake, you'll outshine the bride herself, so pretty you look."

Dru laughed. "Leave off your Irish blarney, Patrick O'Donnell. I've known you long enough to keep your empty flattery from turning my head."

"A shame you feel that way, for I meant it from the heart." He turned toward Gavin. "It's not fair you should have so many beautiful women at the Lucky Strike, mate, while I've got nothing but brothers to look at." He motioned with his head for Gavin to follow, then hooked Emily's hand through his left arm and Dru's through his right. "Come in out of the cold. We've merrymaking to do this day."

While Patrick squired the ladies inside, Gavin led the team and wagon around to the stables. As he unhitched the horses, he wondered at the odd tension he felt around Patrick. The two of them were good friends. Was he suddenly jealous of the wealth of the O'Donnells? No. That wasn't it. He was content with the Lucky Strike.

Still, he hadn't wanted to come to the wedding, and he dreaded going inside and listening to Patrick lavish compliments on the womenfolk.

Womenfolk? Or just Emily?

Setting his jaw, he headed for the house.

■ ■ ■ ■

Dru hadn't exaggerated when she said folks would come from miles around to see an O'Donnell get married. The large house seemed in danger of bursting at the seams with people, young and old alike, all of them in good spirits as they gathered close to hear the tiny, dark-haired bride promise to love, honor, and obey the strapping, red-headed groom.

After the ceremony, servants carried platters of food to the long tables set along one wall of the great room in the center of the house. People milled about, chatting with neighbors, sharing gossip, eating and laughing.

Names swirled in Emily's head. Too many to keep straight. In the past two hours, Patrick had introduced her to nearly every person who lived within a hundred miles of Challis. There were a few from even farther away, like the man with sagging jowls and narrow eyes who stood opposite her now.

"If you'll excuse me, Miss Harris, Senator Brewer," Patrick said. "I see that my brother Jamie wants a word with me."

Senator Brewer rubbed the whiskers on his chin. "Where are you from, Miss Harris?

I venture you are not from around here."

"I'm from Boise City."

"You don't say. Harris." He frowned. "Harris. Do I know your family? I certainly should if they live in my district."

"I was raised by my sister and her husband, Maggie and Tucker Branigan."

"You're Judge Branigan's sister-in-law? Well, well. I had no idea he knew the O'Donnells." He lowered his voice. "It never hurts to have wealthy friends when one is in office. I'll have to have a talk with that brother-in-law of yours. If he were to run for higher office and had the support and money of the O'Donnells behind him, there'd be no stopping him. I can see why he sent you to represent him."

Emily took a sudden dislike to the senator. "Tucker doesn't know the O'Donnells, sir. I'm the governess for the Blake family."

"A governess? Out here?" Bushy eyebrows rose on his wrinkled forehead.

She could almost read the questions running through his mind: Was Judge Branigan in financial trouble? Was Emily in some sort of disgrace, sent away where few people would see her? Was there a scandal brewing? Something that might be politically advantageous to know? It made her blood boil.

"Excuse me, Senator. I'd better make sure my young charges aren't up to any mischief. You know how children can be."

"Of course. You go right ahead about your duties."

What a disagreeable man. When she wrote to Maggie and Tucker again, she would inform them of this encounter.

She moved through the throng of people in the great room, unconcerned about Sabrina and Petula. The children of the wedding guests were all being attended by members of the O'Donnell staff in some other room in the house. She'd only used them as an excuse to leave the senator's company. In fact, what she wanted most was a few minutes alone. She hadn't attended a gathering this large in over a year. The room felt too close, the air too thick.

She made her way out of the great room, through more guests who mingled in an adjoining sitting room, and finally found herself in the hallway of the east wing. An open door at the end of the hall beckoned to her. She hurried toward it.

As she stepped into what turned out to be a sunny solarium, she came to an abrupt halt. Gavin stood near the long bank of windows, his expression pensive as he stared outside. She took a step backward, planning to leave.

Perhaps she made a sound, for he turned and looked her way. His gaze stopped her departure.

"I didn't know you were in here." Why did she say that? She didn't need to explain.

He jerked his head toward the windows. "Come look." His tone seemed ominous.

Emily moved to the windows, leaving several feet of space between herself and Gavin, even though she wished to stand close beside him. Seated on a bench in the garden was Sabrina, her face a portrait of misery. Emily followed the girl's gaze toward a gazebo where Trevor O'Donnell leaned against the railing, smiling down at a pretty teenaged girl in a pink dress. As they watched, Trevor straightened, removed his suit coat, and draped it around the girl's shoulders.

"I'd like to break his jaw," Gavin said.

Emily understood then, and her heart went out to him, despite herself. "Brina would never forgive you if you did."

"He's broken her heart."

"It will mend. She's only nine."

Gavin sighed as he turned his back toward the window and looked at her. "I don't know how to be a father to girls."

"Nonsense. You're reacting as any father

would in similar circumstances."

"You think so?"

Emily's first instinct was always to encourage someone when they were down. Her words to Gavin had been nothing more than that. Words meant to encourage. She'd constructed a barrier between them several weeks earlier, a barrier meant to protect her from her own feelings. But now, as she realized how deeply worried he was, as she recognized how much he loved Sabrina — how desperate he was to be a good father to the girl, how scared he was that he would fail — Emily's guard lowered.

"Yes, Mr. Blake. I think so. You're a good father. Brina and Pet adore you."

He looked at her in silence, his eyes thoughtful and unwavering.

Her breathing grew shallow as she met his gaze, silence surrounding them. She couldn't let her resolve weaken further. She had to stay strong. He had been so cool with her since she declared her desire to go home to Boise, and that was exactly how she wanted things to remain between them. For both their sakes.

She lifted her chin and said with as much dignity as possible, "I think I'll return to the party."

"You've had a good time today?" he asked

before she could turn to leave.

She nodded, stayed by his words.

"I won't be able to give Sabrina a wedding like this one when her time comes."

Her resolve failed her. "She won't need a big wedding. All that will matter to her is that she loves the groom and that her family is with her."

More silence and then, "Thank you, Miss Harris."

If she didn't leave now, she might begin to cry. Her thoughts and emotions were all a jumble. She was confused about her feelings for this man. But where could she turn for guidance? Oh, if only Maggie were here. If only she could ask her sister what —

"Ah, so here you are."

She turned toward the sound of Patrick O'Donnell's voice, grateful for the interruption, thankful for any excuse to escape.

Patrick stood in the solarium doorway, Dru holding his right arm. "We've come looking for you both."

One look at Emily's face and Dru knew that something had changed between those two. She had almost given up hope in the weeks they'd been back home. She'd begun to wonder if she'd mistaken Emily's feelings. But there it was in her eyes, clear as day to anyone who had eyes to see. Could Gavin see it? No, she didn't think he could.

I must talk to her. I must tell her it's all right. I must talk to them both. I cannot wait any longer.

Patrick said, "Gavin, I think Dru would like to go home. She's feeling tired."

Gavin moved toward her in an instant. "I was afraid this would be too much for you."

"It wasn't too much for me," she lied. "It did me good to be here. But it is growing late, and I would prefer to arrive home before dark."

Emily said, "I'll get the children and meet you in the front hall." Then she hurried out of the solarium as fast as decorum allowed.

God, please don't let me be too late. I feel certain she is the one you mean to love my daughters and to love Gavin. Please don't let me be too late.

SIXTEEN

It was nearly dark by the time the family arrived home, the first stars already visible in the east. Dru stirred and lifted her head from Emily's shoulder as the wagon rolled to a stop in front of the house. Gavin jumped down from the wagon seat, then took his wife in his arms and carried her inside.

Emily turned to look behind her. "Wake up, sleepyheads. We're home. Let's get you inside and into your own bed."

Sabrina groaned and rolled onto her side beneath the blankets, snuggling closer to her sleeping little sister.

Emily reached down and gently shook the older girl's shoulder. "We're home, Brina. Time to get inside. It's cold out here." Holding her skirt out of the way, she stepped down from the wagon and went to the back of the vehicle, waiting for Sabrina and Petula to join her there.

They didn't budge. She was about to climb into the wagon bed when Gavin reappeared.

"You'll ruin that pretty dress of yours, Miss Harris," he said, stopping her. Then he hopped into the back of the wagon. He lifted Petula first.

"Give her to me, Mr. Blake. I'll carry her inside while you get Brina."

He hesitated a moment, and she felt him watching her. What was he thinking? She wished she knew.

He knelt on one knee and passed the child from his arms to hers. Emotion formed a lump in her throat as she carried Petula into the house. This all felt too right. The four of them home from an outing, the children tired, her carrying them to bed with Gavin.

Only there weren't just four of them. There were five — and she was the fifth. She was the one who didn't belong.

Once in the children's bedroom, Emily sat on the edge of the bed and helped Petula out of her coat, shoes, and dress while Gavin did the same with her sister on the opposite side of the bed. Although still half asleep, Petula managed to sit up and raise her arms when told to. But the instant her nightgown slid over her head, she turned and crawled under the covers, her arms clutching her pillow close. Emily leaned down, straightened the blankets over her shoulders, and kissed the girl on the forehead.

"Good night, Pet," she whispered.

When she straightened, she saw Gavin drawing the covers over Sabrina. As Emily had done with Petula, he leaned low to kiss Sabrina's forehead.

"Sleep tight," he said.

Emily's heart beat an odd rhythm in her chest. Oh, how she wished —

No, she wouldn't wish it. She wouldn't think it.

"I'll walk you to your cabin, Miss Harris, and make sure you've got a fire for the night."

"It . . . it isn't necessary. I can —"

"I've got to unhitch the team anyway. It's no bother."

It would have been easier if he'd stayed angry with her. It would have been better if she'd remembered she didn't even like him much.

They walked in silence toward Emily's one-room cabin. When they entered it, they discovered the temperature inside was nearly as cold as outside, the fire in the stove having long since burned down to a few coals. Gavin built it back up in no time.

■ ■ ■ ■

Dru knelt beside the bed, hands folded, head bowed.

"Help Gavin, Lord. Draw him by your Spirit. Teach him to trust you. Touch his heart and heal it."

Tears splashed onto her knuckles, then slid slowly over her fingers to the comforter beneath her hands.

"When I'm gone, Lord, knit a new family together. Bring this house alive with love. It's seen too much heartache already. I want my girls to be happy. I know that Gavin and Emily care for each other, but they're trying so hard not to care because of me."

She drew a deep breath as she looked toward the ceiling.

"I haven't gone about this the right way. Help me make it right before I go."

Gavin turned from the stove. Emily stood in the center of the room, clutching her coat collar close about her throat, her face lit by the firelight from the open stove door.

"It should warm up in here pretty fast," he said.

She nodded.

He glanced about the darkened room.

"Do you have everything you need?"

"Yes."

He cleared his throat. "Listen, I know I haven't been . . . I've been a bit gruff with you since we left the basin. I . . . I'd like to say I'm sorry. It isn't your fault."

"It's all right, Mr. Blake. I understand."

He doubted she did. For that matter, he wasn't sure he understood himself. The reason seemed to shift from day to day, moment to moment. Was it because he thought her too much like his mother, selfish and spoiled and desiring an easier life, one she could have with her prosperous sister and brother-in-law in Boise? Or was it because Patrick O'Donnell had showed interest in her? O'Donnell, who could give her that easier life right here in the Challis area. Or was it because Gavin found her so tender with the children, so gentle with Dru, so full of life and laughter? So irresistible, when all reason and all rules of common decency told him he should not find her so.

"I'd better take care of the horses."

In three strides he could reach her. In three steps he could gather her in his arms and pull her close and kiss those sweet lips. Everything inside screamed for him to do just that, but somehow he managed to turn on his heel and walk away from her.

"Good night, Miss Harris."

"Good night, Mr. Blake," he heard her say as he pulled the door closed behind him.

He'd lost his mind. That was the only explanation for the things he felt, for the things he wanted. He'd lost any shred of common sense, and Emily Harris was responsible for it.

SEVENTEEN

Emily dreamed that Gavin had kissed her. She dreamed he'd held her close and whispered words of love. She dreamed that he'd stayed with her. Dreams that seemed real and possible. Dreams that made her feel guilty, even in sleep.

After dressing the following morning, she checked her reflection in the mirror atop the bureau and pinched her cheeks between forefingers and thumbs, trying to put a hint of color in her pale complexion. But there was nothing she could do about the look of shame in her eyes.

"I'm a horrible person," she whispered. "How could I let this happen?"

What she wanted was to crawl back into bed and stay there all day. But she couldn't. She had obligations to Dru and to the children. She'd given her word that she would take care of them, and despite the fragile state of her heart, she wouldn't let them down.

Oh, Maggie, I wish you were here. You could tell me what to do.

At the door, she took her cloak from the peg and threw it over her shoulders.

Gavin . . . His name echoed in her heart.

Pulling the hood over her head, she opened the cabin door and hurried toward the main house. Just as her hand touched the latch, she heard the clatter of hooves and turned to see Gavin ride his gelding out of the barn. If he saw her there, he never let on.

Just as well.

She lifted the latch and entered the kitchen.

"Look what you did!" Sabrina's shrill cry brought Emily up short.

Before her stood Petula, already in tears, egg yolks spotting her leggings and broken shells surrounding her feet.

Emily shrugged off her cloak and hurried forward. "Don't cry, Pet. We can clean this up in no time."

"Ma wanted an egg for breakfast," Sabrina said, glowering at her sister. "And Pet just broke the last of them. The hens won't lay any more until tomorrow. Pet ruined Ma's breakfast."

The younger girl began to sob. "I . . . I

did . . . didn't mean . . . mean to drop them."

Emily pushed tangled brown hair away from the child's face as she knelt beside her, unmindful of the gooey mess on the floor. She kissed Petula's cheek. "Hush now. Shh. Your mother will understand. We'll make her something she'll like much better than eggs."

"What?" Petula sniffed, then rubbed her sleeve beneath her nose.

"I don't know. Why don't I go ask her?" She gave the girl an encouraging smile as she rose to her feet. "Brina, would you please help Pet clean up the floor while I see what will tempt your mother's appetite?"

Sabrina looked none too happy, but she nodded in agreement.

"Miss . . . Miss Harris?" Petula pointed. "Look."

Emily's gaze dropped to her skirt, the pale blue wool now stained yellow. "Don't worry, Pet. It will clean." She wasn't sure that was true, but she couldn't bear it if Petula started to cry again.

She turned and walked to Dru's bedroom. As she paused before the door, memories of last night's dreams came rushing back — and with them, the guilt. If only she could take her dreams and thoughts into captivity as the Bible commanded her to do.

She leveled her shoulders, drew a deep breath, and pushed open the door. "Dru?" The room was shrouded in shadows.

"Is everything all right out there?" The woman's voice was barely more than a whisper.

"Yes." Emily crossed the room. "Just a little tiff between sisters." She stopped beside the bed. "But I'm afraid there won't be any eggs for breakfast. Pet dropped them."

"It doesn't matter." Dru released a sigh. "I doubt I could have eaten more than a bite."

"I saw Mr. Blake ride out. Will he be back for breakfast?"

"No. He'll be gone the better part of the day."

Emily frowned. "Should he have left you alone?"

"I told him to go. I knew you would be in soon. I was hoping we could talk, you and I, and sometimes men are just underfoot."

"We can talk as much as you like." It seemed to Emily that the woman in the bed had withered away to nothing. "But you should try to eat something first."

"Perhaps later. Come back after the girls

have their breakfast. There are things I need to say."

"Of course, Dru. Whatever you'd like."

"I'll just close my eyes and rest until you return. I'm so tired today."

After preparing the children's breakfast, Emily went to her cabin to change out of her soiled gown. Upon her return, she found Dru fast asleep. Since Dru usually read to the children from the Bible on Sunday mornings, Emily sat with them near the fireplace and read parables from the Gospel of John, then led them in prayer.

Several times throughout the morning, she returned to the bedroom to check on Dru, but the woman never stirred, her breathing so shallow it barely existed. Worry began to gnaw in Emily's chest, and she prayed for God's guidance, unsure what to do. She also prayed for Gavin to return.

It was shortly after one o'clock when a knock sounded on the door. When Emily opened it, she found Patrick waiting on the stoop, hat in hand.

"Good day, Miss Harris. I hope I've not come at an inopportune time."

"Not at all, Mr. O'Donnell. Please come in out of the cold."

With a nod, he stepped past her.

Emily held out a hand to take his hat. "Gavin isn't here, but he should return at any time."

"It's not Gavin I've come to see."

"I'm afraid Dru is resting."

"It's not her I've come to see either."

Perhaps it was the schoolboy look of hope on his face that gave his intentions away. Emily wasn't sure how to react, not when her heart was already in a tug of war over her feelings for Gavin.

"Won't you sit down?" she said softly, motioning toward the chairs near the fireplace.

The time she had spent with Patrick the previous day at his brother's wedding had been pleasant. Although a large man, he had an air of gentleness about him that appealed to her, as did the merry twinkle in his eyes and his infectious grin. She thought she could like him a great deal — if not for Gavin Blake.

Then again, perhaps she could use Patrick's interest in her to her advantage. Perhaps he could become a shield between her and Gavin. Maybe his interest would protect her from herself and the feelings she shouldn't entertain. And perhaps she might learn to return his affections. It would be better for everyone if she could.

"I'm glad you came for a visit, Mr. O'Donnell. I enjoyed my time at your home yesterday. It was a beautiful wedding."

"It was at that. My brother is a lucky man to have found himself the perfect wife." A smile pulled at the corners of his mouth. "I'd be happy indeed if the same could be true for me."

Dru could see Charlie. He waited for her, smiling, arms open wide. A warm, comforting light surrounded him. Once she reached him, her pain would cease, her weariness would dissipate. She would be able to laugh again and run through the woods and fall down with Charlie in the grass. Once she joined him, she could be free of concerns.

He beckoned for her to hurry.

I'm coming.

But something held her back. Something unfinished.

Soon, Charlie. I'll join you soon.

She struggled up through the darkness, an arduous, tiring journey.

Relief rushed through Emily when she saw Dru's eyes flutter open. "Hello there." She forced a smile onto her lips. "You've been asleep all day. Are you hungry?"

"No, I'm not hungry." Dru lifted her hand.

Emily took hold of it, cupping it between both of hers. "Mr. O'Donnell came for a visit and was sorry not to give you his regards in person. He said he'll come again soon." She paused as she leaned closer. "Let me get you some broth. You should eat, even if you aren't hungry."

"No." Dru shook her head. "Don't go."

She sank onto the edge of the bed. "What is it you need?"

"I have little time left and too much yet to say."

Emily opened her mouth to protest but was stopped by the look in her friend's eyes.

"There's so much I wanted to do before I joined Charlie."

She swallowed the lump in her throat and tightened her hold on the frail hand within hers.

"Gavin's a good man, Emily. We've loved each other in our own way. But he wasn't meant to marry me. I've been unfair to him." Dru closed her eyes. "I need you to understand how things are between us."

"I do understand. There's no need to explain."

"No, you don't understand."

Emily stroked the back of Dru's hand, certain that whatever the other woman wanted to tell her, she didn't want to hear.

"Gavin has never loved me as a man loves a woman. I never expected him to."

"Oh, Dru. You shouldn't —"

"Listen to me, please. I've told you that he married me because I was dying and my daughters will need someone when I'm gone. He was my husband's friend. He was my friend. And so he did the only thing he could to help. He married me."

Emily nodded, even though Dru wasn't looking at her.

"Gavin is the kind of man who gives his word and never goes back on it. He's like a rock that way. He's true to his friends, through and through. He's tenderhearted, although he tries not to show it. He's got a lot of love bottled up inside him, just waiting to be poured out on others. He can be stubborn and gruff, but it's just a cover for the tenderness inside him that he doesn't want others to see."

Tears trickled from the corners of Dru's eyes and splashed onto the sheets. "You care for him. I know you do. He needs that. He needs you to care. He will need you even more when I am gone."

Tears blurred Emily's vision, but she stubbornly blinked them back.

"Emily . . ." Dru opened her eyes once more. "Don't forget your promise. You'll stay through spring." She smiled sadly. "Unexpected things bloom in the spring. Perhaps I'll be able to see it from heaven."

"Don't talk that way, Dru. Maybe the doctors are wrong. Maybe you'll live for years and years."

"Promise me you'll stay, Emily. Give me your word."

"I promise. I won't leave. I give you my word, but —"

"Ask Stubs about Gavin. Make him . . . make him tell you everything he can."

Emily wasn't well acquainted with death, but she could see its shadow slipping over Dru's face.

"I'd like to see Brina and Pet now. Will you help me sit up? Will you comb my hair?"

"Yes, of course. I'll help you. I'll do whatever you need."

"You're a special young woman, Emily. I'm so glad God brought you into our lives."

Gavin tossed a flake of hay into the gelding's stall, then made his way toward the house. His mood was as heavy now as when he'd ridden out of the barn that morning. Nothing had changed in the hours he was gone. Everything that he'd wanted to escape was with him still.

When he entered the kitchen, he felt the

strangeness, the heavy silence of the house. Then he saw Emily standing in the doorway of the bedroom he shared with Dru.

"Gavin."

Cold tentacles of dread reached around his heart.

"It's Dru."

Quick strides carried him out of the kitchen and across the parlor. He brushed past Emily and into the dimly lit bedroom, stopping before he reached the bed.

Dru's arms were around Petula's shoulders as she kissed the child's forehead. Then she lay back against the pillows, obviously exhausted by the effort. Her eyes met Gavin's, and she offered a tiny smile. "Here's your pa. It's time I talked to him. And then I must rest. Good night, my dear daughters. I . . . I love you so very much."

"Ma," Sabrina said in a choked voice, "can't we stay a little while longer?"

"Not now, Brina." She sighed as she closed her eyes. "I need to speak to your pa."

Gavin watched as Sabrina took hold of Petula's hand and led her little sister away from the bed. When Sabrina looked at him with eyes so like her mother's, he felt immobilized by the pain written in them. She understood what was happening.

"Come along, girls," Emily said. A moment later, the door closed with a soft click.

Dru opened her eyes once more. "I waited for you."

He moved forward on stiff legs.

"Hold my hand, Gavin."

He knelt on the hard floor and did as she'd asked.

"You've been a good friend. To me and to Charlie."

"Dru —"

"No, let me do the talking. There's so little time." Her gaze, although weary, was tender. "From the moment I first laid eyes on Charlie, I knew there was something special between us. Nothing in this world would've kept me from being his bride. Not anything. I loved him that much."

He nodded, his throat tight.

"You know I'm not afraid to die, Gavin. I know where I'm going, and it's a better place. And I'll be with Charlie. My only regret is leaving my girls, but they've got you and Emily now. They'll be fine. Just fine."

Her eyes closed again, and she was silent for a long time. Gavin tightened his grip on her hand, as if to keep her bound to this earth.

"Don't be afraid to love someone like I

loved Charlie. It makes everything in life worthwhile."

"You two had something special."

"You could have it too."

Gavin shook his head. "I'm not as good a person as you are."

"I think you could love Emily."

He stiffened. "Dru, I —"

"You were wrong about her, Gavin. She belongs in this place. She's young and strong and loves Brina and Pet so much. She could love you too if you let her."

Gavin stood and walked across the room, brushed aside the curtains to look outside, then turned toward the bed again. "I don't need her to love me. I just need her to look after the girls."

"You're a stubborn man, Gavin Blake." Dru pushed herself up on the pillows. "As bullheaded as any cattle you've got on the range."

"Maybe so, but it's just the way I am."

With a long sigh, Dru sank back on the bed, the energy she'd expended draining her. Eyes closed again, she said, "You deserve love, Gavin. I wish it for you. So does God."

Silence fell across the room, and Gavin realized she'd fallen asleep. He returned to sit beside her, watching the shallow rise and fall of her chest. He shouldn't have said what he did. He shouldn't have upset her. She was weak enough already without using what little strength she had to call him stubborn and bullheaded. And it wasn't right that she had to die. She was the kindest woman he'd ever known. It wasn't right for her to be stricken with cancer and taken from this world at her age.

The wind rose outside, whistling under the eaves of the house. A lonely, mournful sound. And Gavin could no more silence it than he could stop Dru's life from ebbing away.

Emily sat on the sofa, Sabrina on one side, Petula on the other. They'd long since given up any pretense of play. Instead they sat in silence, the girls clutching favorite dolls, staring into the fire.

Emily prayed some, tried to pray more, fought back tears.

It was well past the children's bedtime when the bedroom door opened and Gavin looked out. His face was drawn, his eyes filled with defeat. "Girls, your mother would like to see you again."

Sabrina slid to the floor first, then reached for Petula's hand. Together they entered their mother's bedroom. Emily rose and followed them as far as the doorway, where she leaned her left shoulder against the jamb.

"Let me hold you," Dru said, her words barely carrying to Emily. "One on each side."

Gavin helped drape her arms around the children, his wife too weak to do it on her own. The gesture was the last straw for Emily. She couldn't hold back the tears any longer. They streaked down her cheeks and fell onto the floor.

Plop . . . plop . . . plop.

No one spoke for thirty minutes or more. The girls sniffled now and then, and Dru kissed their heads, first one, then the other, then again and again and again. Sorrow pressed hard upon everyone in the house while death waited at the door.

At long last, Dru said, "I love you, Brina. I love you, Pet. Don't ever forget how much I love you."

Sabrina said, "We won't forget, Ma."

Gavin reached out to brush strands of hair from Dru's forehead.

She gave him a little smile. "What happened in the past . . . can't be changed . . . but the future can." Her eyes fluttered closed. "Gavin . . . I wish you love."

Emily pressed her right hand against her

heart, as if to stop it from breaking.

"My Lord . . ." Dru whispered the words on an exhaled breath. Then all was still except for the sound of the wind in the eaves.

Somehow Emily fought back another wave of tears, enough so she could enter the room and do what she had been hired to do. "Come along, girls," she said with quiet authority. "It's time you were in bed."

Did the children know their mother was gone? Gavin couldn't tell. They weren't crying now. Their tears had been spent some time ago. He watched as Emily helped each of them from the bed, holding them close against her sides.

"She's with her God," he said softly.

Emily answered, "I know." Then she led the children away.

He looked at Dru's face and was struck by the change in it. Earlier it had been drawn with pain, but now there was no sign of it. She looked younger, lighter, more like the woman she'd been before Charlie died.

He lifted Dru's hand and kissed it, then laid it across her chest.

Gavin . . . I wish you love.

As he heard her parting words repeating

in his mind, a chink appeared in the carefully constructed wall around his heart.

EIGHTEEN

Emily stood on the knoll, her right hand on Sabrina's shoulder, her left on Petula's as the children pressed close against her. Gavin stood on the other side of the grave, his face a controlled mask.

The minister's voice droned on, dispensing words of consolation and hope. Overhead, gray clouds rolled across the heavens, driven by a frigid wind. The weather seemed in keeping with the sorrow that blanketed the friends and neighbors who had gathered to bid Drucilla Blake farewell. As Reverend Keating's final prayer was carried to the mourners on the wind, the snow began to fall.

People departed quickly after that, hurrying toward their buggies, horses, and wagons.

Gavin made no move to leave, not even after the last person had offered his condolences and gone. Emily's heart ached for him. What words could she offer that would lessen his sorrow? How could she be of help? She longed to make a difference but didn't know how.

"Come along, girls," she said softly. "We must get inside."

As the three of them turned, Emily saw Patrick O'Donnell waiting at the bottom of the slope. A lump formed in her throat. She longed for someone to comfort her the way she was trying to comfort her two charges, and she knew Patrick would willingly become that person to her if she would let him.

Slowly, Emily guided Sabrina and Petula toward the house. When they reached Patrick, he fell into step beside them, not saying a word. They walked until they reached the front door, and then Emily stopped and looked back toward the knoll. The snow was falling in large gentle flakes, but she could still see Gavin's silhouette against the hillside.

"Miss Harris?"

She turned toward Patrick.

"You'll take cold if you stand out there much longer. Come inside and warm yourself by the hearth. You'll do no one any good should you take a fever."

She nodded, cast one final glance over her

shoulder, and entered the house.

"Give Gavin time," Patrick said.

That's what Dru had said too. Give him time. But there was so much more she longed to give him. She wanted to give him her heart. She wanted to share his grief, help him carry the burden of sorrow. Didn't he understand —

"Come here, lass." Patrick drew her toward the fireplace with a hand beneath her elbow. Once there, he helped her out of her cloak before urging her to sit in a nearby chair. "I'll be of whatever help I can be." He sat in the other chair before taking her hand. "Please let me be of help, Miss Harris."

A strong shoulder to lean on would be a wonderful thing. It was clear that Gavin had no intention of offering his shoulder — or anything else — to her. And why should he? He'd just lost his wife. She felt as if she could shatter into pieces. How was she to keep her promise to Dru with things as they were?

Patrick's fingers tightened around her hand. "I'm here for you, lass. Whatever you need, I'm here for you."

"Thank you, Mr. O'Donnell," she whispered as fresh tears began to fall.

The front door slammed shut, and Emily

looked over her shoulder to meet Gavin's troubled gaze. His dark hair was dotted with flakes of snow, and his face was red from the cold. Without a word to either Emily or Patrick, he moved on toward his bedroom, the door closing firmly behind him.

Emily removed her hand from Patrick's grasp. "Thank you for your kind words, Mr. O'Donnell. I appreciate them." She stood. "Now I must go to the children. It has been a difficult day, and they need me."

She found the two girls curled up together on the bed. Sabrina was stroking her sister's hair and whispering, "Don't cry, Pet," while large teardrops streaked her own cheeks.

Maggie had talked to her in just that tone of voice when they were young. Orphaned and living with a cruel uncle, there had been many occasions for them to huddle together, the two of them against the world. Or so it had seemed.

Whenever Emily had been unhappy or frightened, Maggie would play the "Good Things" game. They would hide in the attic, where Uncle Seth never thought to look for them, and together they would think of all that was good and happy and bright. Margaret Ann, Emily's favorite doll. Cuddles, the stray dog that had befriended them. Blue skies. Picnics on hot summer days. Polly, the iceman's Clydesdale.

Maggie had been both sister and mother to her, but Emily had longed to be part of a happy family. And she'd been lucky. Coming to Idaho on that wagon train so many years ago had given her the family she'd longed for. New brothers in Tucker and Neal Branigan. A new sister and best friend in Fiona Branigan. New grandparents. And later her adorable nieces and nephews. She'd been granted so many things good and happy and bright.

How long would it be before Sabrina and Petula could play the "Good Things" game? Could she help them find the happiness their mother wanted for them?

Emily crossed the room and sat beside them on the bed, pulling a blanket over them. She stroked their hair and murmured words of comfort. She silently prayed for God to protect their small hearts, to help them heal. And eventually, as the shadows in the room deepened, both girls drifted off to sleep.

Emily was surprised to find Patrick still seated by the fire when she came out of the children's room. He rose from his chair the moment she appeared.

"I thought you'd gone." She walked toward him.

"I couldn't leave until I made sure you were all right."

She sighed. "I'm all right. Just tired." She sank onto the chair nearest the fire, her gaze locked on the orange flames. "I was remembering how Maggie, my sister, used to make me feel better when something bad happened to us. We used to try to think about good things, pretty things. Like a fine horse pulling a shiny black carriage. Or a lady's hat with a purple ostrich feather. Or maybe a winter snowfall. Sometimes we'd play the game for hours."

"Did bad things happen often, Miss Harris?" He sat down once again.

"Yes. My parents were dead, and the uncle who came to raise us was a hateful man. There was no love in his heart for either of us. But God was good. Maggie and I had each other, and later God brought other people into our lives who loved us."

"I'm glad of that. I'd not have you sad if I had my way about it, and that's the truth."

She turned her head to look at him. "I don't want Brina and Pet to ever feel unloved or alone, either. I want to protect them from sorrow. I promised Dru . . ." She let her voice trail into silence.

"Grief takes many forms, Miss Harris. I believe you will find a way to help them navigate through it."

His kind words acted as a balm on her hurting soul, and she wondered, given enough time, if she could ever feel more for him than simple friendship.

November 20, 1883

Dear Maggie,

We laid Mrs. Blake to rest today. There was a biting wind and the skies were gray. Despite the threat of snow, many people attended the funeral. Mrs. Blake was loved by all who knew her.

The day before she died, we attended a wedding at the home of a neighbor. The O'Donnell house is fashioned after a wealthy estate in Ireland, I'm told. There are four O'Donnell brothers, and it was the second oldest who was married that day. It was such a festive affair. I never dreamed we would be facing death within such a short time. I suppose death always takes us by surprise, even when we are told the person is dying.

Mr. Blake has shut himself away in his grief, although he has tried to comfort the children as much as he can. And I am doing my best to relieve their pain.

Mostly I hold them and read to them and try to keep their minds occupied. I have often wished for your wise counsel. There are times that I feel completely unequal to the task before me. At other times I believe this must be why God sent me to stay with this family.

Please pray that the Lord would grant me wisdom. Pray that hearts will heal. Mr. Blake is not a man of faith, which was a heartache for his wife while she was alive. Perhaps God will use this loss to draw Mr. Blake to him.

My love to all. I will write again soon.

Your sister,
Emily

Nineteen

The days and weeks drifted by, little noticed by Gavin. Sorrow and regrets weighed him down. Logical or not, he blamed himself for Dru's death. If he'd worked harder, been more successful, had more money. If he'd taken her to see one more doctor. If he was smarter or better educated. If any of those things were true, then maybe she wouldn't have died.

And he could have been a better husband in the time they were man and wife. True, their marriage had been one of convenience, never consummated and never meant to be. True, their mutual affection had been based upon friendship and nothing more. But if he'd tried a little harder to love her in a deeper way, maybe she wouldn't have longed for Charlie. Maybe she would have fought harder to live.

He saw the children through a fog and found it almost impossible to speak to them, to even touch them. They needed him — he saw it in their eyes — but he felt unable to reach out to them. He was frozen on the inside. At least they had Emily. She cared for them. She comforted them. And maybe she would have comforted him too if he could let her.

He couldn't let her.

While Gavin wrestled with his inner demons, winter arrived in earnest. It blanketed the Salmon River Range with thick layers of snow, sometimes with lazy crystals drifting to earth, sometimes with vengeful blizzards, winds howling across the mountains and valleys. Temperatures fell below zero at night and often lingered there until noon. The skies seemed eternally gray, like a mirror of the sadness that gripped the Blake home.

Emily was almost thankful for the fullness of her days. She took care of the house and the girls, preparing meals, washing and mending clothes. She made sure the children kept up with their lessons, more to keep their minds occupied than for the learning itself. She had made a promise to Dru, and although it wouldn't be easy, she meant to keep it.

Christmas would have been a dismal affair in the Blake house, if not for Patrick's help. He became a frequent visitor to the Lucky Strike in the weeks after the funeral, and Emily was grateful for all he did for them. He took her and the girls on an outing to chop down a Christmas tree, then helped them string popcorn and make paper garlands for decorations. He took Emily into Challis in his sleigh so she could buy gifts for the children to go under the tree on Christmas morning, and he bought a large bag of nuts to fill their stockings. He also did his best to give what comfort he could to Gavin, but his friend paid him no heed.

Emily hadn't expected Patrick to visit on Christmas Day, but a little after one o'clock, he arrived at the front door.

"Merry Christmas, Miss Harris."

"Mr. O'Donnell, what a pleasant surprise. Please, come in from the cold. Let me get you some coffee to warm yourself."

"It's a fine day. The sun is out again, and the snow is sparkling. I thought perhaps you might join me for a sleigh ride. Surely Gavin and the young ones could spare you for a time."

"Well, I —"

"Don't be saying you have work to do. It's Christmas, after all. Even a governess deserves some time off today."

From the kitchen doorway, Gavin said, "Patrick's right, Miss Harris. We can manage on our own for an afternoon. Go and enjoy yourself."

She was dispensable. Gavin didn't need her, didn't want her, had rejected her time and again, only tolerated her because it had been Dru's dying wish that Emily stay with the girls until spring. If she'd had any hope that Gavin might learn to care for her as she cared for him — as Dru had wanted, Emily had come to believe — the past few weeks had shattered it.

"I'll get my wrap," she said softly.

Before she could take more than a few steps toward the kitchen where she'd hung her coat earlier that morning, Gavin brought it to her. "Enjoy yourself," he said.

The threat of tears made her throat ache. "Thank you."

"No need to rush back. I can look after Brina and Pet."

If she didn't leave right now, she might let him see how much his words hurt. She didn't want that. She turned toward Patrick, who took the coat from her hands and helped her into it before opening the door.

"We'll return in an hour or so," Patrick told Gavin.

Gavin didn't reply.

Once Emily was seated in the front seat of the sleigh, Patrick covered her with a fur-lined lap robe. Then he joined her on the seat, taking up the reins and slapping them against the team's rumps. The sleigh slid away from the house, accompanied by the jingle of bells on the harness.

It was a beautiful Christmas day, the sky so blue it almost hurt the eyes, the snow glittering in the sunlight. The cold against her cheeks revived Emily's spirits.

"Look there," Patrick said, breaking the silence that had stretched between them. He slowed the horses to a halt.

Emily followed the direction of his gaze to a herd of elk, a hundred or more, moving slowly but steadily across the valley about half a mile ahead of them. The sound of horns clicking against horns carried to them on the breeze. Several elk — a few with massive racks spanning four or five feet across — stopped and stared in their direction, then continued on their way, as if to say that humans were of no importance.

"The Indians call the elk *wapiti*," Patrick told her. "It means 'white,' referring to their tails."

"I've never seen so many in one place before." She turned and gave him a smile. "They're breathtaking."

He leaned close. "If you'll allow me to say so, Miss Harris, so are you."

She liked Patrick a great deal. He was generous and amusing, candid and tender. That he would like to be more to her than a friend had never been in question, but he had never pressed her. She thought that was about to change.

"Miss Harris . . . Emily . . . you know that I care for you."

A girl could do much worse than Patrick O'Donnell for a suitor. Much worse. And he was ever so thoughtful. Hadn't he shown her countless courtesies in these past weeks? When she'd had no one else she could turn to, there he had been.

"Sure and I've been hoping you might consider me for a husband."

How should she answer? She had always said she would only marry for love and for no other reason. But marrying for love wasn't possible now. For the man she loved didn't love her in return.

Patrick pulled her left hand from the muff she held on her lap, then slid a ruby and emerald ring onto the tip of her finger, pausing to ask, "Will you marry me, Emily?"

"Patrick . . ."

"I swear I'll do all in my power to make you happy."

"It's so soon after Dru died. I couldn't leave Brina and Pet now. Their hearts are broken. And I cannot accept this." She removed the ring from her finger and pressed it into his hand. "It's too soon."

"Fine. You needn't wear the ring. You needn't upset the children. But tell me you'll marry me. We'll wait as long as you wish to wed. Say you'll marry me, Emily. Tell me when that can be."

"I promised the Blakes I would stay until spring, until the cattle go back to the basin."

"Mid-June then. It's a good time for a wedding."

"But I —"

He stopped her words with a kiss.

She wanted to be stirred. She wanted her heart to react. She wanted her pulse to race.

"Go on, Emily. Say you'll marry me," he whispered, his lips still near her own. "Say it."

Gavin didn't want her. Probably didn't need her. Most likely wouldn't miss her when she was gone.

"Say it."

"All right, Patrick. Yes. I will marry you."

He kissed her again.

Don't be afraid to love, Dru had told Gavin.

Don't be afraid to risk it all, was what

she'd tried to tell him. Don't be afraid to trust and give. Don't be afraid to take in return. Don't be so embittered by what someone did in the past that you can't look for the good in others. Don't believe that every woman is like Christina Blake, selfish and spoiled. Believe, instead, in the best in people.

It all became crystal clear in Gavin's mind as he lay in bed, sleepless and searching for answers.

Don't be afraid to love. Really love. Love with everything — heart, body, mind, and soul. Don't be afraid to love.

I think you could love Emily . . . She belongs in this place . . . She could love you too if you let her.

He'd had Dru's blessing. More than her blessing. Her prayers. He knew that now. Should have known it then. Should have understood that this had been Dru's desire even before they went to Boise to hire a governess.

He got out of bed and went into the parlor. Hot coals glowed red in the fireplace. He checked the mantle clock, 2:00 a.m. He tossed more wood into the fireplace and waited for it to flare to life.

Dru had wanted more for him than he'd wanted for himself. Because she'd loved

Charlie with her whole heart, she'd wanted the same for Gavin. More, she'd wanted her daughters to be raised in that kind of home, where the parents loved completely and fully.

She was right. He was bullheaded.

Gavin walked into the kitchen and looked out of the window toward the one-room cabin that had been his home while Charlie was alive. Emily was asleep in there now.

She could love you too if you let her.

Could she? Could Emily love him if he let her?

Maybe. Maybe he should find out if Dru was right.

Emily awakened before dawn. She wouldn't be needed in the house for several more hours, but there was no point trying to go back to sleep. Her thoughts were already churning. She needed to write to Maggie and tell her about Patrick's proposal. Her sister would want to meet him before their wedding day. Would Maggie and Tucker come to Challis or would she and Patrick need to travel to Boise? Of course, no one could find fault with the good-natured, kindhearted Patrick O'Donnell. Everyone who knew him liked him. One couldn't help but fall victim to his Irish charm.

But there was an ache inside Emily. She wanted more than kindness, more than goodness.

She wanted Gavin.

With a moan, she tossed aside the blankets and rose from her bed. She drew on a robe as she walked across the room to the window. Brushing aside the curtains, she stared across the yard that separated her cabin from the main ranch house. Stars twinkled in the clear black sky, the light reflected in the mantle of snow that covered the ground.

What would Gavin think when she told him of her engagement? Would he be happy for her? Or would he be glad to be rid of her? Perhaps he would think nothing of it at all.

A light flickered inside the children's bedroom. Were they awake so early, even after all the excitement of Christmas Day? One of them could be ill. They had partaken rather liberally of the candy Patrick had brought with him yesterday.

She turned from the window and pulled on stockings and boots, followed by her cloak.

The serenity of the scene she had looked upon through the window had been misleading. When she opened the door, she was met by a wall of frigid air. Her lungs complained as she dragged in a frosty breath. Pulling her cloak more tightly about her, she hurried across the yard, the snow crunching beneath her footsteps. In her hastiness, she strayed once from the hard-packed trail between the buildings and broke through the crusty surface, her leg sinking in snow almost to her knee. She caught herself just in time to prevent a nasty wrenching.

By the time she reached the house, the light had disappeared from the children's room. Quietly, she opened the kitchen door and let herself in. She was almost to the children's bedroom door when Gavin's voice stopped her.

"The girls are fine. I just looked in on them."

She sucked in a breath of surprise as she turned toward the fireplace. He stood in front of it, the light flickering behind him.

"You're up early," he said.

"I saw the light in the children's room and —"

"You couldn't sleep?" He took three steps forward.

"No." She could make out the outline of his face now, the bold cut of his jaw, the line of his nose, the deep set of his eyes.

"Neither could I." His voice sounded different, stronger, more like Gavin. "I was thinking about Dru."

Her knees weakened, and she sat in the nearby chair.

Gavin returned to the fireplace, hunkering down as he added more fuel to the fire. The flames licked the wood, curled around it in a hot caress, then reached toward the chimney. The glow of the fire played over his hair, still tousled by sleep.

The intimacy of the moment — the two of them, man and woman, alone in this parlor in the dark of night — made her breath quicken. When he rose and came toward her, she closed her eyes, concentrating on the thundering of her heart even as she heard the other chair creak as he settled onto it.

"I was thinking about Dru," he repeated after a lengthy silence. "About what she hoped for the future for everyone she loved."

Emily had wanted things too. She had wanted this man. She had wanted a future with him. "I told Dru I would stay until June. I'll keep my promise." It was too late for a future with Gavin, even if he'd wanted it. She had given her pledge to Patrick.

"Maybe you could come with us when we take the cattle to the summer range. Maybe

226

you could stay longer than June." He paused. "The girls will miss you if you go away."

"I'm sorry. I can't." She opened her eyes to look at him. "I . . . I'm getting married in June." She hadn't meant to tell him this way, but the need to shield herself against the desires of her heart forced the words from her.

"Patrick," he said softly. "I should have known."

"He's been so kind to us these past weeks. And yesterday, when he asked me to marry him, I —"

Her words of explanation were cut off when he stood and pulled her to her feet. She had no time to protest, no time to try to pull away, before his mouth claimed hers. She had been kissed before. Patrick had kissed her only yesterday. But she'd never been kissed like this, never in a way that made the world spin like a child's top. All that existed for her was the feel of his arms as he embraced her, the taste of his lips upon hers, and the terrible knowledge that she was no longer free to love him.

As quickly as the kiss began, it ended. Gavin took a step backward. "Patrick has the means to give you everything money can buy." His voice sounded gruff. "But is that enough, Emily?" He turned and walked away.

She sank onto the chair a second time and wept.

Twenty

Patrick pulled the fur blanket over Emily's lap. "Ready?"

She nodded.

He glanced behind them at the two girls snuggled beneath another lap robe in the back of the sleigh. "Are the lasses ready?"

"Yes," they cried in unison, both of them wreathed in excited grins.

"Good. Let's go!" He picked up the reins and smacked them smartly against the rumps of the dappled-gray team. As the sleigh slipped across the yard between house and barn, Patrick waved at Gavin who stood near the barn door.

He was glad Gavin had refused the invitation to join them. There would be other times to be a good friend to the poor man. Today he preferred to think of the happier times that were to come. Today he preferred to be alone with his betrothed.

He glanced to his right, a pleasant warmth

spreading through him as he looked at Emily. The cold air had added splashes of pink to her cheekbones and the tip of her nose. Pretty enough for a Currier and Ives lithograph in her fur-lined bonnet and white muff.

It was still hard for him to believe that she'd consented to be his wife. Every time he'd seen her over the past week, he'd wondered if she would tell him that she'd changed her mind. Wonder of wonders, she hadn't. And today, the first day of the New Year, they were going to announce the news to his family. It had been hard not to tell his brothers before this, but somehow he'd managed to keep his promise to Emily, just as he hoped to keep all his promises to her for the rest of his life.

Patrick wasn't running with blinders on, of course. He knew he didn't own the fair maiden's heart. Not yet. Not fully. But she was fond of him, and that was a good start in his mind. From what he'd seen, married folks who began as good friends seemed happier longer than some who married in a blaze of passion.

Still, the months leading to June stretched impossibly long in his mind. They couldn't be over too soon for his liking.

■ ■ ■ ■

Emily stared at Killarney Hall as the sleigh sped toward it. The stone house seemed even more impressive today than on her first visit here. It sprawled against the backdrop of mountains, the exterior a solemn gray against the pristine whiteness of winter.

As if he'd read her thoughts, Patrick said, "Killarney Hall is fashioned after the estate of an old English baron in Ireland. My parents came to America while I was still a lad, but my da never stopped missing the emerald-green valleys or the cool, misty mornings of Ireland."

"Where are your parents now?"

"Buried, both of them, beneath the aspens." He pointed up the slope of the foothill. "Three years ago now."

"I'm sorry," she said, wondering that she hadn't known this before they became engaged. They'd spent many hours together, but she'd never asked questions, never tried to know him better than what he offered on his own. She hadn't been curious enough to ask questions, and the realization shamed her.

I want to care for him. I want to make him a good wife. There are so many reasons that I should love him.

But her traitorous heart yearned for another even now.

"Emily? Have you heard a word I've said?"

She looked at Patrick. "I'm sorry. My mind was wandering."

"Are you ready to go in?"

She hadn't noticed the sleigh had stopped. "Yes, I'm ready." There was no going back now, and that was for the best.

As Patrick, Emily, and the children stepped into the entry hall, a servant — dressed in a black suit, white shirt and collar — appeared to take their wraps. "The family is waiting for you in the salon, sir."

"Thank you, Crandall. Do you think Cook might be able to find a piece of cake for the lasses?"

Sabrina's and Petula's eyes lit up with eagerness.

"I think so, sir. If you'll follow me, young ladies, I'll take you to the kitchen."

"May we, Miss Harris?" Sabrina asked.

Emily nodded. "If you promise to mind your manners. You too, Pet."

"We will," they said in unison.

After the girls disappeared into the bowels of the house with the butler, Patrick offered the crook of his arm. "Are you ready?"

She forced a smile onto her lips. "I'm ready."

All four of the O'Donnell brothers were brawny men, none of them standing under six-foot-two. Each of Patrick's younger brothers had red hair, although the shades varied slightly, from Patrick's carrot red to Trevor's rich auburn. They also had the same open, friendly faces and the same laughing eyes.

It was a bit daunting, walking into their midst. She felt overwhelmed by their size and enthusiasm as they crowded close, paying her outrageous compliments and saying it was about time Patrick brought her back to Killarney Hall.

It was Pearl, Shane's bride of a little more than six weeks, who relieved some of Emily's apprehension. "Get back, you big ox." Pearl pushed Shane on the shoulder, forcing him to take a step back. "Can't you see she's about to suffocate?" She took Emily's arm and pulled her away from the four brothers. "Don't mind them. They take some getting used to, but they're a good-hearted lot."

Emily glanced over her shoulder. Each of Patrick's brothers wore satisfied grins. She thought they must have guessed the reason for today's visit.

"You should visit us more often, Miss Harris," Pearl continued. "Patrick can come for you in the sleigh whenever you'd like."

"Thank you. I —"

"Come summer," Patrick interrupted, "you'll be able to see Emily whenever you want. She's going to be living at Killarney Hall . . . as my wife."

"I knew it!" Jamie shouted.

"Sure if I didn't see it coming!" Shane slapped his older brother on the back. "Congratulations, Paddy."

Trevor gripped Patrick by the upper arms and gave him a shake. "We'd given up hope you'd find the courage before you were too old, brother."

Pearl gave Emily a hug. "I'm so glad, Miss Harris. Now I won't be the only woman in the family. We'll be sisters, you and I."

"Please. Call me Emily."

The brothers surrounded her before she could say anything more. She received a bear-like hug, followed by a kiss on each cheek, from each of them. Finally, she was claimed once again by Patrick. He led her to a sofa, then sat beside her, his arm around her shoulders. As the brothers and Pearl took nearby seats, he regaled them with stories of his courtship of the lovely Emily Harris, much of it dramatically embellished. The room was filled with laughter as the minutes ticked away on the mantel clock.

Emily felt like a terrible fraud. Since Patrick loved her, the whole clan would love her. That was apparent. But she didn't deserve their easy and effusive affection. They believed she loved their brother in return, that she would marry him for all the right and proper reasons, that she would make him happy. She wished she did love him. It would make things so much easier. But she was determined to learn to love him. She knew she would in time.

"Sir." Crandall's imperious voice broke into her thoughts. "Cook reports that dinner is ready. Shall I inform her you are adjourning to the dining hall?"

"Yes, Crandall. Do so at once." Patrick turned a solemn look on Emily. "It's the devil to pay if the O'Donnells aren't ready when the food is. Cook rules her corner of the house with a vengeance. You'll meet her later and no doubt win her over with your sweet smile."

She wasn't sure whether or not he spoke in jest. "I'll do my very best."

Patrick stood and drew her up from the sofa.

"Wait," she said as the others rose too. "I

have a favor to ask of everyone."

They all looked at her.

"I . . . I haven't yet told Sabrina and Petula of my engagement. It's too soon after they lost their mother. Please, let us not mention it within their hearing. I want to wait until the time is right."

Patrick gave her shoulders a gentle squeeze. "Sure and we understand. We'll not say a word."

She gave him a grateful glance. All would be well with them. She knew it would.

TWENTY-ONE

"And this will be our bedroom, once you're Mrs. O'Donnell."

Patrick shoved open the door, revealing the chamber with its large four-poster bed, gleaming wood floors, and cherrywood bureaus. Persian rugs were scattered around the room. Upholstered chairs sat in a cozy semi-circle before the fireplace. Heavy draperies framed the large windows.

Emily felt a hard lump form in her belly as she stepped into the room. "It's beautiful."

"Not nearly as beautiful as you." He closed the door behind him.

She knew she would feel his hands on her arms any moment, knew that he would turn her toward him, that he intended to kiss her. There was no avoiding it this time. Except for the day she'd accepted his proposal, she'd managed to forestall anything more than a few pecks on the cheek.

She'd kept the children nearby as a safe-guard.

But they weren't with her now.

"Emily."

It happened just as she'd expected. He turned her to face him, pulled her close into his embrace, and brought his head low to kiss her. He held her tenderly, lovingly. His lips were warm upon hers.

She waited to be stirred. She wanted her world to be knocked askew. She wanted Patrick's kisses to be as memorable as the kiss she'd shared with Gavin.

Gavin . . . Go away. Leave me be.

She pulled back from Patrick, feeling warmth rise in her cheeks. Kissing one man. Thinking of another. It was wrong, and she was ashamed.

Patrick stared down at her for a few moments, then amusement lit his face. "There's no need for embarrassment, my love. We're to be wed."

"I . . . I'm not —"

"Aye, I can see I'll have to move slowly. But you needn't fear me."

"I'm not afraid of you, Patrick. Truly I'm not. It's just that . . ." *It's just that you're the wrong man.* "It's just —"

"No need to explain. I understand. And I know that you'll get over your shyness with time. I'm a patient man."

But he *didn't* understand. *Couldn't* understand. And how patient would he have to be if she continued to long for another man in his place?

Joker scratched at the door and whined, then returned to his master's chair and rested his muzzle on Gavin's thigh.

"They ought to be home soon." Gavin stroked the wolfhound's head. "Too quiet around here when they're gone, isn't it?"

Joker groaned, as if in understanding.

Gavin returned his gaze to the fire, his thoughts drifting as he watched the hypnotic flickering of the flames. He remembered the way Emily had looked the day of Shane O'Donnell's wedding. She'd fit right in at Killarney Hall, perfectly suited to one day be its mistress. She fit in there much better than here. It was a truth he'd always known, right from the first time he saw her in Boise City. But he no longer wanted it to be true.

He shouldn't have kissed her. That had been a grave mistake on his part. The moment he'd heard she was to marry Patrick he should have walked away. He'd never expected her to stay anyway. Never wanted her to stay. Dru had wanted it, and he'd let that confuse him. That was all.

Patrick was a good sort, not to mention he was as rich as King Midas, thanks to his late father's success in the gold fields. Emily would be happy with Patrick. What woman wouldn't be happy, living in the lap of luxury? Wouldn't he want the same for his daughters?

"She won't need a big wedding," Emily had told him as they'd watched Sabrina's heartbreak over Trevor. "All that will matter to her is that she loves the groom and that her family is with her."

Gavin shook his head. Easy enough for Emily to say. After all, she would soon be married to the head of the O'Donnell clan.

"Look, Miss Harris!" Petula cried from the back of the sleigh, her voice filled with excitement. "Look at the deer!"

As Emily twisted around, she saw Petula jump onto the seat, her arm pointing behind them. "Sit down, Pet. You shouldn't be —"

Before the warning was all the way out of Emily's mouth, the sleigh jerked hard to the right. With a scream, the child bounced over the back of the sleigh.

"Patrick, stop!"

He pulled back on the reins.

The moment the sleigh came to a rest, Emily shoved off the lap robe and jumped to the ground. She stumbled in the snow, falling to her knees. "Pet!" She scrambled to her feet and raced back along the sleigh tracks.

"My arm," Pet whimpered. "My arm hurts, Miss Harris. It hurts bad."

Before Emily could lift the girl into her arms, Patrick's hand on her shoulder stopped her. "Don't move her yet. Let me have a look first."

"Is she gonna be all right?" Sabrina came to stand next to Emily. Her face was ashen, her eyes frightened as she whispered, "She's not gonna die, is she?"

Emily dropped to her knees and hugged Sabrina. "No, Brina. Pet's going to be fine. You'll see." She understood the child's fear. Both her father and her mother had been taken from her in a short period of time. It wasn't surprising that she might fear an accident would take Petula from her as well.

Patrick turned toward Emily. "I believe her arm's broken. It doesn't look right to me." He frowned. "We're almost to the ranch. I'll take you there, then head for town to get the doctor."

Petula continued to whimper in pain as Patrick lifted her from the ground and carried her toward the sleigh, Emily and Sabrina close on his heels. As soon as Emily was seated, he passed the child into her waiting arms, then hurried around to the opposite side and got in. Moments later, they were hurtling across the frosty countryside.

"It hurts," Petula said amidst her sobs.

"I know, Pet. But it won't hurt for long. We're almost home, and then we'll get you taken care of."

Gavin stepped through the doorway at the same moment the sleigh pulled into the yard. Perhaps it was the expression on their faces or the hectic way they'd arrived, but he seemed to know something was amiss even before his gaze fell on the whimpering little girl in Emily's arms.

"What happened?"

Emily answered, "Pet fell. We think her arm is broken."

"It hurts, Pa."

Gavin took the child from Emily. "We'll get it fixed, Pet. Hold on. We'll take care of it."

Emily and Sabrina disembarked and followed Gavin toward the house.

"I'll be back with the doctor as quick as I can," Patrick called to them.

Once inside, Gavin laid Petula on the bed in the children's room, propping her head with a pillow. Emily removed the girl's shoes before pulling a comforter over her legs.

"We need to take your coat off," Gavin said.

"No, Pa. It'll hurt too much. I don't wanna move it." Petula squeezed her eyes shut. "It hurts bad."

Gavin's gaze met Emily's. She felt the same helplessness she saw in his eyes. "We could cut it off," she suggested softly.

"It's her only coat."

His reply felt like a slap, and she wanted to sit and cry along with Petula.

"Children mend mighty quick from a thing like this." Dr. Forester led the way out of the children's bedroom. "She'll have some pain at first, but her arm will heal up fine. Just keep her quiet until it's good and mended."

"For how long?"

"About six weeks. Maybe not even that long. Children tend to heal faster than adults."

Gavin tried to imagine Petula staying still for six weeks. "Easier said than done."

Dr. Forester chuckled. "Do the best you can." He turned toward Emily, who stood just outside Petula's bedroom. "The laudanum should help her sleep for several more hours. Watch the clock and don't give her more until I said."

"I'll be careful. Thank you."

The doctor faced Patrick. "Well, Mr. O'Donnell, since you insisted on bringing me here, I'm afraid you'll have to drive me back to Challis. But if you don't mind, could we try a more sedate pace? I'm an old man."

Patrick chuckled as he looked past Gavin to Emily. "I'll be back in a day or two to look in on the wee lass. You take care of yourself."

Gavin thought Patrick would have liked to say more, if the moment and place had been more private. As it was, he simply nodded again and pushed his hat onto his head as he followed the doctor out the door. Gavin went with them and waited until they'd pulled out of the yard before going back inside. He stopped in the doorway to the children's bedroom.

Seated in Emily's lap, Sabrina said, "Stay with us tonight, Miss Harris. Please. I don't wanna be alone with Pet. What if she wakes up and starts crying again?"

"Of course I'll stay. I'll make my bed on the floor so I'll be close if either of you needs me." As if sensing Gavin's presence, she looked toward the doorway. "That is, if it's all right with your father."

He wasn't sure it was all right. He wasn't sure he wanted Emily Harris under the same roof, both day and night. He had enough trouble sleeping as it was. She already haunted his thoughts. But he couldn't think of his own comfort at a time like this. He had to think of Sabrina and Petula. They wanted Emily nearby. They loved her. Trusted her. Needed her.

"You won't have to sleep on the floor," he said. "I'll set up a cot. I imagine they'll want you in here for a while." Gavin turned on his heel and left.

"Miss Harris, may I have a few words with you before you retire?"

Emily tucked the blanket over Sabrina's shoulders before straightening and turning toward the bedroom doorway. "Of course, Mr. Blake. I'll be right with you."

Gavin disappeared from view, but Emily waited a few moments to calm her rattled nerves. It had been a stressful day, meeting Patrick's brothers, then Petula's accident. Her emotions had swung on a pendulum, from one extreme to another. She wasn't sure she had the strength to be alone with Gavin right now, but what choice did she have?

He waited for her before the fireplace,

hands shoved into the pockets of his trousers, firelight flickering behind him. A lamp on a side table provided the only other illumination in the room.

"Miss Harris, I need to apologize to you."

"Apologize?"

"For the other night."

Her heart skipped a beat as she remembered that brief time in his arms.

"It shouldn't have happened."

He didn't explain what "it" was. He didn't need to.

"It isn't my business who you choose to marry. I'm grateful that you'll continue to care for Brina and Pet until that time comes."

"I promised I would."

"And you keep your promises, don't you, Miss Harris?"

"Yes."

He took a step forward.

She took a step back.

"You don't have to be afraid of me," he said, so low she almost didn't hear him.

I'm not afraid of you, Gavin. Her heart tripped again. *I'm afraid of myself.*

"Good night, Mr. Blake." She turned toward the safety of the children's bedroom.

"Good night, Miss Harris."

Another snowstorm blew in from the northwest during the night. Emily lay on her cot in the children's bedroom and listened to the mournful wail of the wind, a sound indicative of the way she felt. Lonely. Hollow. Empty. Despairing.

Oh, God . . .

As those words — a pitiful cry for divine help — drifted into her thoughts, she was forced to admit how long it had been since she'd tried to pray. Really pray. Had she sought God's will before she accepted Patrick's proposal? Had she looked for answers in his Word before deciding to take this job or promising Dru she would stay until spring? Had she asked for God's help when it came to her feelings about Gavin? Or had she simply rushed headlong into life and then hoped God would clean up her mistakes in the aftermath?

She covered her face with her hands, wishing she could go back in time and start over. What a poor Christian she was. What a terrible witness. She'd much rather be like Dru. The woman's faith had been so strong, and never once had Dru ceased to pray for those she loved. Emily had learned much from her in the two months they'd lived together.

Sleepless, restless, she rose from the cot, drew on her robe, and slid her feet into her slippers. Then she left the bedroom and made her way to the kitchen. Rather than lighting a lamp, she opened the door to the stove and stirred the banked coals to life, adding fuel when it was ready. By the light from the stove's belly, she filled the kettle with water and set it to heat on the stove, hoping a cup of tea would soothe her spirits.

"Couldn't sleep, Miss Harris?"

She gasped softly as she spun toward the table, a hand over her heart. Gavin sat in one of the chairs, a darker shadow in the dark room.

If he knew he'd startled her, he didn't let on. "How's Pet? Is she keeping you up?"

"No." She drew a steadying breath. "She's sleeping all right."

"I broke my nose when I wasn't much older than Pet. Fell out of the loft in the barn. My pa didn't bother with sending for a doctor. He just grabbed hold of me and shoved the bone back into place. Hurt like the dickens. A broken arm's gotta be worse."

With the fire growing hotter, Emily closed the stove door. "She'll be over the worst of it in a day or two."

"It's good that you're here. She'd be lost without you. Both Pet and Brina would be lost without you."

She wished she could see his face and considered lighting the lamp. No. Better to leave them in the dark. Better she not be able to look into his eyes. Better that he couldn't read her emotions.

"They love you, Miss Harris."

"And I love them."

"They'll miss you when you go."

And I'll miss them. I'll miss you, Gavin. Her heart beat so fast she wondered if he could hear it from the other side of the kitchen. "I'm going to have a cup of tea. Would you like some?"

He was silent awhile before answering. "Thanks. I would."

A match struck. The lamp on the table came to life, chasing shadows into the corners.

Emily forced herself not to glance behind her. Instead, she took down two cups and placed them on the worktable, then reached for the tin that held the tea. Not until the water in the kettle had come to a boil and the tea had been steeped did she look in Gavin's direction. "Would you like milk and sugar?"

"No." He shook his head. "I'm fine with it as is."

She carried the two cups to the table, setting one before him before moving to the opposite side of the table and sitting on the chair. Outside the wind continued to moan and the house to creak. Here in the kitchen they were warm and cozy.

Gavin seemed content with the silence between them, and Emily didn't rush to fill it with her own voice. Instead, her thoughts drifted back to her own childhood, to the loneliness and fear she had known living with her Uncle Seth. She'd taken her fears with her when she and Maggie joined the wagon train, bound for Oregon, but Tucker Branigan had somehow reached through her anxiety. He'd been able to make her laugh, sometimes even through her tears. That's how Gavin was with his stepdaughters.

Sabrina and Petula would be fine when Emily left this house to marry Patrick. Gavin loved them, and although he seemed to think he wasn't up to the task of fatherhood, she believed he would always do well by them. They were happy children, despite the loss of their father and mother. Did Gavin know it was because of his love for them, his steady nature, that they weren't afraid all the time, that they could laugh despite their sorrows? If he didn't know, he should.

"Mr. Blake?"

"Yes?"

"Brina and Pet love you. God was good to bring you into their lives."

Gavin stared into the cup held between his hands. "You believe God had a hand in all of this?"

"Yes."

He looked at her across the table. "So did Dru. She had a strong faith."

"I know."

"My mother called herself a Christian." His voice hardened. "But I never saw her live what she supposedly believed."

"Not everyone who calls Jesus 'Lord' shall enter into the kingdom of heaven. We must do the will of the Father."

Conviction tightened her heart. She couldn't be doing God's will, loving one man and planning to marry another. How on earth would she ever put things to right?

Twenty-Two

Sipping the bitter coffee in the tin cup, Gavin tipped the chair back on its two hind legs until it leaned against the bunkhouse wall.

"Jess oughta be in tomorrow." Stubs filled his tin cup with whiskey. "Unless last night's storm forces him to hole up in the line shack."

Gavin grunted his response, only half-listening to his old friend.

"How's Pet? She doin' okay?"

"She's hurting some, but that won't last long."

"How 'bout Brina? She was pretty shook up over the little one's fall."

"She's fine. Miss Harris is keeping them occupied with crafts or schoolwork or something."

"She's a fine young woman, Miss Harris is. Good with those girls."

Gavin hadn't come to the bunkhouse to

talk about Emily. In fact, he'd come here to try to forget her for a while. His gaze shifted to the whiskey bottle in the center of the table. This was one of those times he wished he hadn't sworn off liquor for good. It might be a relief to drink himself into oblivion, the way his father had done every night for the final years of his life. Which was the very reason Gavin wouldn't give in to the temptation.

"You know" — Stubs rubbed his grizzled chin, his expression pensive — "I been thinkin' how rare it is that a man meets just the right girl for him. It's been my observation that most folks settle for something less. Like you and Dru. A nicer woman I've never known, but if she hadn't been ailing and needed a pa for her girls, you two wouldn't've tied the knot. You'd've gone on as friends."

Gavin didn't care for the direction Stubs was going, but he said nothing to stop him.

"You gave that woman all the caring she could've asked for. She was lucky to have you, as her husband and friend. Yes, sir. Lucky, she was. And Dru knew it too, don't think she didn't."

"She deserved better than I gave her."

"You're too hard on yourself, Gavin." Stubs shook his head. "Way too hard.

There's all kinds of love in this world. All kinds. Kind you got for them girls you adopted. Kind you had for Dru. I reckon there's even the kind you have for an old coot like me. Yes, sir. All kinds."

Gavin closed his eyes, wishing his friend would stop talking.

"Dru never stopped lovin' or missin' Charlie, but she loved you in her own way too. And you know what she wanted most for you? She wanted you to find what she and Charlie had. Told me so herself. Told me that after she was gone, she hoped you would marry again, but that you'd do it for love next time."

Gavin let out a long sigh. "I know, Stubs." He thought of Emily, the way she'd looked in the middle of the night, sitting across the kitchen table from him, lamplight illuminating her pretty face, reflecting in the pale hair that fell about her shoulders. "But sometimes the things a man wants can't ever be his."

"Sometimes," Stubs agreed softly, then added, "and sometimes they can be."

January 2, 1884

Dearest Sister,
    I hope this letter finds you well. Please

give my love to Tucker and to my darling nieces and nephews. I have missed you all so much, especially on Christmas when I knew you were all gathered around the tree. I could see each one of you so clearly in my mind. It was almost as if I were right there with you. Almost but not quite.

I am sorry I haven't written in several weeks. So much has happened since my last letter to you that I hardly know where to begin.

Christmas was not as dreary an affair as I feared it might be, thanks to one of our neighbors, Mr. Patrick O'Donnell. I told you about the wedding that we attended at his home outside of Challis in November. Mr. O'Donnell made certain the Blake children had a tree with trimmings and gifts to open on Christmas morning. He has been a good friend to this bereaved family.

I am thankful I can tell you that Mr. Blake's grief over his wife's death seems to have eased somewhat. He is attentive to his children once again. I have always enjoyed watching Mr. Blake with Sabrina and Petula, and the girls adore him. I am reminded of how kind Tucker was to me as a child. I must have tried his patience far more than I knew, and yet Tucker never showed me anything but love. That's how Mr. Blake is with these girls. They are blessed to have him as their father.

Petula took a tumble while we were out in the sleigh yesterday, New Year's Day, and broke her arm. Oh, how it frightened me when it happened. The poor dear was in quite a lot of discomfort last night, but seemed much improved today. The doctor set her arm in a splint, which isn't at all comfortable, and has advised us to keep her as quiet as possible for the next few weeks. As I write this letter, she is napping on the sofa near the fireplace, having fallen asleep while playing with her favorite doll. For now at least she is following doctor's orders.

Her big sister is sitting on the floor nearby, reading her McGuffey's Reader. Sabrina is very bright and a good student. I wish I had brought more books with me when I came from Boise, for I fear she won't be challenged for long by the ones we have here.

I heard talk while in town in December that a school may open in the fall. That would be a blessing to all the families in the area. Perhaps I will apply for the position as teacher.

Emily worried her lower lip as she pondered what to write next. No, not what to write, for it had to be said, but how to word it.

That last sentence must take you by surprise, dearest Maggie, learning that I might not return home to stay this summer. But there is a reason for it. Mr. O'Donnell has proposed marriage, and I have accepted his offer. I cannot leave the Blakes for a few more months as I promised Dru that I would remain as the children's teacher and governess until spring when the cattle return to the Stanley Basin. Therefore, Patrick and I won't marry until at least June. I know that you will like him when you meet him. Of course, I want the wedding to be held in Boise, and I trust you will want the same.

Tears welled unexpectedly as she imagined her wedding, surrounded by her loving family. What would Maggie think if Emily confessed she wasn't in love with Patrick? She would ask her to reconsider. Maggie would ask her why she didn't love him. And so she wouldn't make any confessions. She was determined to love the man who loved her. Surely God would want her to honor her promise to wed just as he would want her to honor her promise to stay with the Blake children until spring.

Maggie, I ask that you please pray for me. In most every way, I am happy and content with my life here. But I have spent little time in prayer and rarely take the time to read my Bible. I feel cut adrift from the Lord, yet seem unable to change the pattern of the things I do or the things I think that cause me to feel that way. I want to know, I need to know, that I am in God's will, but I cannot seem to hear him. He feels so far away.

I see that Petula has begun to stir so I must close this letter and prepare it for the post. I trust that the stagecoach will still make it to Challis despite the snow we have received. Please write to me as soon as you can. I long for news of you all.

With love, your ever-devoted sister,
Emily

Twenty-Three

Gavin pulled on his coat. "I'll be gone for several days. Stubs will be here if you need anything. He'll milk the cows and feed the chickens and livestock, so you won't have to worry about those chores."

Emily tamped down the fear she'd felt since he told her he was riding out to check on the herd. She told herself it was worry about being solely responsible for the girls, but she was more afraid for Gavin. Afraid he might get caught in another blizzard. Afraid he might get lost or hurt. Afraid she might never see him again.

"In weather like this, the cattle can just bunch up and wait to freeze or starve to death. Jess might need a hand."

"Where will you stay at night?"

"There's a number of line shacks on this range. I'll sleep in one of them." A frown drew his brows together. "Will you be all right on your own?"

"Of course." Oh, what a liar she was. "The girls and I will be fine."

"Duke and Duchess are coming with me." His hand rested on the latch. "Joker will stay here. He might not be very smart, but he'd let you know if something was amiss."

She nodded.

"I figure I'll be back by Sunday, but don't worry if I'm not. No telling what I'll find when I get out there."

I'll worry every moment you're away. "I won't."

He wrapped a wool scarf that Dru had knit for him around his neck, pulled his hat down low on his forehead, and opened the door. For a fleeting moment, he glanced back at her. Then he was gone, the door closed behind him.

Emily felt the emptiness close in around her. Sunday seemed a decade away.

Several days later, the high country was still in the frigid grip of winter. But the threat of new snow had disappeared, and in its place came clear blue skies and a bright yellow sun, a sun that gave little warmth but brightened the parlor and kitchen of the Lucky Strike ranch house.

While Emily was busy with the butter churn — a task she had mastered under

Dru's careful tutelage — Sabrina read to Petula from a children's storybook. " 'Many years ago there lived an emperor who cared so much for fine clothes that he spent all his money upon them.' "

"What's an emperor?" Petula asked.

"Like a king. Right, Miss Harris?"

"Yes, that's right, Brina. An emperor is like a king."

Sabrina continued, " 'He gave no thought to his soldiers nor to the affairs of his empire.' "

"That's selfish. Who'd want a king like that?"

"I don't know. Probably nobody, but that's how the story goes. Now just listen."

Emily smiled to herself, enjoying their sisterly banter, and glanced through the small glass window in the over-and-over to see how the cream was doing. Dru had taught her to watch for the little grains of butter — about as big as number six shot — which would tell her it was time to add water. Seeing them, she opened the cover, threw in some cold water, and continued churning.

" 'He had a new coat for every hour of the day and spent most of his time riding through the streets that everyone might see his handsome clothes.' "

"He'd need lots and lots of coats to keep warm if he was riding through the streets in Challis in the winter."

"Pet, quit interrupting the story." Sabrina's voice rose in frustration.

"I don't like it anyway. The king's stupid." Petula slid off of her chair and came into the kitchen. "Miss Harris?"

"Yes, Pet."

"Are there really places in the world where it never snows? Where it's like summer all the time? Mr. Stubs says there is, but I didn't believe him."

"He was telling you the truth."

"Have you ever been someplace like that?"

"No. I've only read about them in books. But I've talked to people who've been to such places."

"Can you imagine, Pet?" Sabrina came to stand beside her little sister. "A place where it never snows. No sleighs to fall out of and break your arm."

Emily shook her head, silently warning them not to fight, then carefully poured the buttermilk from the churn into a large pitcher.

"Can we have some, Miss Harris?" Sabrina asked, eyeing her favorite drink.

"Help yourself."

While Sabrina got down two cups and

filled them with buttermilk, Emily dumped a large quantity of clean, cold water in with the butter to wash it, then turned the churn and tipped the water out. The muscles across her shoulders complained, but she ignored them. She wasn't finished yet. She would have to rest later.

Maggie wouldn't believe Emily could churn butter, not even if she saw it with her own eyes. Somehow Emily had avoided learning how to do many household chores while growing up. She wondered now if Maggie had sheltered her just a little too much when she was young. Someone had done the laundry and churned butter and baked bread, back before the Branigans could afford to hire a cook and a maid, but it hadn't been Emily.

No wonder Gavin had thought she wouldn't last. She probably wouldn't have if Dru hadn't been so patient with her.

Emily emptied the contents of the churn onto the butter worker, a shallow wooden trough with a fluted roller that moved up and down the channel when the handle was turned. She poured generous amounts of water over the butter as she worked it, squeezing the moisture off with the roller, making sure the butter was washed clean.

In her memory, she heard Dru's warning:

"If it's not absolutely clean, the butter will never keep."

When she was certain there was no milk left in the butter, Emily salted and worked it some more, then flung it in handfuls into an earthenware crock. After pounding the salted mixture again, she rammed it hard with a wooden tool.

Again she heard Dru's voice: *"You must drive out all the water and air, Emily, so the butter won't go rancid."*

Satisfaction flowed over her. She'd remembered everything Dru had told her. Perhaps it was silly to feel so proud — women had been churning cream into butter for centuries — but this was the first time she'd done it all by herself, without any supervision, and it felt good.

One more proof that, despite Gavin Blake's thoughts to the contrary, she *was* cut out for this place. If not in the beginning, then now.

She was washing the worktable when a knock sounded at the front door. She could guess who it was. Patrick. Another storm had kept him away for a time, but this day's clear skies had guaranteed he would call upon her again.

"Good day to you, lass," he said to Sabrina when she opened the door. He pulled off his hat with one hand, his other arm behind his back. His gaze flicked to Emily and Petula in the kitchen. "And how is that arm, Pet? You've been much on my mind."

"It's getting better. Still hurts but not as bad as before."

"And you're not giving Miss Harris any trouble, minding the doctor and all?"

Petula frowned. "I've been good. Haven't I, Miss Harris?"

"Yes, indeed. You've been very good, Pet. Both of you have."

"Well then, it's glad I am to hear it, for I've brought along some new friends for you and your sister." Patrick drew his arms from behind his back, producing the two porcelain-faced dolls he held in his hands.

Sabrina's eyes went wide with awe. "Those are for us?"

"Aye. That they are." He handed both dolls to Sabrina. "Take one to your sister now."

"Thank you, Mr. O'Donnell." Sabrina clutched the figures to her chest and carried them to the kitchen. In a moment, she and Petula were seated on the floor, both of them holding a doll in their laps.

Patrick's gaze returned to Emily. "It's good to see you. Sure and you're looking lovely today."

She swept loose strands of hair off her forehead with the back of one hand. "There's that blarney you're so famous for." She smiled. "I was churning butter earlier. We were nearly out."

Patrick walked across the room. "Best time for that is in summer when the grass is lush and green. It's hard to get much milk from a cow in the dead of winter."

She felt slighted, although there was no reason for it. Dru had told her the exact same thing.

"You should be sitting in a garden filled with spring flowers, rather than churning butter." He took hold of her hand and raised it to his lips. "Once we're married, you'll not have to do such things again."

Emily opened her mouth to respond but was interrupted by Sabrina's voice.

"Married?"

She turned toward the corner of the kitchen where the girls sat with their new dolls. The stricken expression on Sabrina's face told her she'd been mistaken not to tell them sooner. If not for Petula's accident . . . No, that wasn't what had kept her silent this long. It had been her own indecision. It had been the feelings she had for their father, feelings that rightfully belonged to her fiancé.

She withdrew her hand from Patrick and walked toward the children. After a moment's hesitation, she pulled a chair from the table and sat on it, her hands folded in her lap. "Yes, Brina. It's true. Mr. O'Donnell and I are to be married. But it won't be until the summer. I'm going to be staying right here with you until then. I . . . I didn't tell you before this because it seemed too soon. There have been enough . . . changes lately without you worrying that I'm going away too."

"Does Pa know?"

"Yes. He knows."

"And he's going to *let* you marry Mr. O'Donnell? He's going to *let* you leave us?" With a betrayed cry, she jumped to her feet, ran to the bedroom, and slammed the door behind her.

Emily's breath caught in her throat. Why hadn't Patrick guarded his tongue? Why hadn't she talked to the children sooner about her plans?

"Miss Harris?"

She blinked back tears. "What is it, Pet?"

"You won't really go away. You're gonna stay with us, aren't you?"

"For now, I'll stay. But when I —"

"Don't you love us?" Petula's voice broke as she asked the question.

"Oh, Pet . . ." Emily slipped from the chair, kneeling on the floor and drawing the child into as close an embrace as her splinted arm allowed. "Of course I love you. I love you very, very much. And I won't be far away at all. Remember how quickly we can get to Mr. O'Donnell's house in the sleigh?"

"It's still too far." Petula sniffed. "Will you . . . will you go with us to the basin? Ma always . . . always liked it there."

"Summer is a long way off," she whispered so only the child could hear. "Let's talk about it then."

Petula sniffed again.

"Why don't you go see if Brina's okay?" She gave Petula another squeeze, and then held her away so she could look in her eyes. "Tell your sister that I didn't mean to hurt either of you by keeping a secret."

Petula nodded and started to walk away. Then she stopped and looked back. "Maybe we can change your mind before summer. Ma always said we shouldn't never give up hope." She gave Emily a woeful smile, then hurried to join her sister in their bedroom.

Emily drew a deep breath as she rose to her feet. "Seems I made a mess of things."

"I thought you would have told them by now."

"I meant to."

He came toward her. "Why didn't you?"

She shrugged. "There just never seemed to be a right time." It was a poor excuse, and she knew it.

"Well, at least Gavin knew before this."

She remembered the night she'd told Gavin she was engaged to Patrick. She remembered him pulling her to her feet and into his arms. She remembered his mouth upon hers and the devastating emotions that had swirled through her, that swirled through her even today. And she remembered his words that had cut like a knife: *"Patrick has the means to give you everything money can buy. But is that enough, Miss Harris?"*

A shiver ran up her spine.

Patrick drew her into his arms. "I love you, Emily Harris, and there's no mistaking that I do. I'd have everyone in the territory knowing it too. I'm sorry the news has upset the lasses, but I'm not sorry that we can talk about it plainly now. You'll see. It will all be for the best."

She accepted his kiss, but inside her a storm was brewing.

Twenty-Four

Gavin spent four days with Jess. When another storm blew through, they holed up in a line shack, but once clear skies returned, they rounded up the cattle from the gullies and foothills and started them back toward home. There was little grazing to be found for now, even along the hillsides where the wind often blew the snow away.

Once the herd was under way, Gavin told Jess to take the dogs and the cattle on without him. He was going to make sure they hadn't left any cows behind. But cattle weren't the real reason he was reluctant to go home. He needed some time to himself. Time to think. His head was a mass of confusion. Nothing much made sense to him these days.

When he and Charlie Porter first settled in this long, narrow valley, they'd built four line shacks at the farthest corners of their grazing land. In comparison with the mammoth ranches he'd seen in Wyoming and Montana, the Lucky Strike wasn't very big, but it still covered more acres than could be effectively managed from the ranch compound in the worst of winter weather.

The line shack Gavin rode toward that day was at the northeast end of the range, miles from Challis, miles from the ranch house, far enough from just about everything but the wind and the snow and the trees. He reached the shelter as daylight began to fade.

This particular line shack was built up against the mountain, the backside of it dug into the southern slope. The back wall and part of each of the two side walls were formed by earth. The remainder was made of logs chinked with mud. Inside there was a cot, a table, and one chair, plus a small stove for cooking and heating.

Gavin didn't remove his coat when he first entered the shelter. It would be a while before the fire took the chill off the room. It never would be truly warm, no matter how hot the fire, but it was better than outdoors and for that he was thankful.

It was while he heated beans in a pan for his dinner that he thought of her again. No surprise. It happened all the time. He couldn't escape thoughts of Emily, not even out on the range.

It was unfair of him to accuse her of marrying Patrick for his money. As much as he wanted to return to the belief that she was selfish and willful, like his mother, he knew it wasn't true. She'd proven him wrong in a hundred different ways since the afternoon when they met in that Boise hotel. She was a young woman — a beautiful woman — who worked hard, loved Dru's girls, and kept her word.

He sank onto the cot and covered his head with his hands.

He'd never wanted a wife. He'd never wanted to end up like his father, a man broken in spirit by the deceptions of a woman. He'd never wanted to see a child thrown away by the very person who should love and care for him the most. He'd been content to go through life on his own, making friends but never risking his heart.

But something inside him had changed. The changes had started with Charlie and Dru, seeing them as they were, loving, faithful, true. More changes had come when his heart had been stolen by two little girls. And then had come Emily. It was as if she'd broken through to a place inside him that no one had found before, and now he didn't know how to close up the barrier again. He didn't even know that he should.

The smell of scorched beans drew him back to his feet. With a towel around the handle, he pulled the pan from the stove and carried it outside where he dropped it in the snow. A hiss rose with the steam. He stood there, listening to the sound and feeling like his heart was as burned as the beans in that pan.

God, if you're out there, if you hear me the way Dru always said you could, show me what to do.

Emily was seated by the fire, reading one of the children's schoolbooks, planning for her next week of lessons, when Joker rose to his feet and trotted toward the kitchen door. She saw his ears cock forward and heard him whimper.

Her pulse quickened. *Gavin's back.*

She rose and followed the dog into the kitchen where she brushed aside the curtain at the window. Although the sun had long since set, the full moon and cloudless sky made the snowy landscape almost as bright as day. No sign of horse and rider in the yard. Disappointment sluiced through her.

Joker whimpered again, this time scratching the door with his paw.

"All right. Go chase a rabbit if you want."

She opened the door. "Don't get lost."

The wolfhound was off in a flash, but before he reached the barn, Duke and Duchess galloped into view.

He is *back.*

Emily grabbed her coat from the peg and slipped it on as she stepped outside into the cold night air. In the stillness, she heard the sounds of cattle. It was all she could do not to run out to meet him.

Only Gavin wasn't to be met. It was Jess Chamberlain who rode his horse into the yard moments later. And no one followed him.

"Mr. Chamberlain?"

He looked her way, nodded, then dismounted and walked across the yard. "You shouldn't be standin' out in the cold, Miss Harris." He removed his hat as he spoke.

"Isn't Mr. Blake with you?"

"No, ma'am. He's looking for any strays. From my count, I don't think he'll find many, but he was set on looking anyway."

Emily did her best to control her tone of voice, hiding her disappointment. "I see. How long do you suppose he'll be?"

"Few days, I imagine."

"Oh." She gave him a fleeting smile. "Well, I won't keep you. I'm sure you're tired and cold and would like to go to the bunkhouse.

Good night, Mr. Chamberlain."

He put his hat back on and bent the brim at her. "Evenin', Miss Harris." He strode back across the yard and led his horse into the barn.

Emily drew a slow, deep breath as she turned and reentered the house. Warm air from the parlor invited her to return to the fireside, which she did as soon as she'd removed her coat. She sat in the same chair, but she didn't take up the schoolbook again.

Why hadn't he returned when he'd said he would? Couldn't he have let Jess look for strays?

She folded her hands in her lap and bowed her head. *God, I'm so selfish. I want Gavin here. I want him with me. I would even send Jess back into the cold and snow in order to have my way. That's unkind. Besides, Gavin doesn't feel the same about me. He'll never feel the same, and I must face that truth. Father, help me learn to love the man I'm to marry and stop longing for something I will never have.*

Gavin thought about his childhood as he lay on the cot in the line shack, listening to the wind whistle around the corners of the shelter. There hadn't been much to his father's farm in Ohio — a few hardscrabble acres, a pigsty, a broken-down team of mules, and a three-room house complete with field mice. His father hadn't enjoyed much success as a farmer, even before he'd taken to drink. He'd never had success in his marriage either, but he'd loved his wife anyway.

Gavin grew up hearing stories of how his father, Timothy Blake, met Christina Cowell while visiting cousins in Pittsburgh. Timothy was a young man and handsome, in a rugged sort of way. Christina was a great beauty but from a poor immigrant family. Somehow Timothy managed to woo and win her, and they married quickly. Soon thereafter, Timothy took his new bride back to his farm, a place Christina hated on sight — hated almost as much as she grew to hate the man she'd married.

Gavin was born nine months after their wedding day. That was perhaps the last happy day of his father's life. After that, Christina made it clear she would bear no more children. She said she refused to become a mousy farmer's wife with a passel of children hanging onto her skirts, her looks gone and her life over.

When Gavin was a young boy, he tried almost as hard as his father to make Christina Blake love him. But he'd wised up sooner than the old man. His mother had married to escape her poor beginnings. She hadn't expected to still be poor once she had a husband, and she'd made certain she wouldn't stay that way.

Gavin sat up on the cot and leaned his head in his hands. He didn't want to think about his parents. He didn't want to remember the cool way his mother had rebuffed his childish attempts to win her affection — or even just her attention. He didn't want to remember his father — unshaven, unwashed, eyes blurry, a bottle of cheap liquor nearby. He'd put it all behind him years ago. Or at least he thought he had. But he'd obviously failed, for those feelings had all come rushing back, thanks to Miss Emily Harris.

Would he become as pathetic as his father because of a woman? God help him if the answer to that question was in the affirmative.

TWENTY-FIVE

The O'Donnell sleigh slid silently over the snow as the pair of horses pulled their passengers toward Challis. Emily and the girls were glad beyond words to be out of the house. They'd been cooped up much too long by bad weather and Petula's broken arm. To make matters worse, Gavin hadn't returned yet with the last of the cattle, and his absence was keenly felt in the household. Although the girls seemed to have forgotten that for the moment. Sabrina and Petula chattered and giggled and reveled in their escape from lessons and chores.

"Someday," Patrick said to Emily, speaking low enough that only she could hear, "we'll be taking children of our own for a ride in the sleigh. Sure and I look forward to the day."

There were so many reasons that she should love Patrick with her whole heart. He was a wonderful storyteller and could captivate his listeners for hours. He was generous to a fault, and he had a surprising patience. And most important of all, he loved God.

Lest she think too highly of him, his brothers had made a point of warning her that Patrick had the infamous O'Donnell temper that could flare in an instant but be gone just as quickly. If that was true, she'd seen no sign of it. He'd never been angry with her. Not even when he should have been.

He's so good to me, and he loves me.

"The stage will be up from Boise City today," Patrick said, "trusting the roads are passable between here and there. Perhaps there'll be a letter in it from your sister. That would lift your spirits."

She pulled her left hand from her muff and took hold of his. "Do I look sad, Patrick?"

"Aye, Emily, you do."

"Well, I'm not. Just lost in thought, I suppose."

"When we've done our shopping, what say we have a piece of Mrs. Benson's famous chocolate cake at the restaurant before we start back to the ranch?"

"Yes!" came simultaneous cries from the backseat of the sleigh.

Patrick laughed, and the sound brought a real smile to Emily's lips.

What was she worried about? She cared for this man, and if she didn't love him passionately now, that would come. Their wedding wouldn't take place for another five months. Much could happen in that brief span of time.

In Challis, Patrick drew the horses to a halt in front of the mercantile. He hopped out of the sleigh, then helped Emily disembark and step to the boardwalk outside the store entrance. Moments later, the girls had joined her there.

"How about a nickel to spend as you like?" Patrick reached into his pocket.

"You'll spoil them," Emily said with a shake of her head.

"Not so very much. It's only a nickel."

Emily looked into Sabrina's and Petula's expectant faces and knew she'd lost the battle already. Once Patrick had made the offer, she hadn't the heart to take it back. And perhaps he was right. It wouldn't spoil them so very much.

She leaned down to look each of them in the eye. "One piece of candy at most. You can buy whatever else you can afford, but not a lot of candy. Agreed?"

They nodded.

She straightened and looked at Patrick. "All right then."

"I'll take the lasses inside, and you can check the post for letters from your sister."

"Thank you, Patrick. I won't be long."

"Take as long as you like. We've a store to explore."

A small chime sounded above the door as she entered the Post Office. The man behind the counter, spectacles perched on the tip of his bulbous nose, looked up at the alert.

"Good day, Miss Harris."

"Good day, Mr. Hutchens. I've come to see if I have any letters."

"You're in luck. The coach arrived yesterday. You've got two letters awaiting you. I'll get them. And there's a bit of mail for the Lucky Strike as well."

Moments later, Emily sat on a bench in the Post Office, opened the first of her letters — this one from her friend Fiona Whittier — and began to read.

December 31, 1883

Dear Emily,

I regret my poor correspondence. You put me to shame because I have already received two letters from you this month.

I cannot believe how much time it

takes to care for an infant. Maggie told me she sent news of the safe arrival of our daughter, Myrna Joy Whittier. She is already eight weeks old. Can you believe that? It seems all I have done since her birth is change her diapers and give her baths and nurse her and rock her. I look forward to an uninterrupted night of sleep, which everyone has promised will happen soon. Oh, how careless I was of those long, leisurely nights before Myrna was born. But I am not complaining. I think she is wonderful, and I am blissfully happy. James is a doting father (if a bit clumsy). I fear he will spoil her terribly before she is even a year old.

James's mother stayed with us for several weeks to help with the baby, and it made us realize that we shall very soon need a larger house. This one will not be big enough as our family grows. (My husband wants half a dozen children at least.) James thinks we will be able to afford a larger house in another year. His business is doing so well. His mother says all the men in the Whittier family are successful by nature.

I must close this letter, as Myrna is demanding my attention. Perhaps the next time I write, I will have something more of interest to tell you. Do write again soon.

Your devoted friend,
Fiona

Cheered by the letter, Emily folded the stationery and returned it to the envelope. Half a dozen children? She wouldn't be surprised to learn Fiona wanted twice that many. She'd been created to nurture.

Still smiling, Emily opened the second letter, this one from Maggie.

January 1, 1884

My dearest Emily,

Another new year has dawned, and my thoughts today are sentimental ones, thinking back over the years and pondering all of God's blessings that my family has enjoyed. I hope that this day finds you and the Blakes well.

We went too long without receiving a letter from you, but Tucker told me that the high country roads aren't always passable this time of year and not to worry. I was so relieved when I heard from you at last. I loved knowing you were in such a beautiful setting and was thankful to hear that you were happy.

Then came your letter about the death of Mrs. Blake. How my heart broke for those two girls. You and I know only too well what it means to grow up without a mother. I'm sure you are of great comfort to them.

As you requested, I am indeed praying that God will give you wisdom, and I pray that Mr. Blake will have his eyes opened to the Savior's love.

But Emily dearest, are you quite certain you want to stay with the Blakes until spring? There must be another capable woman living in the area, someone who could love and tend the children and allow you to return to your family.

Your nieces and nephews miss you, Sheridan most of all. And Matthew Foreman has asked about you several times since you left Boise. That poor young man is completely besotted with you, and I don't believe he has given up hope, despite your refusal of him.

The weather here in the valley has been mild this winter. A number of storms have blown through, but the snow hasn't lingered more than a few days at a time. However, the mountains are coated in white and look quite lovely.

I will close now and hope that this letter will reach you without great delay. I send my love along with Tucker's and the children's. We are counting the weeks until you are home again.

Your loving sister,
Maggie

The last words were difficult for Emily to read through the tears welling in her eyes. After setting the letter aside, she dried her cheeks with her handkerchief.

"Bad news, Miss Harris?" the postmaster asked.

"No, Mr. Hutchens. I'm just a little homesick is all." She gave him a tremulous smile. "My sister wrote the letter less than three weeks ago. The roads must be much better than they were."

"That they are. That they are."

Emily put the mail into her pocketbook and rose from the bench. "Good day to you, sir."

"And to you, Miss Harris. Tell Gavin that me and the missus are thinking of him and how sorry we are for his loss."

"I'll do that."

The chime sounded above her head again as she left the post office.

■ ■ ■ ■

Gavin rode into the yard at the Lucky Strike in the afternoon, eight days after he'd departed. He hadn't accomplished much after Jess drove the herd toward home. In the remaining days, Gavin had found only a half dozen stragglers hiding in the draws and gullies of the foothills. The rest of the time he'd spent wrestling with memories of his mother and father and trying to figure out what to do about his feelings for Emily Harris, now that she was engaged to another man. Should he talk to her, tell her he was falling in love with her, that he couldn't stop thinking of her? Or was the better thing to leave her be? If she loved Patrick, why complicate things for her? Staying silent, keeping his distance seemed the honorable thing to do. If he'd ever had a chance to earn Emily's affections, he was too late now.

He was in the barn, loosening the cinch on his gelding, when Stubs joined him there.

"Right good to see you back, Gavin. The girls missed you."

He grunted an acknowledgment that he'd heard the cowpoke's words but didn't look up.

"Reckon they'd have been out here already, but they've gone to town with Miss Harris."

He yanked the saddle off the horse's back and turned toward Stubs. "Did Patrick take them?"

"Yep. Went in that fancy sleigh of his. About an hour or so ago. Maybe more."

"Has he been over here a lot while I was gone?" He dropped the saddle onto a rack.

"Every couple days or so." Stubs cocked an eyebrow. "Problem with that?"

Gavin shook his head. "Just wondering."

"I expect him and Miss Harris have lots to talk about, what with planning a wedding come the spring."

"I expect so." He ran a brush over the gelding's back.

Stubs cleared his throat. "You know, Gavin. I think you oughta —"

"I know what you think, Stubs. It isn't going to happen."

"Are you —"

"Just leave it be, old friend."

Silence, then, "If that's what you want."

"It is." Gavin tossed the brush into a bucket and led the horse into a stall where he could be watered and fed.

"Sure but you're looking more sad now, love, than before you went into the Post Office." Patrick put his index finger beneath Emily's chin and tilted her head up so their gazes would meet. "Was there bad news in your letter?"

"No." She shook her head, at the same time drawing a step away from her fiancé. "No bad news. I just miss my sister."

"Of course you do. Have you thought of taking a trip to Boise when the roads are better? We could go together. Introduce me to the family."

"I couldn't possibly do that, Patrick. I can't leave Brina and Pet."

"Gavin could spare you for a couple of weeks."

She shook her head again. "No. I promised Mrs. Blake that I wouldn't leave until the cattle are taken back into the basin."

Patrick studied her awhile in silence, a silence that made her squirm on the inside, uncomfortable with what he might read on her face, see in her eyes. But she didn't look away, no matter how much she wished to.

It was Petula who rescued Emily, stepping in between the two adults. "Look what I bought, Miss Harris." She held up a box. "It's a set of checkers for Pa. He's got a board but some of the checkers got lost so he couldn't play no more."

"That's 'cause you were playing with the

checkers outside when you weren't supposed to," Sabrina said. "You're the one
who lost them."

Emily gave the older girl a warning glance,
then bent down to look Petula in the eyes.
"That's very nice of you to spend your
nickel on your pa."

"It wasn't the whole nickel. I got a pep-
permint stick too. But just one, like you told
us."

"Good girl." Emily ran a hand over Petula's hair before turning toward Sabrina.
"And what did you buy with your nickel?"

"A Scholar's box, to keep my pencils and
eraser in." Like her sister before her, she
held up her purchase for inspection. "It's
almost exactly like the one you've got at
home, Miss Harris."

"Very nice. It is a lot like mine. Only yours
has a lock. Mine doesn't."

Patrick laid a hand on her shoulder. "Your
supplies are already in the sleigh. Shall we
have that cake now?"

"Yes!" the girls cried together.

"It will spoil all of our suppers." Emily
smiled despite herself. Who could not
respond in kind when looking at the joy
written on Sabrina and Petula's happy
faces?

And besides, what did it matter if they

spoiled their supper this once? It wasn't as if she needed to do much cooking with Gavin away.

TWENTY-SIX

"Pa's home!" Sabrina cried as the sleigh pulled into the yard.

Emily's heart thundered in her chest, and she wondered if Patrick would guess she was as excited as the children to know Gavin was home again.

Sabrina and Petula were out of the sleigh the instant it stopped. They dashed across the yard to the barn where their father stood in the open doorway. He lifted them both, one in each arm, holding them close to his sides.

Somehow, Emily forced herself to do nothing more than wave at him, acknowledging his return. Then she allowed Patrick to help her from the sleigh and the two of them carried the purchases into the house.

"Sure and the lasses are glad to have their da at home."

Emily set her basket on the kitchen table.

"Yes, they've missed him a lot. A week is a long time when you're their ages."

"Dru knew they would be in good hands with Gavin after she was gone."

"Yes."

Patrick turned her to face him. "They'll not lack for anything when you're no longer their governess."

Tears burned her eyes but she fought them back, swallowing hard. "Of course not. He loved them long before my arrival."

"It won't be as if you can't see them whenever you wish, Emily, once you're living at the hall as my wife. It's not all that far to the Lucky Strike."

That's where Patrick was wrong. She wouldn't be able to see the children whenever she wanted, because seeing them would mean seeing Gavin too. And she didn't think her heart would be able to bear that. Perhaps, in time . . .

Patrick shook his head as he chuckled softly. "It is clear there'll be no cheering you up, my girl, no matter what I say. So I will take my leave of you and you can read your sister's letter a second time." He drew her close and kissed her.

When their lips parted, Emily put her arms around him and pressed her cheek to his chest. "Thank you," she whispered.

"For what?"

"For being so kind and understanding." She drew away from him. "You're the kindest of men, Patrick O'Donnell."

"That's what I've been telling you all along." He grinned, a look that brought a smile to her own lips. Who could resist the famous O'Donnell charm? Even when she knew Patrick was talking blarney. "Ah, there's your smile," he said — and leaned down to kiss her again.

Cold air swirled into the room, and Emily took a step back to look in the direction of the kitchen door.

Gavin locked gazes with her for a fraction of a second before closing the door, turning, and shrugging out of his coat. When he faced them again, he said, "The girls tell me I'm indebted to you, Patrick."

The Irishman waved off Gavin's thanks. "Next time I come over, I'll have to challenge you to a game of checkers."

"You'll lose if you do."

Patrick chuckled again. "We'll see." He looked at Emily. "I'll see you soon."

She walked with him to the front door and remained on the stoop, hugging herself against the cold, until he was back in the sleigh and driving from the yard. After a quick wave farewell, she reentered the house.

"You shouldn't have let Patrick give them money," Gavin said, standing in the kitchen doorway.

She stiffened at his gentle but definite reprimand. "It was only a nickel apiece."

"Nickels can be hard to come by around here, depending on the price of beef on the hoof."

She could have told him that she had tried to dissuade Patrick, albeit not very hard. Instead she said, "I hadn't the heart to deny them. I'm sorry. I'll know better next time."

Silence stretched between them. Not that Emily's head wasn't filled with things she would like to say. Words she wanted to say but couldn't. Words she had no right to speak aloud.

"I'd better gather my things and take them to my cabin. Now that you're back, I'm not needed in the girls' room at night. Pet is sleeping peacefully again."

"I appreciate the care you've given the girls, Miss Harris."

How formal they were with each other. How distant. Whatever they might have had seemed irrevocably lost.

Emily nodded as she crossed the parlor. She passed close enough to Gavin that he could have reached out and stopped her. Close enough that she might have turned and stepped into his arms. But he didn't reach out and she didn't turn. She moved right by him and into the children's bedroom.

She had spent two and a half weeks in this bedroom — from the first night of Petula's accident — sleeping on a less-than-comfortable cot. Little by little, more of her belongings had migrated from her one-room cabin and into the main house. Now it was time to return them to the place they belonged — to the servant's quarters. For that's all she was, really. Just the governess and teacher and occasional cook and maid. Just that, when she wanted to be so much more.

January 20, 1884

Dearest Maggie,

I was so glad to receive your letter. Even more delighted that it reached me so soon. In under three weeks. I'm hopeful that means you have also received my last letter to you. I have been quite homesick for many more reasons than I could express on paper.

Mr. Blake was away for just over a

week, so I was in charge of his house as well as the children. We got on rather well, I believe. Of course, we were not completely alone. One of the ranch hands was here, taking care of the outside chores.

Petula is getting better and has adapted to using only one arm. Much better than I could do, I am sure. For the most part, Sabrina is a kind and attentive sister, but sometimes she gets irritated. I suppose she is jealous of the extra attention Pet receives because of her injury.

As I write this letter, Mr. Blake and the children are playing checkers (father against daughters). The game pieces were a gift from Petula, which she gave him upon his return from the range several days ago. They cost four cents at the local mercantile. I don't think I've ever considered what could be bought for under a nickel before.

Patrick suggested that he and I come to Boise for a brief visit, but I told him I could not leave the children. I promised Mrs. Blake that I wouldn't. Not until spring. But when the time comes, I know you will like Patrick. He is such a good man.

You would like Mr. Blake too, and you

would adore his daughters. As do I.

Your loving sister,
Emily

Twenty-Seven

"Mr. Martin? May I speak with you a moment?"

Emily wasn't sure why she was finally following Dru's request. Whatever it was that the woman had wanted her to know about Gavin, it couldn't be of any importance now. Emily was engaged to Patrick, and Gavin didn't much care, one way or another. Still, she'd awakened this morning with the need to know, with the need to hear whatever Stubs would tell her, if for no other reason than to honor a dying woman's wish.

Stubs lowered the horse's hoof to the ground and peered at Emily from beneath the brim of his battered hat. "What's on your mind, Miss Harris?"

Emily stepped into the stall where he was working. "I . . . I wanted to ask you about Mr. Blake."

He lifted an eyebrow. "What about him?"

This was more difficult than she'd expected. "Before she died, Dru . . . Mrs. Blake . . . told me to ask you about Mr. Blake. She said you were to tell me everything, including the things she never knew."

"She did, huh?"

"Yes. It seemed important to her."

Stubs leaned his back against the stall rails and bumped his hat off his forehead with his knuckles. "What about you, Miss Harris? Is it important to you?"

She wished she could say no. Her life would be so much simpler if it weren't. "Yes." Emily didn't dare look at Stubs while she waited for his response. She feared he'd guessed too much about her feelings already.

"Would you mind walkin' with me to the bunkhouse? I could use a cup of coffee."

She nodded her assent, and together they left the barn. A cold wind whipped at her skirts, sending a chill up her spine and along her arms. She hugged herself, wishing Stubs would walk a little faster. But as with his speech, Stubs took his own good time.

Once inside the bunkhouse, Emily sat on the bench on one side of the table in the center of the room while Stubs stoked the fire in the pot-bellied stove.

"Coffee?" he asked without turning around.

"No, thank you."

He poured himself a cup, then turned from the stove. "I wasn't more'n fifteen when I went to work for Timothy Blake — that was Gavin's pa. My folks were gone, and I didn't have a place of my own or nowhere to go. Gavin's pa was a nice enough fella back before he took to drinking, but he never had two nickels to rub together."

Stubs brought his coffee to the table and sat opposite her. "Gavin was about three when I first got there. Cutest little tyke you ever saw. And Mrs. Blake, Christina . . ." He shook his head and whistled through his teeth. "What a beauty she was. Stopped men in their tracks, she did. Timothy worshipped the ground she walked on, and that ain't no exaggeration. But she hated that farm and she hated being poor. Hated her husband too, even though he treated her like she was a queen. She didn't pay Gavin no mind either. Never wanted to hold him or be with him. Cold, that woman was. Real cold."

Emily felt her heart breaking for the little boy whose mother didn't love him.

"You remind me a bit of Christina. Not that you look like her, but you've got the same color of hair and eyes and are about the same height. Don't suppose Gavin ever told you that, did he? No, he wouldn't tell you that."

"But I'm no great beauty."

"And that there's the main difference. I've never seen you put on airs. You don't seem to know you got the power to break a man's heart with a toss of your head or a casual glance. Christina knew the power she had, and she used it. She wanted to be rich, and she wanted off that farm. Didn't matter to her that she had a husband and a little boy."

Emily recalled Gavin's gruff behavior toward her when she was first hired. Was this why? Because she resembled his mother?

"I can't say for positive, but I think Gavin found his ma and her rich lover together while his pa was away. Guess there wasn't any reason for her to sneak around and pretend after that. She left the farm in Mr. Hannah's company, bold as you please. Just up and walked off and left her husband and son. Gavin was about ten, maybe twelve years old at the time. She never saw her boy again 'til after his pa died. Mr. Hannah's money bought her a divorce and even respectability, and she wanted no reminders of her old life, not even from her own flesh and blood."

"Poor Gavin."

"Timothy Blake drank himself to death, but I left long before that happened. Gavin told me his pa didn't care what happened to the farm after his wife left. Just let it go to rot. Gavin did his best to do what needed done, but he was just a boy still."

Emily swallowed the hot lump in her throat.

Stubs took several sips of coffee before he continued. "Christina soured Gavin good on women. I suppose he didn't want to come home one day to find his woman in bed with another man."

"How could she do that to her family?"

"Promises didn't mean nothing to Christina Blake. She was beautiful and selfish and cared only for herself." Stubs shook his head. "Easy to understand why Gavin decided he'd never marry."

"But he married Dru."

Stubs smiled. "That was different. Charlie was Gavin's friend. Closest thing he could've had for a brother. They were like this." He held up two crossed fingers. "After Charlie died, it fell to Gavin to look out for the family. He was glad to do it too. He loved Dru and the little girls. And lookin' out for them would've been good enough if Dru hadn't got the cancer. When she knew she was dyin', she asked Gavin to marry her so her girls would have a pa when she was gone. She didn't want them to be orphans."

"But he loved her. You said so, and I could see it whenever they were together."

"Sure he loved her. We all did. Couldn't help but love her."

Emily agreed with a nod and a wistful smile.

"But Dru and Gavin didn't have a real marriage," Stubs said.

Emily recalled what Dru had said to her once, not long before her death — *He married me because I asked him to, not out of some great passion.*

"I'm thinkin' she hoped he'd learn to love you the way she'd loved Charlie. But I guess that ain't possible now, you being engaged to marry Mr. O'Donnell and all. He's a good sort. I've seen how attentive he's been to you since Dru died. No wonder you've come to care for him."

She did care for Patrick. But not enough. Not nearly enough.

"Thank you for telling me all of this." She rose from the bench.

Stubs gave her a questioning look. "What're you gonna do now, Miss Harris?"

She walked toward the bunkhouse door. "I'm going to try to make things right."

Pulling the collar of her coat up to cover her ears, Emily hurried from the bunkhouse to her cabin. Once inside, she sat on the foot of her bed and stared at the floor.

How do I make things right? How can I unravel the mess I've made of things? She covered her face with her hands. *How do I make things right?*

Thoughts raced through her mind. Thoughts of Dru. Thoughts of the children. Thoughts of Gavin. And finally, thoughts of Patrick.

Patrick. She lowered her hands and straightened. Nothing could be made right until she broke her engagement to Patrick. No matter what else happened, she couldn't marry him, hoping she would learn to love him. She couldn't marry him feeling as she did about Gavin. It wasn't fair to any of them. Most of all, it wasn't fair to Patrick. He deserved better.

Through the kitchen window, Gavin saw Emily leave the bunkhouse and walk to her cabin, her coat collar pulled up against the cold. She hadn't spent much time in the main house since his return with the strays. While she never neglected the children or failed to give them their lessons, it was clear she had no intention of remaining in his company any longer than necessary.

Which was for the best. That was what he wanted. Wasn't it? If she was to marry Patrick, better he stay clear of her. Better he concentrate on changing his feelings.

He was about to turn around when a sleigh pulled into the yard. It looked like Harvey Ball's pair of matched roans in the traces, but it definitely wasn't Harvey holding the reins. The driver was a stranger to Gavin. Or was he? There was something vaguely familiar about him.

The man got out of the sleigh, then helped the woman who had been seated at his side to disembark. They both wore fur hats and heavy winter coats. Stylish ones. Not the sort of thing a person ordered from the mail-order catalog or bought at the local mercantile.

As the couple moved toward the house, Gavin left the kitchen and walked to the front parlor door, opening it before they could knock.

"Mr. Blake," the man said when their eyes met.

"Yes?"

"I'm Tucker Branigan and this is my wife Maggie. We met last September in Boise."

"Oh, yes. Forgive me. I didn't recognize you." He took a step backward. "Won't you come in?"

"Thank you." The couple moved past him into the parlor.

"Brina," Gavin called. When his daughter appeared in the bedroom doorway, he said, "Run get Miss Harris. Tell her that her sister and brother-in-law are here."

"We hate to intrude," Maggie Branigan said. "We would gladly go to Emily's cabin, but we weren't sure —"

"It's no intrusion." Gavin held out his hands. "Let me take your coats and then you can sit down near the fire."

"That's kind of you." She removed her fur hat.

"Emily didn't tell me you were expected. She'll be glad to see you."

Tucker Branigan helped her wife out of her coat. "We didn't tell her we were coming. We wanted to surprise her."

Maggie nodded, then said, "May I say that we were sorry to hear of your loss. Emily was very fond of your wife."

"Thank you." Gavin took their coats and hats and carried them into his bedroom, placing them on the bed. As he turned again, he heard the kitchen door close.

"Maggie! Tucker!"

He stopped in the doorway to his room and watched as the sisters embraced.

"I can't believe you're here." Emily's voice cracked with emotion. "But the roads. They must be awful. I'm surprised you got through."

Tucker said, "The passes were open, and there's not as much snow to the south."

"How long will you stay? Where are you staying?"

Maggie laughed, and Gavin was struck how very much like Emily's laugh it sounded — and how much he'd missed hearing her laughter lately.

"We took a room at the boarding house in town, and we plan to stay a few days at least. Perhaps more."

Gavin hadn't seen Emily look this alive, this happy, in weeks, and he had to admit it warmed his soul to see it.

He moved into the parlor and motioned toward the chairs. "Please, everyone. Sit down. Make yourselves comfortable." From the corner of his eye, he saw Sabrina and Petula watching the adults. "Come here, you two, and meet Emily's family."

"Oh, yes." Emily motioned them to stand before her, then placed her left hand on Petula's left shoulder and her right hand on Sabrina's right shoulder. "Maggie and Tucker, these are my students. Pet and Brina, this is my sister and her husband,

Mr. and Mrs. Branigan. They've come up from Boise for a visit."

Gavin wanted to remember them just like this — Emily, Sabrina, and Petula. They looked like a family. A happy family. Almost like a mother and her daughters.

Maggie leaned down to meet the girls at eye level. "It's a pleasure to make your acquaintance. Emily has bragged on you a great deal in her letters. You must both be very well-behaved and smart."

Sabrina and Petula exchanged glances and giggled.

Emily sat beside her sister on the sofa and the two embraced again. Then Emily asked after her nieces and nephews.

"Everyone is well. Sheridan misses you. We all do. But you know that."

"And Fiona and her baby?"

Maggie laughed. "Fiona is enraptured over little Myrna. She can talk of nothing else but how sweet the baby is and when she first smiled and when she first laughed. The sun rises and sets by that child as far as she is concerned. And James is nearly as bad."

Gavin stood off to the side of the fireplace, watching and listening to the two sisters, their faces animated as Emily asked about other mutual friends and Maggie answered.

He noticed that Tucker didn't attempt to participate in the conversation. Instead he leaned back in the chair and smiled as he observed them. There was something about his look, something about his posture that said he'd often sat and listened to them have similar conversations. Had listened and enjoyed himself.

Lucky man.

When Emily seemed at last out of questions, Maggie glanced toward her husband and said, "We were rather hoping to meet Mr. O'Donnell. Is it too late in the day to call upon him? How far from here is his home?"

A slight frown pinched Emily's brow as she checked the watch pinned to her blouse. "It might be better if we do it tomorrow. It is growing late in the day."

"If you think that's best." Maggie's gaze shifted to Gavin. "Mr. Blake, would you mind terribly if we took Emily back with us for the night? We've already arranged for a room for her at the boarding house. We don't want to take her from her duties but we —"

"It's all right, Mrs. Branigan. Of course you want to spend time with her. She should stay with you at the boarding house for as long as you're in Challis. That's why you came. We can manage without her." He gave the children an encouraging nod. "Can't we, girls?"

They can manage without me . . . Those words ran through Emily's head time and again as the sleigh carried them toward town. *They can manage without me . . . They can manage without me . . .* Could Gavin have made it any clearer how unimportant she was in his life or the lives of his children?

In an effort to distract her thoughts from the grim refrain, Emily asked about more of their friends, and Maggie obliged her curiosity. But once the rented sleigh and horses were returned to the livery and they were seated at a table in the restaurant, Maggie asked her, "What's troubling you, Emily? Something is. I can see it in your eyes. I could read it in your letters. It's one of the reasons we came to see you."

As much as Emily wanted to pour out her troubles to her sister, she couldn't do so. Not yet. Not until she'd talked to Patrick. Not until she'd made things right. So she shook her head and said, "I've just missed you all very much."

Maggie didn't look convinced, but she let it slide. They spent the remainder of the evening talking of many things but never

about Gavin Blake or the feelings she had
for him.

TWENTY-EIGHT

When the rented sleigh reached the top of the hill, Tucker reined in the team and looked over his shoulder at Emily. "Is that it?"

She nodded. "Yes, that's it. Killarney Hall."

"You didn't exaggerate, did you?" He whistled softly. "It is a castle."

Nerves fluttered in Emily's stomach, making it hard to do more than nod. She'd lain awake most of the night, rehearsing the words she wanted to say to Patrick. Even so, she felt unready. Maybe she'd been wrong not to confide in Maggie first, not to get her advice. And yet, that hadn't felt right to her. She had gotten herself into this predicament. She would have to get herself out of it.

The moment the sleigh pulled to the front of the Hall, the door opened and Patrick stepped into view. When he recognized Emily, he grinned and strode toward them. "Emily, love. This is a surprise." His gaze lingered on her like a caress.

Oh, this was going to be so hard, telling him she couldn't marry him. She didn't want to hurt him, but that was exactly what she had to do. "Patrick, this is my sister Maggie and her husband Tucker Branigan."

"A good Irish name if ever I heard one." Patrick nodded at Tucker, then offered his hand to Maggie to help her out of the sleigh. "Emily didn't tell me you were coming."

"She didn't know. We surprised her yesterday afternoon."

While a servant took care of the horses and sleigh, Patrick ushered his guests into the house. They were soon joined by the rest of the O'Donnell brothers and Shane's wife. More introductions followed. More idle pleasantries. Coffee was served along with pastries. And all the while, Emily's insides were twisting into intricate knots.

"Have the two of you settled on a date for the wedding?" Maggie asked.

Patrick reached for Emily's hand. "Sure and I haven't been able to get an answer from her on that yet." He squeezed her fingers, giving her a smile. "But the wedding will be just as soon as possible, I will tell you that."

Emily felt the blood drain from her head. Her lips numbed and the skin on her face prickled. She leaned toward Patrick. "May I speak with you privately?" Her gaze shifted to Maggie. "You'll excuse us, won't you?"

Her sister inclined her head. "Of course." But her eyes were filled with concern.

Emily stood and led the way out of the sitting room. She had no particular destination in mind, but soon found herself in the solarium, looking out the windows as she'd done the first time she came here, Gavin by her side.

"Emily? What is it, love?"

She turned to face him. "I'm sorry, Patrick. I shouldn't have brought Maggie and Tucker with me."

"But why ever not, love? It's natural they'd want to meet me."

"Oh, Patrick." Tears welled in her eyes, but she blinked them away, refusing to let them fall. "I should have come to see you alone. You deserve better than what I've given. But I can't . . . I was wrong to ever —"

Understanding dawned in his eyes. "So that's the way of it."

She lowered her gaze to her left hand. "I was wrong to have accepted your proposal,

Patrick." She removed the engagement ring he'd given her, the one she'd started wearing — at Patrick's insistence — once the children knew her plans to marry him. "But I thought . . ." She held the ring toward him. "I thought —"

"You thought you could learn to love me."

She nodded, and now there was no holding back the tears. They dropped from her cheeks and made tiny splashes upon the tile floor.

"Don't cry, love. I knew I was reaching beyond my grasp when I asked for your hand."

"That's not true, Patrick."

He took her in his arms, and she let him. He patted her head and her back, as if soothing a child. "I'm thinking maybe I was too late to win your heart. I'm thinking it may have already belonged to another."

He knows. He knows I love Gavin.

Gavin looked at the trunk that he'd set on the floor inside the boarding house door. Everything Emily had brought with her from Boise was now in that trunk, although not packed as neatly as when she came.

"You'll see that Miss Harris gets this," he said as he handed an envelope to Mary Smith, the boarding house proprietress.

315

"I'll see to it, Mr. Blake." Her eyes were filled with curiosity but somehow she refrained from asking what she shouldn't.

Gavin was thankful for that.

He turned and left the boarding house. If he was a drinking man, he would have stopped in the saloon for a bracing shot of whiskey before the journey back to the ranch. As he wasn't, he settled for turning his coat collar up and tugging his hat lower on his head before setting out toward home.

He should have sent Emily packing long ago. He should have released her from her pledge the instant he'd learned of her engagement. What had Dru been thinking when she hired Emily anyway? If not for Dru's romantic notions of marriage and family, if not for Emily's presence in his home, he wouldn't have begun to want things he'd never wanted before.

Most of all, he'd wanted her.

He'd wanted to call her Emily instead of Miss Harris. He'd wanted to see her pale, silky hair freed from the hairpins and falling down her back. He'd wanted her to step willingly in his arms. He'd wanted to drink deeply of her kisses. He'd wanted to see her beautiful face the first thing every morning and the last thing every night.

He'd wanted her.

But he'd set her free, as he should have done weeks ago.

Emily cried all the way from Killarney Hall to Challis, cradled in the arms of her sister. She was so ashamed of herself for hurting Patrick the way she had. She'd used him abominably. He deserved so much better, yet he hadn't condemned her as he had every right to do.

But even as she wept, there was a corner of her heart that felt a little lighter, a little relieved, a little hopeful. Hopeful that another man might look at her a bit differently, once he knew she wasn't engaged.

Her hope died when she and Maggie entered the boarding house, and she saw her trunk on the floor of the entry.

"Mr. Blake brought it by a short while ago. Said you would want it." Mary Smith stepped from behind the counter, holding an envelope toward Emily. "He asked me to give you this."

Emily seemed unable to lift her arm to take the envelope from the woman. She couldn't move, could scarcely breathe. Maggie didn't suffer from the same paralysis. She accepted the envelope on Emily's behalf before taking hold of her younger sister's arm and steering her toward the staircase.

When they reached Emily's room, Maggie asked, "Do you want me to leave you alone while you read it?"

"No. Please stay."

Maggie took a seat on the chair near the window while Emily sat on the edge of the bed and opened the envelope.

Miss Harris,

It is best for everyone concerned that I free you from the promise you made to Dru. You should not be expected to delay your wedding until spring just because my wife asked you to remain in our employ until then.

I have taken the liberty of packing your belongings in your trunk so that you need not return to the Lucky Strike.

Brina, Pet, and I wish you much happiness in your marriage to Patrick O'Donnell, and we will no doubt see you both on occasion.

Gavin Blake

The realization hit like a hammer on her soul. He truly didn't want her. He had packed her trunk and sent her away, not even allowing her to say good-bye. Not to him. Not to the children.

Fighting for breath, Emily crumpled the

318

paper in her hand.

She had grown to love Sabrina and Petula. Did he hate her that much that he couldn't even let her tell them good-bye?

"Emily?"

"I want to go home, Maggie," she said softly. "I want to go home with you and Tucker. Just as soon as we can leave."

"Of course. I'll ask Tucker to make the arrangements."

Twenty-Nine

They set out in the sleigh, Gavin and the girls, well before noon the next day. In no time at all, their exposed skin had turned red from the cold. Their breath made frosty clouds in front of their faces.

"What'll I do while you and Brina skate?" Petula asked. "I could've stayed home if Miss Harris was there. Why hasn't she come back? I thought she was only gonna be in town one night. Didn't she say just one night?"

Maybe Gavin's plan to give the girls an enjoyable afternoon skating on the pond before he told them Emily was gone for good hadn't been the best idea.

"When's she coming back, Pa?" Petula persisted. "I don't like it when she's gone."

He pulled back on the reins, then twisted to look at his daughters on the seat next to him. "Miss Harris isn't coming back."

"Not coming back?" Sabrina's eyes grew

wide. "But she —"

"You know that she's planning to marry Mr. O'Donnell. She couldn't stay with us for good. It was better that she go now."

"But Pa —"

"We'll get along fine, the three of us. You'll see. I'm not a bad cook and we can work together on the other chores that need done. And there's no reason I can't help you with your schoolwork this winter. There's even talk that Challis will have a school come next fall. Won't that be great?"

Petula turned her face into her sister's coat and began to cry.

Gavin felt helpless in the wake of those tears.

Sabrina wiped her nose on her coat sleeve. "Why didn't Miss Harris come and say good-bye?"

Not only did he feel helpless. He felt selfish. He hadn't wanted to see Emily again. Seeing her again, once the decision for her to go was made, would have been too hard for him. He hadn't considered that it would hurt Sabrina and Petula even more not to see her.

"That's my fault, Brina. I . . . I thought it would be easier if I told you after she was gone. I'm sorry. I guess I was wrong." He looked out across the snowy landscape. "Do you still want to go skating or would you rather go home?"

Sabrina sniffed. "Let's go home, Pa."

Home. The problem with home was, Gavin knew he would see Emily everywhere he looked. In the kitchen preparing a cup of tea or baking a pie. At the table, helping the girls with their schoolwork. Mending the children's clothes while seated next to the fire in the parlor. Comforting Petula. Laughing with Sabrina. Stroking Joker's head.

For the first time in his life, Gavin truly understood what life had been like for his father. Understood and pitied him.

The trip from Challis to Boise by stage was rough, cold, slow, miserable. For most of the journey, Emily kept her face turned toward the wall of the coach, her eyes closed. She didn't want to talk. She didn't want to be comforted. She wanted only to be left alone with her heartbreak.

It seemed like years rather than a few months since she'd ridden away from Boise in the back of the Blakes' wagon, on her way to make a difference in the lives of two little girls she had yet to meet. But it had been *her* life that had changed most of all. She would never forget Sabrina and Petula — or their father. Not as long as she lived would she forget them.

She scarcely noticed the passing of time. The five-day stage ride passed in a blur. One day seemed the same as another. She disembarked from the coach when told to. She reentered it when told to. At the stage stops, she picked at her meals but never because she was hungry; she ate to please Maggie and for no other reason. She didn't care to know how many miles they'd traveled or how many miles they had yet to travel. It mattered not at all to her.

Nothing would ever matter to her again.

Although Gavin told himself he'd rather chew nails than go into town for supplies having made the trip with Emily's trunk less than a week ago, he couldn't help wondering if she had stayed in Challis or taken up residence at Killarney Hall. For all he knew, she and Patrick were already wed.

It was none of his concern, one way or the other, he reminded himself as he stopped the sleigh in front of the mercantile. None of his concern.

Then he looked up and saw Patrick come out of the boarding house. His stomach sank. He wasn't ready to see the two of them together, and he hoped she wouldn't exit right behind her fiancé. She didn't, to his great relief.

Patrick saw Gavin. Even from this distance, he could see the other man's frown. Why a frown? Hadn't Gavin done his friend a favor?

Patrick left the boarding house and headed toward Gavin. When he was still some distance away, he said, "You're a bloomin' fool, Gavin Blake."

Gavin stepped out of the sleigh and onto the boardwalk. He wasn't in the mood for whatever was coming.

"What's wrong with you, mate? Have you got no sense at all?"

"I guess you mean Miss Harris."

Patrick's eyes narrowed. "What else would I be meaning?"

"I thought you'd be relieved that she isn't working for me any longer. Now your wedding won't have to wait until spring."

"What the devil are you talking about? She broke our engagement."

Gavin took a step back, as if the bigger man had struck him.

"Are you daft, man?"

"You aren't getting married?"

Patrick shook his head, a look of disgust replacing the anger of moments before. "She wasn't apt to marry me when she's in love with you."

In love with me? Gavin wiped his hand over his face. Surely he hadn't heard right.

"I've a good mind to knock some sense into you with my fists."

"What made you think she was in love with me?"

"I guessed it when she broke our engagement. Should have guessed it sooner, but I turned a blind eye to all the signs, hoping she'd marry me anyway. Hoping I was wrong."

Gavin looked toward the boarding house. "She broke your engagement just now?"

Patrick made a derogatory sound in his throat. "Saints alive, man! She left for Boise days ago. Went by stage with her sister and her husband. I never took you for a fool before this, Gavin, but a fool you are to have let her go."

He hadn't let her go. He'd done something much worse.

He'd sent her away.

Petula awakened Gavin in the middle of the night. "My chest hurts, Pa."

As he sat up, still groggy from sleep, he thought perhaps she meant her heart ached the way his did. Then he touched her and found her skin hot.

"My head hurts too."

"You've got a fever." He got out of bed and lit the lamp. "Better keep you away from Brina so she doesn't get sick too. Crawl into my bed while I get you a glass of water."

She obeyed with a soft moan.

Gavin hurried into the kitchen, returning moments later with the promised drink. He lifted the girl's head and held her while she took several sips. As soon as she was done, she turned onto her side and curled into a ball. Almost at once, she began to shiver.

Poor little tyke.

He tucked the blankets closer around her. Joker nudged his thigh.

"Not now, boy."

The dog nudged him again, then turned and padded out to the parlor. There, he looked back at Gavin and whimpered.

"All right. I'll let you out."

But Joker didn't head for the door. Instead he went into the children's room.

Gavin followed the dog, worry beginning to nag at him. Sure enough, when he leaned over to straighten the blankets, he found Sabrina burning with fever too. She coughed weakly, then rolled her head on the pillow from side to side.

He wished Emily was there. The children were sick and they needed her. *He* needed her. But she was gone. Gone because of his stupidity and stubborn pride.

Gavin returned to his bedroom, scooped Petula from the bed, and carried her back to her own room, laying her next to her sister. Then he went to the kitchen to fetch rags and a basin of cold water. He would send Stubs for Dr. Forester at first light, but until then, he had to do what he could to lower their fevers.

If only Emily was with him.

THIRTY

As soon as the Branigan family arrived at their Boise home, Emily went to her old room, stripped out of her soiled travel clothes, and crawled under the covers on her bed. She would have cried, but her tears were spent. She was completely dried up on the inside. She hurt everywhere, from the tips of her toes to the top of her head. The ache was so bad all she wanted to do was go to sleep and never wake up. To sleep and forget.

God, please help me forget.

Maggie stood just inside the doorway, waiting while Dr. Weick examined Emily. When he turned toward her at last, the look in his eyes sent a frisson of fear coursing through her.

"Doctor?"

He moved toward her, and when he spoke, it was in a low voice. "Your sister is a very sick young woman, Mrs. Branigan. Keep your children away until the danger of contagion has passed."

"What's wrong with her?"

"Influenza."

Influenza — contagious and often fatal, especially to the young and the elderly. "But she'll recover all right. Won't she, doctor?"

"It is difficult to say for certain, Mrs. Branigan. Get her to drink as many fluids as possible. Keep a cool compress on her forehead. Make certain that whoever cares for her washes their hands immediately upon leaving this room." He turned and picked up his black leather bag. "I'll return in the morning."

Maggie didn't show the doctor out. Instead she stepped closer to the bed.

Emily moaned, then mumbled a word.

Maggie thought it sounded like "Gavin," but she couldn't be sure.

Oh, Emily, you must get well. I couldn't bear to lose you. Stay strong, kitten. Stay strong.

A knock sounded on the door, and Sarah, their housemaid, looked in. "Mrs. Branigan, is there anything I can do to help?"

"Yes, Sarah. Move the children's things downstairs, away from this room. They can sleep on the floor of the sitting room. I don't want them coming upstairs as long as their aunt is sick. And Dr. Weick said we must wash our hands upon leaving the sick room. Please remember that."

"Yes, ma'am."

"And could you bring me a basin of water right away?"

"Yes, ma'am. At once."

"Thank you, Sarah."

When the maid was gone, Maggie pulled a chair close to the bed, sat on it, then began to fan the air over her sister's face.

"Gavin . . ." Emily whispered.

"No, darling. It's me. Maggie. I'm right here beside you. You're going to be fine. You're going to get well in no time at all."

Emily moaned softly and rolled from side to side beneath the covers before quieting again.

"I'll be right here if you need anything, dearest. Don't worry. Maggie's here."

Dr. Forester shook his head, his expression grim. "The next few hours will be critical. If she doesn't rally soon, you must prepare yourself for the worst."

Gavin stared down at Petula, looking so small and frail in the bed. "But Brina's so much better now."

"One cannot predict these things." The doctor placed his hand on Gavin's shoulder.

"You need some rest yourself, Mr. Blake. I'll stay with the child. You go and get some sleep. We can't have you falling ill too."

Gavin nodded, but when he left the bedroom, he didn't go to his own room. Instead, he took his coat from the peg by the kitchen door and went outside, welcoming the feel of the bracing cold air on his face. He walked across the yard, past the barn, and on down the road a good half mile before he felt his legs give out. In a flash, he was on his knees.

"God . . ." he whispered. "God . . . God, be merciful. Don't let Pet die. Please . . . help her. Help me . . . God . . ."

His voice trailed off. Words weren't enough. Words couldn't express the desperate cries of his heart. He covered the back of his head with his hands and groaned as he leaned forward, almost touching his forehead to the ground. *God, hear me. Please . . .* He felt nothing. Heard nothing. No answer. Only the cold.

But what did he expect? Who was he that the Almighty would hear his plea? He'd turned his back on the Christian faith when he was still a boy. He'd made no room in his heart for anyone, let alone God. Would his selfishness mean the death of his little girl? He felt his heart might burst with the anguish of that thought.

God . . . Help me, please . . . Oh, God . . .

Strange, the images that flashed through his mind as he knelt there on the snowy ground in the middle of the road. Unrelated pictures juxtaposed one atop the others. His broken and unhappy father, in a drunken stupor. His selfish and uncaring mother, throwing away the framed photograph he'd brought her. Dru with her Bible open on her lap, peaceful despite her losses and her own illness.

His breath came in gasps, and unable to stop himself, he threw his body forward, prostrate on the ground.

God, hear me. Help me . . .

He couldn't have explained to anyone what happened in that moment, as he lay there in the silence. It wasn't as if he heard a voice speaking to him from on high. But suddenly he knew he was not alone, and with that knowledge came warmth and peace and an overwhelming sense of love. The anger he'd felt for so many years, the bitterness, the hatred toward his mother, the shame about his father — they were gone, excised from his heart by a skilled Physician. On the heels of their removal came a certainty that all would be well, that he wouldn't fail as a father, that Petula would recover, even that Gavin might find the love he'd denied himself for far too long.

His heart overflowing with prayers of gratitude, Gavin lay on the ground and let the tears fall.

Emily heard the muffled voices. They were so often there — the voices, whispering words of encouragement. She wished they wouldn't. She wished they would go away and leave her in peace. She wanted to slide into blessed oblivion. Away from the burning in her throat and the weight on her chest that made it so difficult to breathe. She wanted to escape to someplace better.

Sometimes, she saw Gavin through the haze, smiling at her, beckoning to her. Time and again she tried to reach him, but she never could. She never quite could, although she wanted to so desperately.

"Gavin . . ."

If only he would come toward her. If only —

A woman's voice said, "Drink this, Emily."

Fingers slipped behind her head and eased her up from the pillow even as a glass was pressed against her lips. She drank obediently. The tea was warm and soothing to her throat.

"That's good, kitten."

"Maggie?" She opened her eyes.

"Yes, dear. I'm here."

"Where's Gavin?"

Maggie frowned. "I imagine he is on his ranch."

"Where am I?"

"At home. In Boise."

The fog in Emily's brain cleared a little, and she began to remember. Her trunk on the boarding house floor. The stage ride to Boise. "Oh," she said, then closed her eyes and turned her face toward the wall.

Better the dreams than this stark reality.

THIRTY-ONE

Gavin dismounted and strode to the front door of Killarney Hall. After a moment's hesitation, he lifted the knocker and let it fall, repeating the action several times.

The door opened to reveal the O'Donnell butler. "Good day, Mr. Blake."

"I'd like to see Patrick."

"Mr. O'Donnell is at home. Please come in, and I'll tell him you're here."

Gavin stepped inside as requested and removed his hat as his gaze swept around the entry hall. Large oil paintings in gilded frames hung on the walls. A marble table held a bronze sculpture of three running horses. The tiled floor gleamed.

As wife of the eldest brother, Emily could have been mistress of this household. She could have had servants at her beck and call. She could have —

"Hello, Gavin," Patrick said from the library doorway.

Gavin turned toward him. "Hello, Patrick."

"I was sorry to hear Brina and Pet have been sick. How are they?"

"The doctor thought we might lose Pet there for a while, but she's on the mend. Thank God."

"Word has it that the gold camps have been hit hard with the influenza this winter. Quite a large number of deaths, I'm told. It's fortunate we are that that's not the case here."

"Yes."

Patrick motioned toward the library, an invitation for Gavin to join him, and then strode into the room without waiting to see if he followed.

Gavin drew in a deep breath, at the same time wondering if coming here had been a mistake. But there was no going back. He needed answers, and this was the only place he knew to find them.

Help me, Lord.

He entered the library and moved toward the leather chairs near the windows where Patrick awaited him. He sat and placed his hat over his right knee.

"I'm thinking you're here about Emily," Patrick said.

He met his friend's gaze. "Yes."

"Well, spit it out, man. What have you come to say?"

"When I saw you in town last" — Gavin leaned forward on the chair — "you said Emily was in love with me. Did she tell you that when she broke the engagement?"

"No, but she didn't have to. If I'd let myself think on it, I would have known it much sooner than I did."

"And you're sure she won't change her mind about marrying you?"

"If I thought there was a chance, I wouldn't be sitting here with you today. I'd be in Boise, pressing my case. But it's not me she's got a longing for."

Agitated, Gavin rose from the chair and stepped to the windows, gazing out through the glass toward the southwest.

"And if I'm not mistaken," Patrick continued, "it's her you're longing for. What's wrong with you, Gavin? Go to Boise and bring her back."

His pulse leapt at the thought but he tamped it down. "The girls have been too sick for me to go now. I'd be gone too long to leave them in Stubs's care."

"So bring them here. Pearl will be glad to mother them, and it isn't like we haven't plenty of room for them."

Gavin turned around. "Why would you

want to help me, given your feelings for Emily?"

"Because in the end, I want to see her happy. And although I think you're a thick-headed idiot, I want to see you happy too. And it's together I think that will happen." A lopsided grin curved Patrick's mouth as he added, "So call me a sentimental fool."

Gavin failed to see any humor in the situation. "She might not forgive me for sending her away."

"Not if there's any sense in that pretty head of hers, she won't."

"You're probably right."

Patrick grunted in disgust, the smile gone from his face. "Will you give up with so little discouragement? If so, then she's better off without you."

Staring at Patrick, he realized his friend was right. He'd spent too many years waiting for the next disaster to strike. He'd closed himself off in a useless attempt to shield himself from life's hurts. He wasn't going to do that any longer. If there was any chance that Emily might forgive him, if there was any chance she might love him still, then he would do whatever was required to win her back.

The large parlor windows gave Emily a clear

view of the tall cottonwoods and poplars that lined the river. Sunlight streamed through the bare winter branches, revealing deserted bird nests and the tree house Tucker and Kevin had built one long-ago summer. She smiled, remembering watching father and son scramble up the boards they had pounded into the tree at intervals. Maggie had stood below, telling them she would tan the hide off the first one who fell and broke something.

The memory made her think of Petula. Had the little girl's arm mended straight? Was she still wearing the splint?

Shaking off the thoughts of the Blake children, she twisted on the sofa and lowered her legs to the floor. It felt good to be downstairs again, good to be surrounded by familiar things. Why ever had she wanted to leave in the first place? Whatever had possessed her to think she should be a governess for Dru and —

No, she mustn't think of him. She wouldn't think of him. It was over, and life would go on. She was young — or so Maggie had told her countless times — and her heart would mend. No. She wouldn't allow his name to even cross her mind. She would forget that he ever existed.

Emily returned her gaze to the window.

339

There wasn't even a trace of snow in the valley. She had to look to the north, to the tops of the mountains that overlooked the river valley, in order to see a mantle of white. Strange, that she should miss the snow.

Before her thoughts could take another unhealthy turn, a carriage rolled down the drive and stopped in the turnaround, still in plain view of the window. A moment later, the carriage door opened and a young woman stepped from the vehicle, a bundle in her arms.

"Fiona!" Emily rose from the sofa and started across the room.

Sarah appeared in the parlor doorway, blocking her path. "What are you doing up, miss? You know what the doctor said about getting proper rest."

"It's Fiona. She's got the baby with her. Open the door, Sarah, and let them in."

The housemaid put her hands on her hips and said, "I will once you're sitting down with that blanket over your lap."

"All right, Sarah. You win. I'm going. See?" She hurried back to the sofa.

Sarah gave her a triumphant look before turning toward the front entrance to the house. A short while later, she escorted Emily's friend into the room. Emily rose from the sofa and embraced Fiona while Sarah unwrapped the blankets that cocooned the baby.

"I wanted to come sooner," Fiona said as she drew back, "but Dr. Weick forbade it. Not until he was sure there was no more risk."

"Of course you couldn't come. You had little Myrna to think of. Oh, let me see her."

Sarah stayed stubbornly in place. "Not until you sit down again, miss. I'll not have you tiring yourself on my watch. No indeed."

Emily sighed and rolled her eyes in Fiona's direction, but she did as she was told, then held out her arms to receive the baby. "Oh, Fiona, she's beautiful. I'm so sorry I wasn't here when she was born. Look. She's going to have your auburn hair and your green eyes too."

"She wouldn't dare not have them. Her father demanded that all daughters born in our family must have my coloring."

"How is James?"

"He's wonderful, as always."

Wistfulness washed through Emily. "And you're both happy. I can tell just by looking at you."

"Of course, we're happy. But what about you? Your last letter said you wouldn't return until spring, and then I heard you were engaged. And by the way, I'm angry with you for not writing to give me that news yourself. I had to hear it from Maggie. And now you are back home again and your engagement is already broken. What happened?"

Emily looked down at the baby. "Oh, lots of things. I realized that I couldn't marry Patrick. He's the best and kindest of men, but I didn't love him as a woman should love the man she's to marry. Not the way you love James or Maggie loves Tucker. Besides, I was homesick. I missed Maggie and Tucker and the children." She kissed Myrna's forehead. "And look what else I missed while I was away. Myrna is half-grown already."

"Hardly," Fiona replied. "She's only four months old, but she has grown a lot. She couldn't help but grow. She eats all the time."

"Four months. It seems so much longer ago since I left to work for the Blakes."

"Emily . . . you can tell me whatever it is that's troubling you. I'll understand."

"There's nothing to tell, Fiona." She drew a deep breath. "Things just didn't work out the way I thought they would. That's all."

■ ■ ■ ■

It was a long, cold journey from the central mountain country to the capital of the territory. The days gave Gavin many hours to replay in his mind the events of the past few months, and there were times he was tempted to turn around and go back to the Lucky Strike. But every time that happened, he heard Dru calling him bullheaded and stubborn again. He heard Patrick calling him a thickheaded idiot. Those thoughts kept him moving forward, even when he was sure that nothing he could say or do would convince Emily to forgive him, let alone agree to marry him. He hadn't done one single solitary thing to deserve her love.

But neither had he done one single solitary thing to deserve God's forgiveness and love, and he'd received them all the same. If one miracle could happen in his life, why not two?

Maggie had waited patiently for Emily to come to her, but it still hadn't happened. It was time she took matters into her own hands.

"If she's too stubborn to admit she loves him," Tucker had said the previous night, "she comes by it naturally. Seems to me her sister was much the same way."

Maggie couldn't argue with her husband. Stubbornness and pride were two of her greatest faults. Combined they were lethal. She'd nearly thrown away her chance for happiness with Tucker because of her stubborn pride. Seventeen years later, she was more in love with him than ever, and she thanked the good Lord every day for bringing her to her senses in time. What would life have been like without Tucker and the children? She didn't want to imagine it.

Now if only she could help her sister avoid making a similar mistake.

She knocked on Emily's bedroom door, then opened it. "Is it too late for a visitor?"

Propped up in bed with pillows at her back, her sister set aside the book she was reading. "Of course not."

"You had a big afternoon, what with Fiona's visit with the baby. I hope you didn't overdo this soon out of your sickbed."

"I didn't. I'm feeling much better."

Maggie sat on the chair beside the bed and took hold of her sister's hand. "You don't know how relieved I am to see you getting some color back in your face. I was so frightened."

"I'm just glad no one else got sick." Emily

shook her head. "I never would have forgiven myself if the children or you and Tucker had fallen ill because of me."

Maggie squeezed the fingers within hers and took a breath. "Emily, dear, I think it's time you told me what happened while you were with the Blakes."

Emily lowered her eyes, remaining silent.

"All right. Let me tell you what I know." Maggie released Emily's hand. "You are in love with Mr. Blake, and you've been in love with him for some time. Perhaps too long?"

Color brightened her sister's cheeks.

"I thought as much." Maggie wanted to take her sister in her arms, to hold and comfort her as she had done countless times through the years. "Tell me."

When Emily finally looked up, there were tears in her eyes. "I didn't mean to fall in love with him, Maggie. I don't even know why it happened. He was so disagreeable to me from the start. He thought I was some silly spoiled girl who wouldn't be able to handle the work. But I proved him wrong." A sad smile lifted the corners of her mouth, then disappeared as quickly as it had come. "I tried to leave when I realized what I felt for him. I knew it was wrong to have such feelings for a married man. Dru was my friend, and I didn't want to betray her, not even in my thoughts. But she wouldn't let me go. She held me to my promise to stay until spring. Even on her deathbed she made me promise to stay with Gavin and the children until they returned to the basin."

Maggie reached out and patted the back of Emily's left hand, wanting to comfort but not wanting to stop the flow of words.

"I wish you could see the Stanley Basin, Maggie. The mountains are so beautiful they take your breath away. When I was there, the aspen and birch trees were already turning gold, but there were still a few wildflowers in bloom. Purple and yellow amid the waving sea of grass. You can't imagine it. You just can't. I understood right away why Dru wanted to stay there as long as possible." Emily stopped to wipe her eyes with the sleeve of her white nightgown. "Oh, Maggie," she whispered. "I should have come home as soon as we went to Challis. I should have come home. I wish I had."

Alarm tugged at Maggie's heart. "Emily, was he . . . did Mr. Blake ever . . . was he inappropriate with you?"

"No." She shook her head. "But not because I wouldn't have let him if he'd tried."

"Emily!"

"It's true." She covered her face with her hands. "It's true. I loved him so."

Maggie bit her lower lip to keep from saying something she shouldn't. She was here to listen, not to condemn.

"He kissed me once." Emily uncovered her face and met Maggie's gaze again. "Only once."

"When?"

"More than a month after Dru died."

Thank heaven for that. "If you loved Mr. Blake, why did you agree to marry Mr. O'Donnell?"

"I don't know. It was all so complicated. Gavin didn't care about me, and Patrick did. Patrick was kind and gentle. And perhaps I felt guilty for loving Gavin while Dru was still alive." Her voice fell to a whisper. "It felt as if I was glad Dru died. But I wasn't glad. I loved her. Her and the children."

"Oh, Emily."

"Patrick was so good to me after the funeral. To all of us. Gavin pulled away from everyone, even the girls for a brief while, but Patrick was there, helping us in every way he could. I knew he loved me, so I said yes when he proposed. I believed I could learn to love him in time. But that wasn't fair to him. I made such a mess of things."

Maggie stood. "I think we've talked long enough, dearest. You need to get some sleep."

Emily continued as if her sister hadn't spoken. "When Mr. Martin told me what had happened with Gavin's parents, I understood a little better why he . . . why he's the way he is. Why he's so guarded with his heart. But I also realized that I couldn't marry Patrick. Not feeling the way I do about Gavin. I was hoping, once I broke the engagement, that Gavin would realize he cared for me too."

Maggie brushed Emily's hair off her forehead and caressed her cheek. "Get some sleep, dearest."

There was a world of pain in the pale blue eyes that looked up at Maggie. "He didn't even let me tell him good-bye. He didn't let me say good-bye to the children. I wanted him to love me, and I made him despise me instead."

Maggie wanted to hate Gavin Blake in that moment. How dare he hurt her baby sister so? But hate was never the solution. Besides, if Emily loved him, there must be a great deal about the man that was good.

THIRTY-TWO

When Gavin reached Boise, he rented a room at the Overland Hotel and paid for a bath and a shave before inquiring about directions to the Branigan ranch. Once on his way, it didn't take long to get there.

He pulled the gelding to a halt at the end of the long drive that led to the Branigan home. It was a sprawling gray clapboard house, built for a large family, two stories tall with a veranda wrapped around three sides. The house at the Lucky Strike paled in comparison. Familiar doubt surged through him, but he ignored it, nudging the horse with his heels.

He dismounted near the front door and twirled the reins around the hitching post before climbing the steps. On the porch, he paused, removed his hat, and smoothed back his hair. Even after taking the time to clean up, he feared his appearance was still a bit rough. But it couldn't be helped. He knocked at the door and waited. There was a slight commotion from the other side of the door before it was yanked open. Two boys, approximately the same ages as Sabrina and Petula, looked up at him.

"Hello. I'm here to see Emily Harris. Is she in?"

"Who're you?" the youngest of the two asked.

Before he could reply, he heard another voice, this one feminine. "Colin. Sheridan. Ask whoever is there to come in. It's too cold to make them stand outside."

The door swung wide and he caught a glimpse of emerald skirts on the stairway. A moment later, Maggie Branigan stepped into view. The smile of welcome vanished from her mouth. "Mr. Blake." Her tone was flat and cool.

"Mrs. Branigan. I've come to see Emily."

"Please come in." She motioned toward an adjoining room. "Would you like a cup of coffee or tea to warm you?"

"Don't go to any bother for me."

The look in her eyes made him feel like something smelly she'd found on the bottom of her shoe. Not that he blamed her.

"Colin, run up to Aunt Emily's room and tell her she has a visitor. Ask her to join us. Sheridan, go with your brother." Maggie looked at Gavin again. "Please join me." Then she led the way into the parlor. "We may have a while to wait. Emily hasn't been down yet today and isn't dressed." She sat on a rose-colored sofa.

Not dressed? At this hour? He settled onto a chair opposite her.

"Emily fell ill with influenza upon our return to Boise."

"She was ill?" His gaze darted toward the staircase. She'd had influenza at the same time as his daughters. If he hadn't sent her away, he could have cared for her. What if —

"You needn't worry, Mr. Blake," Maggie said, bringing his attention back to her. "She's recovering nicely. What business brings you to Boise?"

"I came to see Emily."

"I find that rather strange, Mr. Blake, considering it was you who sent her away."

There was a greater resemblance between these sisters than he'd thought at first. He recognized the steely resolve in both Maggie Branigan's words and her posture.

"I made a mistake, Mrs. Branigan. We want her to return."

"I see." She rose from the sofa. "It may not be as easy as that, sir."

"I'll do whatever it takes."

"You'll have to." She moved toward the

doorway. "Excuse me while I see about the tea."

"Who is it?" Emily asked Colin when he delivered Maggie's message.

"Don't know. Never seen him before."

Him? Oh, she hoped it wasn't Matthew Foreman. But it couldn't be Matthew. Colin would recognize him.

It was tempting to send her regrets. She'd felt a terrible lethargy ever since her talk with Maggie last night. She would be very poor company for whoever had come calling. Then again, her sister wouldn't have sent for her if she didn't feel Emily should come down.

She donned a simple day dress of yellow linen and tied back her hair at the nape with a ribbon. She scarcely glanced at her reflection in the mirror before leaving the bedroom and descending the stairs.

She was prepared for anyone except for the person she found waiting in the parlor. Could she be seeing things, the way she had when her fever raged? She gave her head a slow shake and closed her eyes. But when she opened them, Gavin was still there. She sank onto the nearest chair at the same moment he rose to his feet.

He needs a haircut.

He studied her with an intense gaze.

He looks tired.

"Hello, Emily."

"Mr. Blake." She hated the breathless sound of her voice. "Where's Maggie?"

He took a step toward her. "She went to see about some tea."

"What are you doing in Boise?"

"I came to see you. I wanted to talk to you."

"To see me." Pain twisted in her belly. "I thought you said everything in your note that was delivered with my trunk."

"I'm sorry for that. I made a mistake. If you'd give me a chance to explain . . ."

She looked at her hands, clenched in her lap. "You don't owe me any explanations, Mr. Blake."

Gavin closed the distance between them. He stopped about a foot away, towering over her, but she refused to look up. She was too tired to look up. She hadn't the strength for this. As much as it had hurt that he'd sent her away without a good-bye, maybe that had been the better way. Saying good-bye to him would hurt too much now.

But he knelt before her, bringing himself to her eye level. "I was wrong, Emily. I hurt you. I shouldn't have sent you away like that, and I'm sorry."

"You're sorry," she said softly.

"The girls miss you. They need you." He paused. "*I* need you."

She shook her head, scarcely hearing him.

"I would have come sooner, but Pet and Brina were sick. They had influenza too, like you. Patrick told me there's been an outbreak of it in the mining camps. You and the girls must have contracted it at the same time."

"How are they?" The question was unnecessary. She knew Gavin wouldn't have left them if they weren't recovered.

"They're well now, but they want you to come back with me."

It wasn't fair of him, using her love for the children against her. "It's better if they don't see me again."

"Well, if not for them, what about your promise to Dru?"

Anger replaced pain and sorrow as she rose from the chair. "You sent me away, Mr. Blake. It's you who forgot your wife's request, not I." She turned and walked toward the doorway.

"Emily . . ."

The tone of his voice conveyed many things. Things she hadn't expected. Against her better judgment, she turned to look at him.

"I've gone about this all wrong. You don't understand. It's not easy for me to put my feelings into words."

It was only guilt for the way he'd dismissed her that had brought him here. Guilt and the need for a woman to watch his children. The thought twisted the familiar knots in her stomach. She wished she could hate him. But she couldn't. She loved him — as much as she'd ever loved him. But she would never tell him so. Not now. "It doesn't matter. We both made mistakes. I forgive you. Does that make you feel better? Now you can return to your ranch with a clear conscience." With shoulders erect and head held high, she walked toward the stairway and the sanctuary of her room. "Good day, Mr. Blake. Please show yourself out."

"I'll be back, Emily. I promise you, I'll be back."

THIRTY-THREE

For a solid week, Gavin called daily at the Branigan home, and for a solid week, Emily refused to see him. Maggie, however, seemed to warm to him with each passing day. Perhaps she began to realize that he was determined, that he wouldn't give up easily. Perhaps she came to believe that he loved Emily and wasn't going away until he could tell her so. By the end of those seven days, Gavin knew he had gained an ally in Maggie Branigan.

But his mission to Boise would still fail unless Emily agreed to see him. And so, as a new week began, Gavin decided to ask for help from someone who wanted Emily's happiness as much as he did.

"I won't take no for an answer," Maggie said, giving Emily a pointed look. "It's time you got out for a bit of fresh air. We'll do some shopping and then have lunch with

Tucker."

"I really don't want to —"

"I don't care what you want. This time you will do as I say. You can't hide in your room for the rest of your life."

Emily didn't intend to stay there for the rest of her life. Only until she knew Gavin had left Boise. Only until there was no risk of seeing him again.

"You're going with me, and that's that. Now put on something pretty to help lift your spirits."

Emily knew when she was defeated. Maggie could not be budged when she was in this sort of mood. And maybe she was right. It would be good to get out. The weather had been unseasonably warm the past few days. A buggy ride might be just what she needed to lift her spirits.

She took a favorite blue dress from the wardrobe and slipped into it, then sat at her dressing table to brush her hair, sweeping it high and securing it with a decorative comb.

Her hand stilled as she remembered the day of the O'Donnell wedding and the comb she had given Dru. How very long ago that seemed. Another lifetime ago. She closed her eyes and allowed the memories to wash over her . . . Dru, frail but happy on the last outing she would have before going home to the Father . . . Sabrina, her young girl's heart breaking over the older boy who paid her no attention . . . Gavin, wanting to shelter his adopted daughter from pain.

"The girls miss you. They need you. I need you."

But missing and being missed wasn't enough.

She gave her hair a final pat. She would not think of Gavin today. She would force him from her mind, once and for all.

"I'm Gavin Blake," he told the clerk. "Judge Branigan is expecting me."

"Yes, sir. Please come with me." The young man rose and led the way to an adjoining office.

The judge's chamber was a large, high-ceilinged room, two walls lined with tall bookcases filled with books. Wood crackled in a wide-mouthed fireplace, throwing dancing fingers of light across the ornate rug. An oak desk stood before tall windows framed with heavy brocade draperies, and Tucker Branigan sat in the chair behind the desk.

"Come in, Mr. Blake." He stood. "You may close the door, Sedgwick. Please see that we're not disturbed."

"Yes, sir."

Tucker motioned toward a chair opposite him. "Have a seat, Mr. Blake."

Gavin crossed the room and sat in the indicated chair, silently praying that all would go well.

"You've made quite an impression on my wife," Tucker said. "A positive one, I might add."

"I'm glad to hear that, Judge Branigan."

"Call me Tucker."

Gavin relaxed a little.

"Maggie seems to think you'll make her sister happy."

"I'll do my level best, given the chance."

Tucker chuckled softly. "Be warned. Emily has the same stubborn streak as Maggie. She won't be easily led where she doesn't want to go."

Gavin recalled those early weeks in the basin, Emily so determined to prove him wrong. "I've seen some of that trait."

A light rap sounded on the door before it eased open enough for the clerk to show his head. "Mrs. Branigan is here, sir. Shall I show her in?"

"Yes, Sedgwick. Thank you."

This was it. The moment had arrived. What could be his final chance to set things right. Gavin rose from the chair and took a couple of steps back toward the wall.

A short while later, Maggie and Emily entered the judge's chambers. Emily wore a gown of shimmery dark blue. Her hair was swept high on her head and capped with a matching bonnet. She didn't notice him right away. Instead she watched as Maggie rounded the oak desk and gave Tucker a quick kiss on the cheek. He saw her expression turn pensive.

"We came to take you to lunch," Maggie said. Then she turned slowly, pretending to be taken aback when her eyes met Gavin's. "Why, Mr. Blake. This is a surprise."

She was a superb actress.

"Mrs. Branigan." Gavin nodded at her as his gaze returned to Emily. "Miss Harris."

He thought she might bolt for the door, but her brother-in-law stopped her.

"Emily, don't go. It seems Mr. Blake has a legal matter that he would like addressed. The matter of a verbal contract."

She blinked. "I'm sorry."

"It has to do with your promise to remain in his employ until spring. Mr. Blake feels you have broken that contract by leaving Challis."

"But he sent me away. You know he did. You saw my trunk and the note."

"I saw the trunk, but I didn't know why he brought it to you. You never showed me what was in the note. Did you show Maggie?"

"No."

"Do you have it with you now?"

"Of course not." She glared at Gavin. "I threw it away."

There it was — her anger. The stiffening of her back and lifting of her chin. The color rising in her cheeks. The spark in her eyes. Glorious. Beautiful. He'd missed seeing this side of her. Gavin suppressed a smile. It wouldn't do for Emily to think he was laughing at her.

"That's unfortunate." Tucker shook his head. "Well, it seems that the only thing to do is leave you two alone to work out a fair settlement. You may use my office while I take my wife to lunch. I expect you to have reached an agreement by the time we return." His voice deepened. "And if either of you leaves before this is resolved, you will be fined and it shall not be a small one. Is that understood?"

"Yes, Judge," Gavin answered.

"Understood," Emily said. Her voice could have frozen fire.

Tucker took his wife by the arm. "Where shall we dine, Maggie? I'm famished."

The moment the door closed behind them,

Emily spun toward Gavin. "How dare you!"

"You wouldn't see me. You wouldn't give me another chance to say what I came to Boise to say. I bungled it the first time. I needed another chance."

She gave her head a slight toss. "I'm not interested in anything else you have to say to me." Then she walked to the windows behind Tucker's desk and stared outside.

How could he do this to her? Accuse her of breaking a verbal contract. That was absurd. Ridiculous. He had sent her away. He hadn't wanted her.

The girls miss you. They need you. I need you.

She was glad the girls and Gavin needed her, but that was no longer enough for Emily. Not enough by half. She had no intention of settling for less than his whole heart. And that, she believed now, was something he would never offer her or any woman.

"We need to sit down and talk," Gavin said.

Startled by the nearness of his voice, she turned to find him standing within arm's reach. Too close. The anger drained out of her. She couldn't stay angry when he was so near. Near enough to touch. Near enough to see the slight shadow of a beard beneath the skin on his jaw. Near enough to see the rise and fall of his Adam's apple when he swallowed.

Near enough to kiss.

She closed her eyes, resisting the thought.

"Your brother-in-law says we must resolve the matter before he returns."

"It was resolved when I returned to Boise." Tears threatened, but she blinked them away. "It was resolved when you sent me away."

"You broke your engagement to Patrick."

"Yes."

"Why?"

"Because I didn't love him, and he deserves a wife who loves him." She looked down at her hands, folded tightly at her waist. "At first I thought I would learn to love him, given enough time, but then I realized I couldn't."

"Why? He's a good man."

"It doesn't matter why." She turned toward the window a second time.

"It matters to me, Emily." His hands alighted on her shoulders, and then, before she could shrug him away, he turned her to face him. She couldn't look him in the eye. "It matters to me because . . . I love you, and I think you love me. I hope you love me."

She found she could look at him after all.

In sheer disbelief. Surely he hadn't spoken those words. She felt the blood draining from her head. Only his firm grip on her upper arms kept her upright.

"I guess I began to love you the day we arrived in the basin and Joker knocked you down with his big, muddy paws."

He gave her one of his rare and wonderful grins and her breath caught in her chest, certain she was imagining things, certain she would awaken at any moment and find she'd been dreaming. She couldn't bear it if that were to happen.

"Emily, I kept my feelings walled up for a lot of years. I'm not quite sure when that wall began to weaken. Probably after Dru started praying for me. Between her and the girls and then you and God, I guess I never stood a chance. The wall had to come down."

The tears returned, and this time she couldn't keep them from falling. Gavin caught one with a fingertip, brushed it away. *Don't let this be a dream. Please don't let it be a dream.*

"I hurt you, and I'm sorry. More than once I hurt you. My pride wouldn't let me admit I cared for you. But now I'm asking for your forgiveness. I'm asking for a lifetime of chances to make it up to you. I'm asking you to stay much longer than spring. I'm asking you to stay for a thousand springs. Make another contract with me." He drew her into his arms. "Marry me, Emily. I don't want to spend another day apart from you. Marry me. Love me."

He kissed her then. Softly at first, a butterfly's breath across her lips. When she inhaled, he deepened his assault in a long, searing kiss that made her senses whirl. She gave herself up to the sensation, matching his embrace with her own. She'd waited a lifetime for this.

Too soon, he lifted his head and stared into her eyes. "Marry me, Emily. Love me."

Speech evaded her, so she nodded.

"You'll marry me?"

She nodded again.

"And you love me?"

She found her voice at last, albeit just enough to whisper. "Yes."

He smiled. "Yes what?"

"I love you, Gavin. I always will."

Lowering his head for another kiss, he smiled. "That's a promise I intend to hold you to."

Epilogue

Stanley Basin, July 1885

"Ma, they're here!" Sabrina galloped her horse into the yard. "They're here!"

Emily lifted her three-month-old son from the cradle that was set in the shade of a tall, leafy tree and waited as the carriage approached. Within moments after rolling to a stop, the entire Branigan clan had spilled out of the vehicle.

Maggie wasted no time in stealing little Nicholas Blake from his mother's arms. "Oh, Emily. He's beautiful. And look at how big he is already. Oh, they grow up so fast. Treasure each moment."

"I do." Emily smiled, thinking how very many moments she had to treasure.

She watched as Gavin helped Tucker unload satchels and a trunk from the carriage. When he saw her watching, Gavin grinned, and joy caused her heart to skip a beat in response.

"I've never seen you so happy," Maggie said softly. "You're glowing with it."

How could she not be happy? God had blessed her in countless ways: Two sweet daughters in Sabrina and Petula; a healthy infant son who was growing by leaps and bounds; and a husband who loved her and never failed to tell her and show her that he did.

A ripple of anticipation flowed through her. She hadn't yet said anything to Gavin, but she suspected there would be another blessing for the Blake family in a little less than eight months.

Maggie eyed her, then leaned closer. "Lo, children are an heritage of the Lord: and the fruit of the womb is his reward. As arrows are in the hand of a mighty man; so are children of the youth. Happy is the man that hath his quiver full of them.' "

"You always could read my thoughts." She looked at her sister. "But don't say a word. I'm not sure yet, and I haven't told Gavin."

The men and the older Branigan children began carrying the luggage to the new cabin Gavin had built last summer for just such an occasion as a visit from Emily's family. As she watched them, Emily imagined the future stretching before them. They would have a house filled with children. From Emily, they would learn their numbers and letters and a thirst for knowledge. From Gavin, they would learn a love for the land and a respect for God's creation. From both of their parents, they would learn a love for the Lord and a love for one another.

She remembered that fateful day, not yet two years before, when she'd read the advertisement for a governess and teacher. She remembered thinking that she wanted to make some sort of difference in the world. In some strange way, she'd felt destined to make a difference.

She thought of the man Gavin had been, so reluctant to love or be loved, so determined not to risk his heart, and she realized she had made a greater difference than she could have imagined when she applied for the job as governess to the Blake children.

Perhaps changing the heart of just one man was the greatest destiny of all.

AUTHOR'S NOTE

Dear Reader:

There are many kinds of heroes and heroines, both in fiction and in life. We tend to remember people who do something extraordinary, something above and beyond what mere mortals think we are capable of. But I believe many of the true heroes and heroines of the Western movement were those brave souls — ordinary people like you and me — who came and lived and loved and died without fanfare. Those are the people I like to write about in my historical fiction.

I first met Emily and Gavin in 1990, and it was my delight to get to revisit their love story all these years later. I have a soft spot in my heart for wounded heroes, like Gavin, and take great pleasure in watching them be redeemed by the love of a good woman, like Emily. That's the unabashed romantic in me.

The Stanley Basin and Sawtooth Valley in the Central Mountains of Idaho contain some of the most spectacular scenery in America. Walled in by four mountain ranges — the Salmon River Mountains, the Boulders, the White Clouds, and the Sawtooths — winter reigns there for seven to eight months a year, with temperatures often falling to 40 or 50 degrees below zero. Summers are short but delightful. The valleys are carpeted with luscious grasses, sage, and wildflowers. Crystal-clear lakes, gurgling streams, and steaming hot springs are abundant. The Sawtooth Wilderness is home to Bighorn Sheep as well as a host of other wildlife. People who choose to live in this secluded corner of the world must be hardy souls — just as their predecessors were — but their reward is the beauty God has bestowed on the mountains, lakes, and rivers that surround them.

In *When Love Blooms,* I took some "poetic license" regarding the bringing of beef cattle into the basin. The lush grasses growing in the Stanley Basin attracted cattlemen several years before settlers came, but Gavin Blake was still about six or seven years ahead of what research shows as accurate. In the summers of 1881 and 1882, a herd of dairy cattle was brought into the basin, the owner packing milk and butter over the narrow trail into the Yankee Fork Mining District. But the dairy cows failed to thrive as the owner had hoped. Beef cattle were a different story. They were brought into the valley in the late 1880s, and they grew fat on the basin's grasses, just as Gavin's cattle did in my story.

As I write this note to readers, I am already at work on my next historical romance, the first of a new series about three young women who find themselves employed in unusual occupations for their day. I hope you'll enjoy meeting these characters as much as I know I'll enjoy writing about them.

In the grip of His grace,
Robin Lee Hatcher
www.robinleehatcher.com

ABOUT THE AUTHOR

Robin Lee Hatcher (www.robinleehatcher
.com) is the author of over fifty-five novels,
including *Wagered Heart, Return to Me,* and
Catching Katie, named one of the Best
Books of 2004 by Library Journal. Winner
of the Christy Award for Excellence in
Christian Fiction, two RITA Awards for
Best Inspirational Romance, and the RWA
Lifetime Achievement Award, Robin lives in
Idaho.

The employees of Thorndike Press hope you have enjoyed this Large Print book. All our Thorndike, Wheeler, and Kennebec Large Print titles are designed for easy reading, and all our books are made to last. Other Thorndike Press Large Print books are available at your library, through selected bookstores, or directly from us.

For information about titles, please call:
(800) 223-1244

or visit our Web site at:
http://gale.cengage.com/thorndike

To share your comments, please write:
Publisher
Thorndike Press
295 Kennedy Memorial Drive
Waterville, ME 04901